Thirteen Gold Monkeys

Benjamin Beck

outskirtspress
DENVER, COLORADO

Dedicated to Devra Kleiman, 1942 - 2010

"Conflict is inevitable. You just have to learn how to manage it."

Preface

This is a story of the early days of the reintroduction of zoo-born golden lion tamarin monkeys to the coastal rainforest of Brazil. We reintroduced these monkeys to help save the species in the wild. Colleagues have been asking me to write a detailed account of this landmark program, but I didn't want to write a dry scientific story that would have to include a lot of detail that would be of interest to only a few other reintroduction scientists and historians. I thought the lessons of aspiration; failure and success; adaptive management and innovation; conflict and cooperation; human strengths and frailties; evil, love, and loyalty; the power and beauty of a rainforest; and the drive of these remarkable monkeys to survive were too powerful to be buried in a droll scientific account. The story reveals for the first time that the fierce passions of a zookeeper and a field assistant for the health and wellbeing of each monkey were the key to making the reintroduction successful. Also revealed for the first time is the despicable poaching of reintroduced tamarins at the hand of a well-known Rio citizen, a crime that killed one monkey and almost destroyed the conservation program.

The characters, and their personalities and experiences, are fictional but loosely based on those who actually took part in the work. The experiences of several people over three decades may have been compressed into those of a single character, so any resemblance to a single person, living or dead, is coincidental. Likewise, the experiences of dozens of monkeys may have been combined into those of 13 individuals that were born in North American zoos and reintroduced to the wild in Brazil in the course of this story.

Geographical places and timelines have been slightly compressed to keep the story flowing. As a scientist I have enjoyed the unfamiliar liberty to exaggerate the sizes of a few animals, and to sensationalize a few animal-human encounters.

But if the reader zooms out to 1,000 feet[1], (s)he will get a scientifically accurate picture of the actors, events, and dynamics of this remarkable story of science and conservation. The major thematic lines are historically correct, and the outcomes are accurately portrayed. Those who want a rigorously scientific account can consult the following scientific article: Beck, B.B., Castro, M.I., Stoinski, T.S., and J. Ballou. 2002. The effects of pre-release environments on survivorship in reintroduced golden lion tamarins. In D.G. Kleiman and A. Rylands (eds.) *The Lion Tamarins: Twenty-Five Years of Research and Conservation* (Washington, D.C., Smithsonian Institution Press, 2002). Pp 283-300. Indeed, *The Lion Tamarins* is *the* source for the big picture.

There is one major exception to the assertion of scientific accuracy: there is no evidence that tamarins can communicate with each other about their hopes, fears, and dreams in English or any other human language. They probably can't express much more than some simple wants and alarms. I put words in their mouths, words that I made up that help me think about how they interpret their experiences. But humanizing them in this way is doing them no favors; they are magnificent in their own right. It's not easy to keep track of the monkeys. Appendix 1 is a "cast of characters".

I am indebted most of all to the approximately 160 golden lion tamarins who gave their lives to this program, and to the dedicated animal keepers, curators, veterinarians, nutritionists, behavioral ecologists, population managers, registrars, educators, volunteers, and directors who helped to breed golden lion tamarins in about 30 zoos and research institutions, get them ready for reintroduction,

---

1   See Appendix 2 for measurement conversions. The reader might dog-ear or bookmark the appendices for quick reference.

tell the story to the world, and provide financial support. Critics of zoos take note: this is a case where zoos walked the conservation talk. Several zoos continue to provide funding for ongoing golden lion conservation in Brazil.

Knowing I will offend some by inadvertent exclusion, special thanks go to (the late) Dr. Devra Kleiman, Dr. Adelmar Coimbra Filho, Beate Rettberg-Beck, Andreia Fonseca Martins, Dr. James Dietz, Lou Ann Dietz, Judith Block, Dr. Alcides Pissinatti, Maria Ines Castro, Dr. Mitchell Bush, and Dr. Richard Montali.

Other key figures included Dr. Lyndsay Phillips, Dr. Lisa Tell, Dr. Jon Ballou, Dr. Jennifer Mickelberg, Dr. Michael Robinson, Dr. Ted Reed, Clint Fields, Dr. David Challinor, Ross Simons, Jeremy Mallinson OBE, Dr. Richard Faust, Dr. Michael Power, Dr. Alfred Rosenberger, Dr. Carlos Ruiz Miranda, Dr. Andrew Baker, Dr. Tara Stoinski, Dr. Charles Menzel, Dr. Carlos Peres, Dr. Laurenz Pinder, Dr. Robert Hoage, John Lehnhardt, Ed Bronikowski, William Xanten, Miles Roberts, Denise Rambaldi, Fernando Fernandes, Dr. Claudio Padua, Dr. Susanna Padua, Dr. Cecilia Kierulff, Dr. Russell Mittermeier, Dr. Anthony Rylands, Nelson Barbosa dos Santos, Paulo Cesar de Silva, Paulo Eduardo Santiago, Jabez Moraes dos Santos, Arleia Fonseca Martins, Elisama Moraes dos Santos, Ezequiel Moraes dos Santos, Sidnei de Mello, Oberlan da Costa, the late Luiz Henrique Cardoso dos Santos, Dionizio Pesamillio, Maria Ines Castro, Rosa Lemos de Sá, Vera Lúcia Ferreira Luz, Joanne Grumm, Cibele Carvalho, Elizabeth Nagagata, Antonio Belermino, Nair Maria Ferreira, and Octavio Jose Narcisio.

Sponsors of the reintroduction work included the Frankfurt Zoological Society; The Wildlife Preservation Trust International; the Smithsonian Institution, particularly its Scholarly Studies, Nelson Fund, and fellowship programs; Friends of the National Zoo; and NHK Television. The Smithsonian National Zoological Park provided time and support for my participation, and for the golden lion tamarin captive breeding and conservation program.

Brazilian federal wildlife authorities granted permits for the work. The name of the agency has changed several times in the past 30 years, but during the time of this story the names were the Instituto Brasiliero de Desenvolvimento Florestal (IBDF) and the Instituto Brasileiro do Meio Ambiente e Recursos Naturais (IBAMA). The United States Fish and Wildlife Service granted export permits for the golden lion tamarins being shipped to Brazil from the United States.

No person or organization on this list is responsible for any portrayals, omissions, or inaccuracies in the story. The buck stops with me.

Chapter 1

Packing For A Trip

The two-leggers turned on the lights in the quarantine ward on Sunday morning at 4 AM, startling the golden lion tamarin monkeys, sleeping in a box in a warm ball with the adults on the outside and infants in the middle. Mom peered out of the box to see Dr. Lisa, the National Zoo's head veterinarian, entering their cage with a long-handled net. The early hour, the appearance of the vet, and the net itself all signaled trouble. Behind Dr. Lisa was Dr. Ira the curator, and Erika, the usually nice zookeeper who cared for the monkeys during the day. They too had nets. This was triple trouble. Dr. Lisa shook the sleeping box and all eight members of the tamarin family tumbled out. The cage door was open and the monkeys were free to escape into the hall of the ward. Nets were waving everywhere, and the monkeys pooped and peed from fright. Then, with startling efficiency, each tamarin was caught in a net and put into one of three plastic shipping boxes that waited on the floor. Ira's yelp was ignored in the confusion.

Mom was put in a box with Venus, her four-month-old daughter, and Vesuvio, Venus' male twin. The 12-month-old twins, the family's "teen-agers", Hera and Hercules, also a girl and boy, were packed with Dad. The young adults of the family, Pandora and Prometheus, were packed in the third shipping box. Each box had a door and windows made of wire mesh, and was stocked with a fluffy pile of hay, some grapes, and quartered oranges. Once packed, the tamarins were put in a darkened room and allowed to settle down.

"I was shipped here from the zoo in Atlanta a few years ago in this kind of box," said Dad. "I have a feeling we're going on a trip."

One by one, the eight members of the "Olympia Family," as they were called, calmed down and began peeping softly. A few dozed off, and Hera even ate a grape.

"It's not like the two-leggers to let us *out* of the cage, and they usually don't chase us around with nets," said Mom. "Do you think they were purposely trying to scare the you-know-what out of us? That would certainly be better than doing it here in the box and then sitting in it during the trip. Anyway, we're all OK for the moment so settle down and get some rest."

But Hera couldn't sleep. She was actually excited about the adventure.

Chapter 2
Up And Away

As the van turned into the National Airport just outside of Washington D.C., Dad said, "I can't see much but I think this is where I came into Washington. This is where the silverbirds come and go, landing and flying off with two-leggers and their stuff. I flew from the Atlanta Zoo in a silverbird, but they made me fly with the stuff, not the two-leggers."

The van pulled up at the cargo terminal. Ira and Erika carried the three boxes inside and did some paperwork at the counter. Then a woman showed up in a uniform and a badge. Ira shined a flashlight into the boxes while the wildlife agent counted heads in the boxes. Erika lured the monkeys to the mesh door with a few slices of banana. The agent said "Eight golden lion tamarins, *Leontopithecus rosalia*; that matches the permit." Ira offered that each tamarin had a tattooed number inside its right thigh for individual identification, but it would be difficult to see.

The agent said: "I don't need to see the tattoos. I trust you." Ira asked if the two-leggers could go to the next room and allow the tamarins to wait for the flight in the quiet darkened room.

"So why are you taking endangered monkeys *out* of the United States?" asked the agent. "Most of the time people are trying to bring animals and feathers and ivory *into* the U.S.".

"Golden lion tamarins are highly endangered," said Ira. "There are only about 150 left in the wild, and they all live in one area in Brazil. But there are almost 400 living and reproducing in zoos, so we are taking some zoo-born tamarins back to Brazil to put them back into the wild."

"Will they be able to find enough to eat, and avoid predators, and find places to sleep?" asked the agent. "What about getting sick or injured?"

"We've been asking ourselves those questions for months," said Erika in her German-accented English, "but reintroduction is a new science and nobody knows for sure." We have been training them to look for hidden food in their cages, and they *are* doing more searching and less waiting for food."

"Well I hope it all goes well," said the agent. "Keep me posted on the progress, OK?" With that, she stamped five different sets of papers, the most important of which was the official permit to export endangered species from the United States.

Meanwhile, in the next room, the tamarins dozed and made soft "I'm-OK-are-you-OK" chirps.

"I bit him," said Pandora, shattering the calm.

"What? Whom?" cried Mom.

"Dr. Ira, when he netted me and tried to take me out of the net and put me in the box."

"Why?" asked Dad.

"I don't really know. I was scared and angry. Maybe his hand closing on my body felt like a predator, like a boa constrictor or a coatimundi, and I was just defending myself."

"What would you know about predators?" said Mom. "Your great grandparents, grandparents, and Dad and I were born in zoos. It's been four generations since anybody in this family even saw a predator."

"All I can say is that he grabbed me like a predator, and I reacted," said Pandora.

"Get those silly notions out of your mind," said Dad. "We're off to another zoo and thank goodness there are no predators in zoos."

But Hera was not so sure, thinking that she had overheard a different plan as the two-leggers talked in the next room. She kept her doubts to herself.

Comforted, the tamarins all dozed. After two weeks of eating only solid food, Venus and Vesuvio eagerly sucked on Mom's nipples. She didn't have much milk anymore, but it was sure calming.

Shortly before 10, baggage handlers took the shipping boxes outside to the waiting airplane. It was really noisy, and the November morning was chilly. The tamarins hunkered down in the straw for warmth and safety. Ira and Erika were nowhere to be seen.

The boxes were put on a moving ramp that carried them up until they were grabbed by a handler in the back of the plane.

"I remember this," said Dad. "They'll close the door and then there will be lots of bumps and noise." Moments later, the airplane did indeed shoot into the sky and headed south. In the coach section, Ira and Erika had their first cup of coffee of the already long morning.

Chapter 3

Happy Landing, Sort Of

After a long stop in Miami (more bumping and swaying, another wildlife agent counting heads and stamping papers), the airplane landed at the Rio de Janeiro airport at 6 AM on Monday. The three shipping boxes were taken to a warehouse at the edge of the runway.

"It's getting kind of stinky in here," said Dad. "I hope we get to the zoo quickly so we can get out and stretch our legs."

"At least it's warm," said Hercules. "Maybe this zoo is in a climate where we don't have to stay inside for days at a time because it's too cold and snowy to go out."

"Hey, I see Ira and Erika over there, talking to some two-leggers with badges," said Prometheus.

Indeed, Ira and Erika were talking to some glowering Brazilian wildlife and customs agents, and the conversation was not going well. Ira's Portuguese, Brazil's native language, was ridiculously imperfect, and the agents spoke no English at all. There were lots of them, all speaking at once and each trying to be the decision-maker. To make things worse, there were reporters and photographers in a waiting room, calling out and straining to see the tamarins. Ira sensed that the customs agents wanted to levy an "import tax", but he already had an official permit to import the monkeys into Brazil and was not ready to pay any money. He and Erika were anxious to see the monkeys and make sure they were OK after the long overnight flight.

The chaos ceased instantly when Dr. Cardoso strode into the room. He was a highly respected and well-known Brazilian primatologist and a textbook alpha male. After a quick huddled conversation with the agents, the papers were stamped. Ira and Erika greeted Dr. Cardoso with respect and gratitude, and the three went quickly to the shipping boxes. Ira's flashlight picked up eight sets of blinking and tired eyes, and he flashed a relieved A-OK to the converging reporters. Never mind that he used the circular thumb-to-index finger circle, which would have been OK in the United States but in Brazil meant something awful about your mother. Viewers of the morning TV news would be amused.

Erika stuck juicy grapes and sweet little bananas into the boxes.

"These grapes really hit the spot," said Mom.

"Yeah, but what are these yellow things?" asked Dad.

"Bananas," chorused Pandora, Prometheus, Hera and Hercules.

"Nonsense," said Dad. "Bananas are little sticky white circles, not dry yellow tubes."

"Didn't you learn anything at the zoo?" said Hera. "You grew up eating *sliced* bananas Dad but these are whole ones. Don't you remember? Erika was trying to get us to peel whole bananas?"

"Why would we do that?" asked Dad. "Don't the keepers have time to cut bananas at this new zoo we're going to?"

Before anybody could answer, Dr. Cardoso, Erika and Ira each picked up a box and headed for a waiting VW microbus. The photographers stuck big lenses up to the boxes, and flash bulbs exploded. Cardoso answered reporters' questions in Portuguese. Finally they put the boxes in the squarish little bus, and roared off. Dr. Cardoso headed back to his lab, telling the Americans he'd see them in a few days.

"What was all that fuss about?" asked Mom.

"Well, we're obviously in a very different place," said Dad. "It's really warm and muggy, and the two-leggers speak a totally different language. We must be going to a really special zoo."

Keeping her doubts and excitement to herself, Hera nodded off, while Pandora chuckled silently about the bandage she saw on Ira's right thumb.

Chapter 4
It's A Jungle Out There

Dr. Peter Madison was driving. He was a Smithsonian postdoctoral fellow, with support to study the behavior and ecology of wild golden lion tamarins. He had worked in Brazil before, spoke Portuguese fluently, and reveled in the food, wine, and culture of the nation. Peter threaded the van through Rio traffic and out into the countryside. Though the highway had only two lanes, the Brazilian drivers shared the shoulders with pedestrians, bicycles, dogs, cows, and horses. Slow-moving, underpowered, and overloaded trucks triggered suicide passing by frustrated motorists, and sometimes there were even five vehicles abreast, racing at high speed in both directions. "Driving on this highway is the most dangerous part of our work in Brazil," said Peter.

They passed through orange groves, sugar cane fields, and cattle pastures, with simple mud houses and elaborate upscale weekend houses. Truckloads of firewood lumbered toward the ovens of Rio's ceramic factories. "There's now only ten percent of the forest that was standing when the Portuguese settlers arrived in the late 1600s," Peter explained. "Habitat loss is the basic reason that golden lion tamarins are so endangered – fewer trees, fewer tamarins. But we think there are about between 150 and 250 tamarins left in the wild. Most live in the Poço das Antas Reserve".

"How do you say that name again, and what does it mean, and what's the difference between a reserve and a national park?" asked Erika.

"*Po-so das Aunt-as*," which means 'mud hole'." A reserve is an area protected by the federal government but tourists are not allowed," answered Peter. "Poço das Antas is the last stronghold for golden lion tamarins, and many unique orchids and birds too," he added, skillfully diving for the shoulder to avoid a car coming head-on while passing a slow-moving truck loaded with pineapples.

Two hours later, after a rest stop, and buying some smoked provolone cheese and a few bottles of Argentinean wine ("There are no stores near the reserve so we have to buy some treats when we can. Otherwise it's just rice and beans."), the microbus passed a small sign denoting the reserve and turned off onto a dirt road. Passing a low wet spot ("We often get stuck here when it rains"), the van pulled up to a heavy wooden gate. Peter dug in the ashtray for a key, and signaled Ira to unlock the gate.

"Hunters can easily crawl through the barbed wire, and there are places where motorcycles can get through, but at least the gate keeps cars and trucks out of the reserve," said Peter.

The road turned worse, slick with red mud and deep potholes. Tall trees, laden with thick flowering vines, crowded in from both sides. The microbus slithered and fishtailed going up the steep hills, and tried to go sideways on the way down.

"This is worse than the silverbird," said little Venus. "When will we get there?"

"I'm not sure where *there* is," said Dad "but I don't think this is a road to a zoo."

"All I can see out the windows are trees," said Hera, thinking back on the overheard conversation with the wildlife agent in Washington.

The bus lurched and tipped sickeningly to one side. The drive wheel whined as it spun hopelessly, searching for a grip in a hubcap-deep puddle of muddy soup.

"Erika, you'll have to drive while Ira and I push," said Peter. Erika walked around to the driver's seat in ankle-deep mud while Ira and Peter headed for the back.

"Put it in low and accelerate slowly." Erika slowly let out the clutch while Peter and Ira pushed. The madly spinning wheel sent torrents of mud backward, covering the men from head to toe. But the bus lurched over the edge of the hole and found some solid ground.

"Between breakdowns and getting stuck five times a day, I often think that golden lion tamarins will go extinct from vehicular failure," said Peter, in a lame attempt at humor.

He took the wheel and drove a few more minutes, finally stopping in a small clearing. He greeted his two waiting field assistants, Carlos and Alicia, in fluent Portuguese.

They opened the back door of the microbus, checked for eight sets of open eyes, and took out the boxes.

"The trail is steep and slippery from this morning's rain. Let us carry the boxes," directed Peter to Ira and Erika. Good idea, as Ira slipped on an exposed root and fell on his butt, no more than 50 feet into the forest. Mosquitoes zeroed in on people and monkeys alike, searching for a blood meal.

"This is no zoo," said Dad, while Venus and Vesuvio suckled furiously, hugging Mom's warm body.

"I've got some news for everybody," said Hera.

Chapter 5

A Room With A View

"We'll go on ahead and get these monkeys to the cage," said Peter to Erika and Ira who were struggling on the steep slippery path. "Follow the little red ribbons tied to the trees, and you'll catch up." Peter and his assistants disappeared silently into the lush forest, and Ira and Erika were left alone, with just the swarms of whining mosquitoes.

"Did he say 'cage'?" asked Dad hopefully.

"There it is," said Hera.

This was a cage like none that these tamarins had ever seen. It was as big as a garage, and 10 feet high. It was surrounded by the forest, and a rocky ledge rose steeply at the back. It had a frame of wood posts and beams, covered by mesh wire. There was an entrance door at the front, and a trap door in the mesh top. The bushes and trees inside had been squeezed in and folded down for the tamarins to climb.

Erika and Ira caught up breathlessly, both now soaked and covered in mud. "Wow, this is amazing!"

Carlos and Alicia grinned proudly as Peter explained how the two had carried in every piece of lumber and roll of wire, and skillfully built the cage while cutting as few trees and branches as possible. He pointed out a trickle of water that tumbled over the rocky ledge. "It's probably not safe for us to drink, but it will be fine for the *micos*, and you can use it for cleaning the bowls and washing."

"*Micos*," said Hercules. "That must be the word for "tamarins" in this new two-legger language. I like it: "we're 'micos' now."

The Cage in the Forest
Photo by Benjamin Beck

Peter and Alicia carried the three boxes into the cage, while Carlos held the door. They opened the doors of the boxes, and retreated. After a minute, Mom put out one arm and put it on the ground, an unfamiliar surface. She rotated her head, cautiously looking up, down and around, softly peeping. A second arm emerged, and then two legs, and she was out.

"All clear," she peeped to Venus and Vesuvio, and they leapt out of the box onto her back, clinging for dear life.

Next came Pandora, then Prometheus, Hercules, and Hera in

strict order of age, each repeating Mom's careful scan, and signaling the OK to the next. Dad came out last.

"This ground feels awful," he said. "I like concrete better". The monkeys climbed the mesh sides of the cage and sat on the horizontal beam that ran around the sides, about five feet off the ground.

Ira and Erika immediately began taking notes about the exit of the micos from the boxes and their initial responses to the new cage. Every 60 seconds, they noted what sort of surface each monkey was using, what it was doing, whether it was moving or still, and which family member he or she was closest to. Carlos and Alicia took three bowls and a bag of fruits from a backpack. Erika carefully cut the bananas into two of the bowls, and added grapes, and pieces of papaya. She went into the cage and hung the bowls on branches inside. She filled the third bowl with fresh water and hung it up too.

Watching that none of the micos would escape, she passed the shipping boxes out of the door to Carlos. Peter said: "We'll clean and disinfect these back at the field station, where we can burn the hay and all of the droppings. We can't risk any chance of spreading American germs to Brazilian animals."

Dad moved close to Mom, and Venus and Vesuvio slid over to his back. "It's good to be out of those boxes," she said, as she tried to figure out how to get to the water bowl." "I'm thirsty and hungry, but how do we get to the bowls?"

"You could jump," said Pandora, "but the branches might break".

"I think I'll just climb down to the ground," thought Mom, "and then climb up that one thick tree trunk. I think I can reach the bowls from there."

"Where are we going to sleep?" asked Dad.

High in one corner of the cage, near the trap door, was a 3-foot section of hollow log. A round hole had been whittled through the bark into the hollow center, and there was a wooden "floor" and "roof".

"I think that log is our 'nest box'," said Hera, already inching toward it on the wooden beam. She stuck her head inside the hole, and then disappeared. Seconds later her head reappeared: "Dry and cozy in here," she twittered, and the others began to check it out.

Dad was unimpressed: "Our wooden box at the zoo was just fine. Why do we need a hollow tree?"

"Listen up," said Hera. "This is obviously not a zoo. When we were waiting in the airport in Washington, I heard the two-leggers talk about *'reintroducing us to the wild.'* I think that means setting us free from cages altogether. I think that's why Erika and Ira were teaching us to search for food while we were in our cage back at the National Zoo. I think that's why they showed us stuffed owls and snakes. And I think that's why we're here. They're going to let us out of this cage soon."

For a few long seconds, only the rainy drizzle and whine of the mosquitoes could be heard.

Then, Pandora, Prometheus, Hercules, and Hera chorused cheerfully: "Cool, we'll be free to go where we want and do whatever we want."

"But what will we eat?" asked Dad, as Venus and Vesuvio slid onto Mom and sought her nipples.

"Don't worry, the forest is loaded with food," chimed the older kids.

"What's this orange stuff?" asked Dad as he stretched from the nest log to a nearby food bowl.

"Papaya," said Prometheus. "At the Zoo, Erika fed it to us whole, with a little window cut into the rind so we could recognize the flesh inside."

"It's really sweet and juicy," said Hercules. "They must have a lot of it here."

"I'll stick to bananas and grapes," said Dad, "and look, we've got the little sticky circles type of bananas here."

"Ouch, these whinerbugs bite and I itch all over," said Pandora, scratching her neck furiously with her hind foot. Suddenly the whole family was scratching.

"Hey, there are ants in the food bowl, and a bird is stealing some bananas," said Dad.

Outside the cage, Carlos was setting up a blue two-person tent in a small cleared area. He quickly made a small table of saplings tied with vines, and made a small bench of leftover lumber.

"It's been a long day," said Ira "and the micos seem to have settled in."

"Let's head back to the field station, get cleaned up, and have some supper," suggested Peter.

They slipped a heavy chain and padlock on the cage door and walked back to the microbus, carrying the reeking shipping boxes.

Chapter 6

Base Camp

The reserve's field station was a converted goat shed that had been abandoned when the reserve was created. Dr. Peter and his team had shoveled out tons of old goat poop, rebuilt the walls and roof, installed some simple plumbing and wiring, dug a septic system, and added a veranda. Fresh, drinkable water was piped from a spring high on the hill behind the station, and a small generator provided just enough electricity to power a few small lights and chargers for two-way radios. A canister of propane fueled a small refrigerator and a stove. Carlos had built some simple storage shelves, chairs, and bunk beds from lumber. He had carved out a huge slab of hardwood from a downed tree for a dining room table, which was to serve for eating, meeting, writing, and examining monkeys (with proper disinfection between functions).

"There's a room with four bunk beds for girls, and another for guys," said Peter, "and there's the bathroom." "Use as little toilet paper as possible and don't flush it down; the septic system can't handle it. Just fold it and put it into the basket next to the toilet. We collect and burn it every morning."

After a moment's hesitation and shoulder shrugging, Erika carried her bags to the girls' room and Ira carried his to the boys'. Erika and Ira were lovers as well as colleagues, but would be sleeping in separate beds in the field station.

Erika's shriek resounded through the house as the first blast of icy spring water hit her. No luxuriating in this shower; it's strictly soap up and rinse off. Today had been cloudy and comfortable, but the evening was cooling off quickly. Erika felt great to be clean and warmed in dry sweat pants and sweat shirt, and thick cotton socks. Ira and Peter followed in order, and the three met at the dining room table. Peter uncorked a bottle of the Argentinean Malbec, surprisingly intense and smooth considering the low price, and sliced some of the smoked provolone onto a plate.

"Here's to a good day," he said, raising his plastic glass.

"Actually, two days for us and the monkeys," said Ira, "but it all went without a serious hitch."

"Where can I wash clothes?" asked Erika.

"Just leave them for Carlos' wife Tina." said Peter. "She'll be happy to have the chance to earn a little extra money. She also cooks and cleans up, and they are saving to buy a house. Right now they are living in an even smaller fixed-up shed next door, with their three-year-old boy."

On cue, Tina appeared with metal pots of steaming rice and bubbling brown beans thick with garlic and bits of bacon. Peter sprinkled an astonishing amount of locally made hot sauce on his beans. "The beans and rice are delicious but need a bit of spicing up."

Erika took a sip of wine and asked: "Is the micos' cage actually in the reserve?"

"Yes, it's right on one edge," answered Peter, gesturing to a faded aerial photo on the wall. "But just over the top of that rocky ledge behind the cage is an old stone quarry. They opened the quarry about ten years ago, when they were building the main highway. They blasted out the rock and then crushed it into gravel. The locals say the noise and vibrations were intense, and dust covered all of the forest and streams. Everything that could walk, crawl, swim, or fly abandoned that whole side of the reserve. It became a biological wasteland."

"But this is a reserve," said Ira.

"The quarry may not have been good for the reserve but the highway was essential for the country's economic development," said Peter. "Fortunately, the quarry is closed now and the forest is recovering. Wildlife seems to be moving back in. We are seeing a lot of birds, and hearing tree frogs. There is a pack of wild pigs called peccaries that is attracted to the ginger plants growing in the swamp near the trailhead, and giant rat-like capybaras are in the swamp too. We wouldn't be surprised to see cougar sign soon."

"What about golden lion tamarins?" asked Erika "Have any wild micos moved in yet?"

"Not that we've seen or heard. That's why your reintroduced group will be so important."

"Let's turn in," said Ira, carrying the dishes to the sink in the kitchen. "We should be at the cage by dawn."

Chapter 7

Settling In

Peter had the water boiling for coffee well before dawn. A Mozart flute concerto played softly from tiny speakers as Erika and Ira came into the kitchen. "Tina left us some hard-boiled eggs, and there's bread, honey, jam, and papayas and bananas. Be sure to pack something for lunch, because Carlos is going to drop you and Alicia off at the cage for the whole day."

Packing food and gear, Ira and Erika went out to the veranda to put on still-wet-from-yesterday boots.

"Be sure to shake out the boots before you put them on," cautioned Peter. "Snakes and spiders like to curl up in warm shoes at night."

"What kind of snakes?" asked Ira.

"The most dangerous is the *fer de lance*," observed Peter as he pounded and shook his boots. "They are not big but they are aggressive and very poisonous."

"What's on your schedule today?" asked Ira.

"Carlos and I are going to set live traps for a group of wild monkeys that we have been trying to follow in the northern part of the reserve. We need to put a radio transmitter on one member of the family so we can find and follow them more easily."

Carlos appeared on cue with a broad smile and a cheery "Good morning." Alicia shoved fruits in her backpack, and the microbus roared off with Carlos at the wheel.

They arrived at the parking pull-off at the first light of dawn, and Alicia led Ira and Erika to the cage. The ginger plants in the swamp were ripped up and crushed. "Peccaries fed here last night," said Alicia.

Nothing stirred at the cage, and Ira's heart sunk. Where were the monkeys? Still asleep? The chain and padlock were still secure, so the three down sat down on Carlos' two-person bench, glad for the shared body heat on this cool morning.

"We'll show you how to start recording data today," said Ira to Alicia, "but for now you can just watch Erika and me."

"Look!" Erika whispered. Two glimmering eyes could be seen in the still-dark recess of the sleeping log. Then an orange head protruded from the hole, and the tamarin began to look around cautiously. Both arms came out, the mico still scanning.

"I'm guessing it's Mom," said Erika to Alicia, "but we won't know for sure until she's out. When the micos had their pre-ship-ment physical exams at the Zoo, we put a distinctive pattern of black circles on each animal's gold tail so we can identify them at a distance."

"How did you do that?" asked Alicia, noting that Ira wrote down the time the first monkey came out.

"With black hair dye and masking tape," said Erika, "and it should last for several months, even with a lot of rain and humidity."

Mom inched over to the wire mesh, just as another head ap-peared at the opening of the nest box. One by one the micos emerged. Dad was last to come out.

As the micos slowly maneuvered to the food bowls, Alicia be-gan to remove their food from her backpack.

"Let's do our food preparation back up the trail where the tam-arins can't see it," said Ira. "Same when we eat. We need to break the tamarins' connection between people and food."

Erika and Alicia took the backpack up the trail, and returned a few minutes later. This time there was only one bowl, and the rest of the food had been stuffed into a dozen little packages made of large folded leaves. The women entered the cage, hung up the bowl, and then, at Erika's direction, wedged the leafy food packages at various places throughout the cage. Erika also wedged a few of the small sweet bananas into different spots. The micos watched intently.

"They need to learn that food does not come in bowls, and is not always found at one and the same place," said Ira. "Another lesson is that food does not come in bite-sized pieces".

One of Erika's Mystery Leaf Packages

Photo by Benjamin Beck

Erika added: "We started this training program at the Zoo, and we have data that show that the tamarins ate less from the bowl and more from these spaced-out mystery packages. Some of them got pretty good at opening whole fruits like bananas and melons too."

"Sitting and waiting for your food to be provided in a particular place at a particular time is a good strategy for little kids and zoo monkeys but it just won't work in the wild," said Ira.

The women rinsed out the water bowl and filled it with fresh water, and then retreated to help Ira with data collection.

The family clustered around the food bowl, gorging on grapes, sliced banana, and (except for Dad) cut papaya.

"Hey, there's not enough food for us all in this bowl," said Mom. "Leave some for your little sister and brother."

But the older kids had found a few whole bananas that Erika had wedged into the cage mesh, and were clumsily pulling them out and peeling them, with big chunks falling to the ground.

Venturing onto a relatively thick branch, Hera ripped into a leafy food packet. Her brothers and sisters gathered around, with the branch bending under the added weight. They fell to the ground and began a vigorous game of chase and wrestle.

"That's a good sign," said Ira. "Stressed animals don't play. They're feeling good."

"We have five categories to describe what kind of surface, or substrate, the monkeys are using," Ira said to Alicia. "There are thick branches and trunks, larger than 5 inches in diameter, relatively thick branches that are 2 to 5 inches in diameter, and thin, flexible branches less than 2 inches across". "Then there are man-made surfaces like the wire mesh and wood frame of the cage and the roof of the nest log, and the fifth type is the ground."

Alicia said "I think I'm getting it: if Hera and Venus are playing on the ground, you'd score them as moving rather than still, playing as the behavior, the ground as the substrate, and Hera would be Venus' closest family member and Venus would be Hera's."

"Exactly" said Ira. "We follow one animal at a time for 10 minutes, making an observation every 60 seconds. Then we follow another animal. Over time, we get a pretty good idea of what they are doing, where, and with whom."

"It's called focal animal sampling," said Erika frostily.

Ira made a mental note to treat both of these very able and smart women with equal attention, at least on the job.

"If you two could take over the data collection, I'll dig a pit latrine," said Ira. He used his machete to cut a narrow path to a spot about 100 feet from the cage. The dense forest would provide total privacy. He made a small clearing, and began to dig with a shovel borrowed from the microbus.

The top eight inches of soil were black and peaty, crisscrossed with dense roots of all thicknesses. He began to sweat as he shaped the three-foot by one-foot ditch. Then he hit a rootless layer of dry red clay, and patiently excavated the ditch to a depth of three feet, standing uncomfortably in the pit itself to finish. He made a pile of excavated dirt at each end, and skewered a roll of toilet paper on a nearby branch.

Then he made use of his new construction, piling just enough dirt on top when he was finished. He returned to the cage and washed his hands in the little waterfall.

Alicia and Erika had become a data collection machine, one observing the focal monkey and one coding the observation on paper. In between, they helped each other with Portuguese and English. Alicia's English was quite good but accented. Erika's Portuguese had been learned in a classroom in Washington, and was not quite appropriate to this situation, where there was little use for asking "Where is the train station?"

The day flew by, sunny, rainless, and relaxed. The monkeys ate and basked and dozed and played. They stretched out luxuriously as other family members picked through their golden hair, removing dry skin, bits of bark and leaf, and the odd fly egg. Erika and Alicia restocked the food bowl and mystery packages in mid-afternoon, and dragged a hollow log into the cage. They scattered food inside the log, and soon the younger micos were running through it.

Sitting atop the log, Pandora stuck her hand under the bark and seemed to be feeling for something. She pulled her hand out abruptly, gripping a small squeaking tree frog. With one chirp, she bit off the frog's head. The others rushed over, sniffing her mouth and the frog's twitching legs protruding from her hand. With a raspy squawk, Vesuvio stared nose-to-nose at Pandora, and she gave the lifeless body to her younger brother. He ran off and ate it greedily.

"Wow," said Mom, "That was impressive. Remember how we used to stick our hands into crevices in the cage at the zoo and catch cockroaches? I guess we just have to learn to stick our hands into different places."

"Wow," said Ira, "Did you see that? We knew they needed meat in their diet as well as fruit."

"We fed them crickets at the zoo," said Erika, "and they also caught cockroaches and ate them."

"How do you code that?" asked Alicia.

"Sticking their hands into crevices and rolled leaves to search for insects and frogs is manipulation of the microenvironment," said Ira. Alicia and Erika rolled their eyes.

"OK, OK, that's too technical. How about 'micromanipulation', which we can code as 'mm'?"

"Works for me," said Alicia.

When they heard Carlos pull into the parking area, they locked the chain on the door of the cage, and trudged up the trail to the waiting microbus.

The boa constrictor lay perfectly camouflaged on dead leaves, a few feet from the cage. Its flicking tongue sampled airborne molecules-of-monkey just as a chef might judge the aroma of lamb shanks braising in a red wine sauce. The two-leggers had no idea.

Micromanipulation
Photo by Benjamin Beck

Chapter 8

When Pigs Fly

It was raining in torrents when two Toyota Land Cruisers sped up to the field station. Jorge, the director of Poço das Antas, and three armed rangers got out and ran for the shelter of the veranda. Peter, Erika, Alicia, and Ira, all freshly showered and changed into dry warm clothes, got up from the dinner table to greet the four sodden officers.

"There are hunters in the reserve," said Jorge. "We've heard gunshots on the other side. We raided a camp with a still-warm fire and the carcass of a dead peccary. Be careful in the forest and don't confront these guys if you meet them."

"Are they sport hunters or out for meat to sell?" asked Peter.

"We don't know yet, and we don't know if they would try to steal your monkeys."

"Come in and have some beans and rice and hot coffee," offered Peter.

Ira caught Erika's glance and said to the group: "I think we should sleep in the tent at the cage tonight. Carlos, can you drive us over?"

Peter nodded to Carlos, and Ira and Erika grabbed ponchos, stuffed their and the micos' breakfast into backpacks, put on still-wet boots (carefully shaking them out), and ran for the microbus.

"With this rain, the road may not be passable in the morning," said Carlos as Erika and Ira got out to begin the walk to the cage in the dark. "We'll get here as soon as we can. Have a good night."

As the sound of the motor receded, Erika said bravely: "OK, we know the trail, our legs are getting stronger, and we have good flashlights."

They walked slowly and silently downhill to the swamp, and

suddenly their world exploded. Screams, squeals, breaking branch-es, gasping breathing, and the strong smell of feces surrounded them. Erika climbed the nearest tree, with Ira pushing her up by the butt. It was over before he could find a tree to climb.

"Peccaries," said Erika. "I recognize the sounds and smell from the time I worked with them in the zoo."

"We must have roused them from sleep," said Ira.

Erika jumped down, and the two hugged, hearts pounding, skin clammy with sweat.

"They have huge, sharp teeth, and can cut each other up quite viciously in a fight," said Erika. "We're lucky they ran rather than stood and fought."

Their pulse actually slowed on the uphill walk to the cage. The chain and lock were secure.

"I'm not walking to the latrine tonight," said Erika. "We'll pee here. Let's hang our ponchos outside, and get into the tent quickly so the mosquitoes don't get in."

She unzipped the door and dove fluidly inside. Ira followed but one of the poles stretching the rain fly got caught in the waist-line in the back of his pants, threatening the whole structure and giving the mosquitoes plenty of time to get in.

"Next time, bend lower" complained Erika. But her crankiness disappeared as they snuggled into the warm sleeping bag.

They overslept, and the micos were already out of the nest tree when they stumbled out of the tent. Using water from their canteens, they brushed their teeth, cat-washed, and dressed. Erika prepared food for the monkeys, putting even less in the bowl and hiding more mystery packages and whole fruits around the cage.

Tearing apart a fallen banana, Hercules and Prometheus, typi-cally for "teen-aged" males, chatted about female anatomy.

"She didn't have a shirt on when she came out of the tent. Did you see that?" observed Hercules.

"Aside from not having much hair, the weirdest thing was that her nursers were on her chest, not in her armpits like Mom's," answered Prometheus.

"Eeyuu, gross!" they said in unison, joined by some of their sisters.

"Enough," said Mom.

Nobody saw the boa, inching toward the cage, tongue flicking rapidly. Inches from Hercules, who was munching a grape that had dropped to the ground, the snake flared its mouth and struck with lightning speed. The micos jumped and fled, chirping loudly but, had it not been for the wire mesh, Hercules would have been the snakes's breakfast.

"Look at the size of that boa," said Ira. "It must be close to 20 feet long and a foot thick." By the time they worked their way around the outside of the cage, the boa, its tiny brain trying to process its first experience with wire mesh, had disappeared into the forest.

"Remember what you said Dad," said Pandora smugly, "We didn't have to worry about predators."

"That thing scares the papaya out of me," said Hercules, still shivering with fear.

"Those stuffed snakes they showed us at the zoo were tiny and didn't lunge," said Prometheus.

All eight micos were hanging on the mesh, chirping loudly, watching the snake slither away. Actually, six hung on to the mesh; Venus and Vesuvio hung on to Mom, sucking vigorously.

"That's the same call we heard when we showed them a stuffed snake at the zoo," observed Ira, scribbling notes furiously. "And right after the first reaction, they all mob around the snake, staying a safe distance away. I'm guessing that's an instinctive reaction, letting everybody know that there is snake danger, and making sure everybody knows where the snake is."

"Great," said Erika, they just have to see the snake before the snake sees them. "

Meanwhile, the boa homed on another unfamiliar smell.

Chapter 9

A Doomed Swamp

Carlos finally picked up Ira and Erika at 5 PM. Alicia was with him. "We had a great day," reported Carlos. "We caught five of the six members of a wild group first thing in the morning. We brought them back to the field station, anesthetized them, weighed and measured them, tattooed them, and marked their tails like you did at the zoo with the Olympia group. We put a radio collar on the adult male and the oldest daughter. They woke up at 3, and were alert so we released them at exactly the same place we had trapped them. The other family member was even waiting for them."

Alicia continued: "We followed them for an hour and they were eating and traveling normally. The radio signal was really clear and made it easy for us to follow them."

"Peter has asked us to meet him at the gate," said Carlos, in a tone that was as gloomy as the thickening clouds.

Peter was in deep conversation with an older man dressed in a clean white shirt, jeans, and rubber knee-high boots. They stood in the swampy wet spot on the road, while bulldozers ground away and chainsaws whined behind them.

As the four walked up, Peter said to the man: "There's a family of about six golden lion tamarins living in this swamp forest. That's about five percent of all of the wild tamarins left in the world! We've seen alligators and orchids in here too."

"I'm going to cut these 60 acres so my cattle will have more prime feeding ground. The monkeys can go into the reserve," said the man.

"They've been trying to go into the reserve but are chased back by other groups who live along the edge. There's no room for them inside. Cutting this forest is a death sentence."

"Tough luck but I own this land legally. You look at this forest and see tamarin heaven. I look at it and see lost money."

Peter said: "I'd like to introduce you to my colleagues Dr. Ira and Erika from the Smithsonian National Zoo in Washington D.C. They are here to reintroduce zoo-born tamarins to the wild, on the other side of the reserve. Ira, Erika, this is Senhor Paulo, who owns all of the ranchland from here out to the main highway. He is cutting this last patch of forest."

"Nice to meet you," said Ira and Erika, sensing that it would be wise to remain spectators in this fast-moving and fluent Portuguese conversation.

"DOC-TOR Peter," said Senhor Paulo, in a voice both respectful and acidic. "I think you care more about your monkeys than you care about people. These cows provide jobs for the poor people who care for them, milk them, process and ship the milk, clean the barns – you get the idea."

"But this forest is protected," Peter protested.

"Nonsense, it's clearly outside the reserve."

"But swamp forest is legally protected even outside a reserve."

"Look around you. What swamp? There's hardly any water in it today. Thousands of acres of swamp forest have been cut around here, and nobody has ever told us to stop."

Peter sighed, and shook hands with Senhor Paulo. "I guess I can't change your mind."

"OK, OK," said Paulo. I'll give you until dawn tomorrow to move the tamarin family out of the forest. You are free to work in there tonight."

The bulldozers and chainsaws stopped, just as the skies opened with torrential rain. The first trickle of water rose over the road as the team got into the microbus and headed for the field station.

Chapter 10

To The Rescue

"Field Station to Headquarters," Peter said urgently over the two-way radio.

"Headquarters, Go ahead Field Station," squawked the reply.

"I need to speak to Jorge. Is he still there?"

"Hi Peter, Jorge here. What's up?"

"Senhor Paulo is cutting that small patch of swamp forest outside the gate, and has given us a chance to rescue the tamarin family that lives there."

"Great, I'll join you in the morning to help."

"It's got to be tonight. Can you round up a few rangers to help?"

"It's technically outside the reserve, so I can't bring rangers, but I'll drive right over and help on my own time."

"10-4, thanks. We'll meet you there in an hour," said Peter.

"Carlos, tie the ladder to the top of the bus, and get our saw," said Peter. "Alicia, round up all of the charged flashlights, and sharpen everybody's machetes. Get us a piece of wire mesh, and a small roll of wire and a pliers."

"Ira and Erika, you're going to have to help. It's raining like mad but fill all of the canteens because this will be hot work. Most important, I want you two to figure out how to get six sleeping tamarins out of a tree nest when we get back."

Thirty minutes later, the five had the equipment packed and were driving toward the gate. They sat silently, thinking of the tasks ahead. It was now pitch black outside. The only sounds were the whine of the bus' engine and the pounding of rain on the vehicle's flat roof.

Jorge had opened the gate and was waiting. "Park the bus here. The swamp is already too high for you to cross. I can make it in the Land Cruiser though."

"OK, here's the plan," said Peter, with his usual calmness and clarity. "We've been following these micos and know where they usually nest for the night; we'll just have to assume they are inside the same hollow tree, about 10 feet up. Ira and Jorge will carry the ladder and put it up against the tree."

"I'll climb the ladder," he continued, "and put the piece of mesh over the hole".

"Alicia, you climb the ladder after me and hand me some cut pieces of wire. I'll loop them around the trunk, and secure the mesh. That will keep the micos from escaping."

"We'll climb down, and Carlos will climb up with the saw and cut off the top of the tree, above the hole. This will be dangerous because we don't know where it will fall."

"Then we'll cut the tree at chest height, catching it as it falls. This will be critical since the swamp is likely to be filled with water and the micos could drown if we drop the tree."

"Erika, your job is to protect the micos. Once that tree is cut, stay as near to the hole as you can, and stop us if we are doing anything that could hurt them."

"Oh, and one more thing – there is a bee hive in the tree trunk, below the spot where the micos sleep. Let's hope they're sleeping too."

"Might as well leave our ponchos. They'll just get snagged," said Carlos.

They stepped out into the black torrent. The flashlights were almost useless.

Peter, Carlos, and Erika went ahead. Erika gave Ira a 'Well-I-guess-this-was-what-we wanted-to-do-with-our-lives' shrug, before she strode into the water, which was now hip-deep. Before long they all were sharing the swamp with alligators, snakes and whatever else they could imagine. Everybody kept their thoughts, and whatever fears they had, to themselves.

Peter and Carlos led the party, their well-sharpened machetes making a barely audible "*ting*" each time they trimmed a branch. Jorge (speaking Portuguese and poor English) took one end of the heavy 16-foot wooden ladder, and Ira (speaking English and poor Portuguese) took the other. Alicia held a light and tried to translate over the deafening rain. They stumbled heavily, tripping on submerged, invisible logs, roots, and vines. Each bend in the trail was a challenge for Jorge and Ira, because the long wooden ladder did not bend. One or the other would have to stop, back up and move off the trail to get around a turn. Sometimes they had to back up ten feet and find a detour, away from the path. The noise of the rain and the language difference challenged Alicia's translation skills, but they finally caught up to Peter, Carlos, and Erika at the base of the nest tree, now in three feet of water.

With nearly wordless cooperation, the plan went without a hitch, and they were headed back to the bus in 30 minutes. Jorge wanted to leave the ladder, but fearing it would be bulldozed in the morning, Peter asked them to bring it out. Jorge, Ira, and Alicia did an encore of the ladder circus.

Jorge returned to reserve headquarters, the Toyota's wheels now nearly covered in rushing water as he crossed a low spot on the road.

The inside of the microbus was a sauna, thanks to the hot night, rain-sodden clothes, and perspiring bodies. Carlos wiped the inside of the windshield with a towel as Peter drove. There wasn't even a peep from the section of the nest tree that lay atop the seatbacks.

Once at the field station, Erika's and Ira's extraction plan began. They moved the nest tree section into the tiny supply closet, which was the only escape-proof place in the house. The log was too long to lay on the floor, so Peter and Carlos began by cutting off the bottom of the log, working by candlelight in the stuffy little room.

They emerged after a few minutes, carrying the lower cut portion and smiling inexplicably.

Erika and Ira went in, shutting the door securely behind them. Erika removed the mesh from the entrance hole, and Ira picked up the now-four-foot section of log and shook it. Three sleepy tamarins tumbled out, stunned and blinking even in the dim light. Erika grabbed two with bare hands. Ira held out two small cubical wire mesh "live traps," and she put one mico in each. He snapped the traps' doors securely, and grabbed the third, who was now sitting on a shelf next to a box of laundry soap. This time Erika held the trap.

"These three look OK but there are supposed to be six," said Ira. "The others must be holding on inside." Ira began to fish around inside the log, his arm in above the elbow, looking much like a tamarin "micromanipulating" for a frog. He felt a head, and worked his fingers down over the mico's shoulders and grasped it under the arms, around its chest. His hand, holding the tamarin, barely fit through the entrance hole, but soon the fourth was securely in a mesh trap.

Groping blindly, he found a fifth monkey. This time the catch did not go smoothly. Ira yelped and extracted his hand with the muscle between thumb and forefinger bleeding profusely.

"That little sucker nailed me."

"So what's new," thought Erika smugly. She deftly extracted the fifth monkey and slipped it into a trap.

There was no sixth mico. They probed and shook the log, and peered inside with a flashlight.

"Only five," they announced as they opened the closet door and entered the kitchen where the rest of the crew waited, sipping coffee.

Chapter 11
A Second Chance

The dining room table was covered in newspapers. Equipment was neatly laid out, and the generator hummed outside, powering one overhead bulb and a single electric outlet.

Peter had been carefully trained by the zoo's veterinarians to administer a tranquilizing drug to the micos and monitor their post-injection condition and recovery.

He injected the first tamarin, and within two minutes, it was sleeping peacefully in the mesh trap.

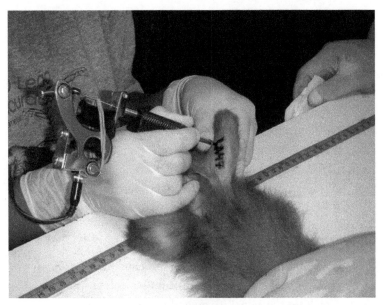

Tattooing a Mico's Leg
Photo by Benjamin Beck

Ira, his hand now bandaged, took the tamarin out of the trap. Erika weighed it: "557 grams." Alicia took notes on a form specially designed to record the results of tamarin "processing," as they called it. Peter took the mico from Erika, and examined it closely: "Female. Probably about 18 months old, not the breeding female because her nipples are small." He dictated a variety of body measurements and observations that Alicia carefully noted, and then shaved the inside of the mico's right thigh with an old-fashioned straight razor. He plugged in a tattoo pen and asked, as it buzzed to life: "What shall we call her?"

"How about 'Swamp 3', saving Swamp 1 and 2 for the adult female and male?"

Peter carefully penned an "S" and a "3", dipping the tip of the pen in ink and retracing the lines several times. He wiped the area with alcohol and observed his work.

"That's permanent," he said.

After Swamp 3 got her tattoo, Peter began to fit her with a small radio transmitter. The transmitter itself hung on a thin bead chain that he clamped around her neck, checking carefully that it was not so tight that it would obstruct breathing or so loose that it would fall off.

"As a young adult, she's likely to be leaving the group soon. This way we will be able to follow her as she searches for a mate," Peter said, ever the patient teacher. "The collar weighs 26 grams, so it's less than 5% of her body weight, which is our criterion. She's almost full grown, so it's unlikely that the collar will get any tighter."

"Check the signal Alicia," he said. "We wouldn't want to find out tomorrow that it's a dud."

"How far will the signal travel?" asked Erika.

"Up to 500 meters, depending on terrain and the density of vegetation," explained Peter. "You could be only 50 meters away and not pick up the signal if you and the monkey are on opposite sides of a hill, but you could pick it up at 500 meters if you and the monkey are on opposite sides of a valley."

Mico with a Radiocollar

Photo by Andressa Sales Coelho

"How long will the battery in the transmitter last?"

"Four months, if we're lucky."

Alicia turned on the shoebox-size radio receiver and unfolded the antenna. The loud "beep-beep-beep" confirmed that everything was working.

The tattoo, while permanent, would not often be visible to a field observer, so they stretched out the mico's tail, and made a one-inch circle half way between the base and the tip of the tail with a black long-lasting hair dye.

"Think of the tamarins' long tails as being divided into quarters. The base is "1," the tip is "5," with "2" and "3" and "4" spaced at one-quarter, one half, and three-quarters of the length," Ira said.

"Suppose there are more than five monkeys in a group?" asked Alicia.

"We can make more than one ring, and can have for example a '1 and 5' for the sixth," Erika answered.

Swamp 3 was given a shot of antibiotics, and was put back into her live trap, which Carlos had cleaned and bedded with hay in the meantime. Processing continued. Swamp 1, the group's adult female, looked suspiciously pudgy, leading Peter to think she might be pregnant. Swamp 4, a male that from his weight was probably Swamp 3's twin, also got a collar. Swamp 5 and 6, both females between eight and twelve months old, were too light to be collared.

It was now clear that it was the adult male, the mate and the father, who was missing.

It was 11 PM by the time the group was processed, the table cleared, the equipment sterilized in alcohol, and the monkeys carefully placed in a quiet corner, their traps covered by clean newspapers.

The biologists took hasty cold showers, which actually felt refreshing but did little for aching legs, and ate cold beans and rice that Tina had set out. There were even a few cool beers.

Everybody thought quietly about the missing male, and how this would affect the family's survival, especially if babies were on the way.

They checked the monkeys at midnight, relieved that they had recovered from the tranquilizing drug. Then micos and the people all crashed thankfully for a few hours of toasty sleep.

Peter's rousing call bouncing off the little house's concrete walls awakened everybody at 5AM. There was little conversation as coffee was brewed, and some cheese, bread, honey and jam were set out. Small sweet bananas were provided for people and monkeys alike. The monkeys peeled and ate them eagerly, peeping softly to ensure contact with their family.

"M'mmmm, this honey is good," purred Erika. "It reminds me of the wild honey my grandmother used to collect in Germany."

Peter and Carlos looked at each other conspirationally. Peter confessed: "It's a good thing the bees were asleep too."

Ira and Erika retreated to the supply closet to reverse last night's extraction. One by one, each trap was opened and its monkey shooed back into the log by gently blowing on it.

When all five had been returned into their familiar nest log, Ira repositioned the wire mesh over the hole. Carlos nailed a little roof on the top to keep it rainproof.

At dawn, the crew left the field station, carrying the log and a sack of bananas.

"We're headed for that ridge on the other side of the swamp," said Peter. "For some reason tamarin groups rarely visit the area."

The rain had slowed, but the path downhill from the field station was slick. The creek in the valley at the bottom was swollen into a dirty, slow-moving lake.

"Carlos built a bamboo bridge across this stream a few months ago. It's submerged now, but you can feel it with your feet," said Peter, as he and Carlos started across confidently, each carrying one end of the 4-foot nest log. One slip, and the monkeys would drown in the deep water.

Ira carried a few live traps, strapped to his back like a pack, just in case, and Erika carried tools and a role of wire.

The "bridge" was two stems of bamboo, lashed to bamboo uprights that had been sunk in the mud. It was 6 inches at its widest, and none too steady. Ira walked sideways, taking tiny steps with his boots planted crossways on the bamboo. Capybaras splashed into the water nearby, startling everybody.

The sun was rising and actually warm as they climbed the hill on the other side, stopping at a splendid tall tree that stuck out above all the others, what botanists call an "emergent tree". Its trunk was 3 feet thick, and wrapped in vines that made it easier for Carlos to climb. There was no ladder this morning.

First he drove a nail into the tree, about 12 feet above the ground. Then he carried the nest log up, and hung it on the nail with a hook he had screwed into the "roof" last night. Alicia handed him pre-cut lengths of wire, and he secured the log to the tree.

"All set?" Carlos asked.

Peter was checking the radios. "Both frequencies work. The signal is loud, because we're close, and the volume is constant because they are not moving. When they are moving, the loudness of the signal changes, because they pass behind trees as they move."

In a few decades, radiotelemetry would become GPS-based and would transmit location information to a satellite and be downloaded later. But this was 1984, and their equipment was state-of-the-art for the time.

"Go," said Peter. Carlos removed the mesh from the hole, and climbed down. Within minutes, the group had emerged and the micos were moving rapidly into the forest looking for food.

"Alicia and I will follow them for a while," said Peter. "Carlos can take you back to the Olympians."

"It's really cool to save them from certain death. At least they have a chance now," said Ira, looking back across the misty valley at the field station.

Chapter 12
Plastic Monkeys

Peter and Alicia caught up with Ira and Erika at the Olympia group's cage at noon.

"The Swamp group look like they lived there all of their life," said Peter. "We maintained contact most of the time, and saw them micromanipulating (the term had caught on) and eating fruit. They were long-calling regularly, indicating that they were staking out a territory."

"Maybe they were looking for Swamp 2," added Alicia.

"They finally settled in for a mid-day rest, grooming and snoozing in the sun," said Peter. "How are things here?"

"They all seem fine, eating well, playing, and looking healthy. No drippy eyes or snotty noses," Ira reported.

Just then, Dad caught a huge cricket on the ground. "This is almost as good as the crickets they fed us at the zoo."

"How did you find it?" asked Mom.

"Easy. I just came down to the ground for a piece of banana and the cricket jumped right in front of me," said Dad.

"Look at that," said Erika. "Even Dad is starting to hunt."

"But in the wrong place," said Peter. "The ground is a dangerous place for a tamarin," he added, and they all recalled the experience with the boa.

"Well, they are eating almost nothing from bowls any more, and they've learned to find and open Erika's mystery packages and whole fruits," said Ira proudly. "They're searching for food all over the cage, rather than waiting for it in one place."

Peter dropped a bomb: "Ira, these are plastic monkeys. Nothing they are doing resembles a wild mico."

Ira looked at Peter as if he had hit him in the head with a board. Anger welled in his throat, and then he felt sad and embarrassed. "What do you mean?" Ira said.

"Look there," said Peter. "Four of them are sitting on the wooden frame of the cage, two are on the roof of the nest log, and two are on the ground. Nobody is using natural vegetation! Prometheus - is that the young adult's name? – just walked on the cage mesh from one side of the cage all the way around to the other side, a good 30 feet, to get a banana, when he could have reached it with a few jumps through the bushes."

"They're spending too much time on the ground, and too much time resting. They aren't long-calling either, which suggests to me that they lack confidence and ownership of the territory," continued Peter.

Ira and Erika were utterly deflated. They had worked for three months to train these tamarins and prepare them for life in the wild, and the world's expert on wild tamarins had just called them "plastic monkeys."

"I don't mean to hurt your feelings," said Peter, "but realities are realities."

With that, Peter, Carlos, and Alicia headed back to the microbus. "We'll pick you up at 4."

When the three were gone Erika and Ira hugged tightly and sought encouragement from each other.

"Erika and Ira do a lot of mouth-sniffing," said Hercules, "and they're not even eating."

Since monkeys and apes don't cry, the micos had no explanation for the tears that welled in the two-leggers' eyes.

Chapter 13
Swamp 2

The atmosphere at the field station was chilly, in more ways than one, as the team took cold showers and cleaned up. Any feeling of triumph at the successful relocation of the Swamp group had been replaced by Peter's sobering assessment of the Olympians.

"We need some cheering up, and some beer to celebrate," said Peter. "Let's pile into the bus and drive to the highway. There's a new Brazilian barbeque just up the road."

The five field workers, plus Tina, and John Wayne, Tina's and Carlos' adorable three year-old son, loved the idea. Tina's beans and rice were returned to the fridge, and Erika and Alicia combed out their hair and put on lipstick. Erika even slipped into a fancier plum-colored REI field shirt. Alicia's shoulder-length black hair gleamed. She grew up in a large family in a small nearby town, and had rarely eaten in restaurants.

They headed for the highway as the sun was setting. The long call wafted over them as Ira locked the reserve gate. Peter picked up his binoculars, which were always with him, and zoomed in on the calling mico.

"I'll bet it's him," said Peter, not having to add "Swamp 2."

There, on the freshly sawn stump of a tree at the edge of the former swamp, sat the forlorn monkey, desperately calling for his family.

"It's too late to try to trap him tonight," said Peter. "He'll be hungry in the morning and will go into a trap quickly."

Brazilian barbeque is all about meat: spicy sausages, chicken thighs, slabs of beef sirloin, fatty short ribs, pork tenderloin, smoked turkey breast, and many other choices, all strongly seasoned, grilled over charcoal, and served sizzling on spits carried around by bustling waiters carrying razor-sharp Tramontina carving knives.

"If you want more of anything, just signal the waiter. It's all-you-can-eat so don't be shy. The salad is well washed too, so tank up on veggies at the salad bar."

"So, how did John Wayne get his name?" asked Erika, between bites of what would become her favorite: grilled beef from the big hump on the back of Brazilian bulls.

Tina and Carlos grinned at each other. "Too many reruns of American westerns on TV at the time, but John Wayne is not a bad role model, is he?"

"He's one of my favorites," said Erika as she helped JW cut up a piece of chicken.

Full of food and beer, everybody but Peter slept in the bus on the way home. Swamp 2 huddled under a fallen branch, and was disturbed by the microbus as it passed in the dark. For all concerned, tomorrow would be a big day.

Chapter 14

Family Reunion

Peter and Carlos drove off at dawn, with six live traps, some bananas, and a thermos of sweet hot coffee.

Erika and Ira made use of the unaccustomed early morning leisure to repack, organize the data they had collected on the Olympia group, and eat a real breakfast of fried eggs and toast. Alicia charged batteries and sharpened machetes, and Tina straightened out the house and washed clothes. John Wayne tottered around, getting in everybody's way, and repeating "mico, mico, mico."

A Trap For Catching and Moving Micos.
Here, Young Twins Cling to Their Father
Photo by Benjamin Beck

"We've been here for six months and haven't really seen a mico," said Tina. "He loves the chickens, and the lizards that cling to the walls, so I think he'd be thrilled to see micos."

"We have to take him over to see the Olympians," said Erika.

The sound of the returning microbus brought every body out to the veranda. Sure enough, Carlos emerged with a mico in a live trap.

"He fell fast for a banana," said Peter. "He only ate one, so I think we can take a chance on sedating him for processing."

In minutes, the monkey had an "S2" tattoo and a tail ring one-quarter of the way from the base to the tip, both sharp and black.

"Can't spare another collar," said Peter. "The group has two already."

Swamp 2 was awake in his live trap and eating by noon.

"Let's see where the group is," said Peter, taking the receiver to the front of the station and aiming the antenna across the valley. The beeps were loud and steady. "They're near the nest tree. Let's move."

The rickety bridge in the valley was above water now, but Ira was still very slow in crossing.

All five members of the group greeted them on arrival at the tree, calling and chirping excitedly. Swamp 4 was walking back and forth on a horizontal branch, with stiffened legs and a conspicuously arched back.

"Uh-oh," said Erika. "That's called arch-walking and it's an aggressive behavior. I don't think he's so happy to see his father."

Carlos opened the trap and Swamp 2 rushed out and up toward the family.

The fight was fast, vicious, and decisive. Within seconds, Swamp 4 was wobbling on the ground, blood seeping from a slash in his right cheek. All of the tamarins were squealing and running around in the tree, in fear and excitement. Soon, the victorious Swamp 2 stretched out on a limb and Swamp 1 began to groom him intensely.

"People caused this," said Erika, "so we should treat his wounds."

"Nope," said Peter. "This is a natural process. He'll have to make it on his own. "

"She's right," said Ira. "He had no chance to run away, to avoid the fight, because of the disruptions we humans caused."

"OK," said Peter. "If the monkeys get hurt due to human action, we can step in but we'll not be shooing off a stalking predator."

Taking that as a decision, Erika scooped Swamp 4 into the little trap and headed off to the field station.

Chapter 15

Bonding

Peter and Ira followed, leaving Carlos and Alicia to monitor the Swamp group. They hastily converted the dining room table to a treatment area, and Peter immobilized Swamp 4 with a skillful injection.

"It looks bad but I've seen monkeys recover from worse," said Ira, gently dabbing the wound with antiseptic. "He's got a few other punctures and scratches, but we don't have to take him to the vet. That gash will heal without stitches. Let's just clean up the wounds, and give him a shot of antibiotics."

The three sat down with cups of coffee after they put Swamp 4 into a live trap to recover, and cleaned off the table.

"What now?" asked Peter.

"He clearly can't go back to the Swamp group," answered Erika, "and I'm not sure turning him loose alone would be wise."

"Pandora will soon be kicked out of Olympians by Mom," said Ira. "She's about the same age as this guy, and it's a great opportunity to mix wild and zoo genes. They're both already marked and collared so we can monitor them easily."

"What makes you think they'll get along?" asked Peter.

Erika answered confidently: "In zoos, if we put a young adult male and an unfamiliar young adult female together, they always bond quickly. You probably just haven't had an opportunity to see this yet in the wild, but I'm sure it will work."

"How do we do it?" asked Peter.

"Could Carlos build another cage like the Olympians', but smaller, out there?" Ira asked, pointing to a grove of promising young banana trees that they had planted between the field station and Carlos' and Tina's little house.

"Sure, we have some leftover wood and wire mesh from the Olympians' cage," said Peter, warming to the idea. "They'll come in for lunch soon, and I'll ask him to start right away."

"We'll drive over to Olys and open the traps," said Ira, referring to more of the little live traps that had already been placed inside the cage to accustom the family to going in them. Erika had wired the spring-loaded doors so they would not snap closed, and she would now only have to remove the wires and put fresh bananas in the traps.

"If all goes well, we'll be back with Pandora by mid-afternoon. Should we also catch and process another one or two to put on collars for the Olympia release?"

"I only have two collars for the Olympians," said Peter. "We'll be using one for Pandora so we can only collar one of the Olympia family. How about the breeding male?"

Ira looked at Erika, and she nodded agreement. Dad was to wear the family collar.

Swamp 4 awakened in his little trap, which had been covered with newspaper and placed on the floor in one corner of the veranda. He began to munch on a piece of pineapple and a small sweet banana, watching the feet of people as they walked in and out.

By 4 PM, Carlos had the cage built and Alicia had furnished it with branches and vines, and even a bowl-shaped wild plant known as a bromeliad, which catches water and attracts frogs and insects. Wild tamarins often search for food and water in bromeliads. Carlos found the short piece of hollow log from which the bee nest had recently been extracted, enlarged the entrance hole, and hammered on a roof and floor to make a nest log for the micos.

Alicia entered the cage with Swamp 4 in the trap, and let him loose. He went to the top, a little scared and disoriented. She quickly backed through the cage door, and the team retreated to watch from a distance.

Swamp 4 slowly explored the cage and the nest log, and ate a few more bananas. Then, looking across the valley to his family's nest tree, he began to make long calls. Tamarins use their loud and melodic long calls to advertise their location, keep contact with other group members, and warn off other tamarin groups.

The five micos on the other side immediately began to long-call in return.

"Let's hope they don't come over here and start a ruckus," said Peter.

Ira and Erika rolled in and proudly took out Pandora and Dad, each in a live trap.

"They were hungry and fell quickly," said Erika. "How is Swamp 4?"

"Probably a little sore but he's sassy," said Peter.

"What are we waiting for? Let's process these two, and then pair up Pandora and Swamp 4," said Ira.

The anesthesia went smoothly, and the radios were attached and functioning well by evening, but the two micos had to be given time to recover completely. It was too late in the evening to take Dad back to Olympians and introduce Pandora to Swamp 4.

Erika and Ira awoke early the next morning and returned Dad to the family. Erika fed the micos, and the two returned to the field station while the family admired Dad's new piece of jewelry.

"That is very impressive," said Mom. "The two-leggers must think you're very important. I wish I had one." She had no idea how badly she would need one.

"They put one on Pandora too," Dad said, "but they kept her at their house."

After a quick breakfast, they took Pandora to Swamp 4's new cage in the banana grove. Spotting John Wayne on the veranda, Erika called him over to watch. He toddled over, took his father's hand and watched wide-eyed as Erika freed Pandora into the newly built cage.

The two micos stared at each other, she from the ground and he from the top of the cage. He arch-walked for two steps, and then relaxed. They met in the middle and smelled each other's mouths.

"What happened to your face?" asked Pandora. No answer.

"The two-leggers call me Pandora. What do they call you?" Silence.

"What zoo are you from?" she asked. He munched a banana and then stretched out on a branch in the mid-morning sun, inviting her to groom him.

A strong new feeling welled up in her, and she began to groom him with care and enthusiasm like never before. She took special care to pick specks of dried blood from his face.

"Does it hurt much?" she asked. He lolled, wordlessly.

Then he sat up and long-called across the valley. She knew the meaning of long calls, and when responses came from the other side, she joined Swamp 4. She felt a growing sense of allegiance to this wounded and quiet young male.

Then it hit her: "He's not quiet when it comes to long calls," she thought. "Maybe he doesn't know any of the two-leggers' language."

The thoughts came rapidly: "Why would he know only tamarin calls?" "Oh, maybe he's not from a zoo – maybe he's a *wild* mico." She stunned herself with this new idea.

John Wayne giggled wildly while the grown-ups looked on with pride and accomplishment.

Just then, Swamp 4 entered the nest log and Pandora eagerly followed. Their radio collars could be heard bumping against the inside of the wooden log, and then there was total silence. The day had passed quickly and the sun began to set across the valley. Parrots flew noisily overhead, returning from feeding grounds to their night roosting site.

"Let's have a glass of wine," suggested Ira.

Chapter 16

Dr. Kay

She always arrived like a hurricane; even if you expected her, you were never fully prepared.

"Pee TER", Eye RA", she trilled loudly from the veranda. The two men got up from the table and walked into the storm.

"Hi Kay." They took turns embracing and cheek-kissing her in the exaggerated Brazilian way. Jorge, who had picked her up at the airport early in the morning, stood back, smiling.

"Do you have any coffee? I couldn't sleep on the plane and I'm not even tired now."

Tina, forewarned, gave her a cup of strong unsweetened black coffee. Kay thanked her in Portuguese. People loved Kay for her willingness to use the language of whatever country she was in, despite a lack of fluency.

"How are things at the zoo?" asked Ira.

"Well, they're still looking for a new director, and I'm really getting tired of being acting director," she replied.

Ira knew they had offered her the permanent directorship several times, but she declined because she wanted to get back to doing research and working closely with scientists and animals. She was first and foremost an ethologist, a scientist who studies animal behavior, and was really good at it too. In the meantime, she was his boss, and Erika's and Peter's as well.

"Kay, let me introduce you to Alicia," said Ira. "She's been helping us and already knows the data-collection system."

"It's nice to meet you, Alicia," said Kay warmly.

While Kay took her bags to the bunkroom and freshened up,

Ira provided a little background for Alicia. "Kay is not only a top-flight scientist but she's a visionary and natural leader too. She's gotten zoos to collaborate on the tamarin breeding program, and has worked with Dr. Cardoso to start the conservation program here in Brazil."

"She's tough and blunt but charming and kind. She is so convincing that she could sell mittens to a giraffe (this Alicia did not understand). She'll respect you and your opinion as long as you're open, honest and hard working. I know you two will get along well together, and you'll learn a lot from her."

Ira knew from experience that you could enjoy great personal and professional benefit as long as you stayed close to the eye of hurricane Kay, but you'd get blown away and sunk if you got too far out.

"So how is the field work going?" Kay asked Peter.

"We've been able to identify six different groups, at least 37 micos in all. We've only been able to capture and process one wild group, and we've got a collar on the breeding male."

"Plus the Swamp group," added Ira. Peter gave Kay a quick account of the rescue and relocation.

"It's amazing Kay," Peter went on. "In zoos you found that a group had only one fully adult breeding male and one female; we're seeing that here too. You discovered that males carry babies; we're seeing that too. You found that they sleep in boxes; here they sleep in tree holes or in dense vine tangles. Your zoo nutritionists found that they needed meat protein, and fed them crickets and baby mice; here they catch crickets and frogs. As artificial as a zoo environment is, zoo tamarins behave pretty naturally."

"Are they territorial?" Kay asked.

"Still collecting data but they seem to be. Groups do a lot of calling and chasing when they meet. Looks like each group defends a territory of about 50 hectares."

Turning to Ira, Kay asked: "And how is the Olympia group doing?"

Ira and Peter exchanged quick glances, and Ira replied: "Pretty well. No sign of illness, and the animals have settled in and are eating well. They are getting better and better at finding food all over the cage, and opening whole fruit. They are catching and eating crickets and frogs. We had a close call with a huge boa – Hercules was saved by the cage but the group responded normally."

"But they seem to be walking too much on the ground, and the wood frame of the cage and the nest log. When they do go on the natural branches in the cage, it's usually just the thick ones," Ira added, a bit defensively.

With scientific directness, Peter added: "Kay, this is the only big difference between zoo and wild tamarins that I've seen. They are not confident and skilled when moving on branches, and pretty much avoid thin, flexible branches altogether."

"Not too surprising," added Ira, "given that in zoos we build cage furniture out of two-by-fours for them."

"I want to see them for myself," Kay responded. "Let me change into field clothes."

Within minutes she emerged, wearing spotlessly clean, crisp field clothes that she had worn over two decades on three other continents. She wore her machete and snakebite kit more like Prada accessories than tools.

As they pulled out of the field station, Alicia pointed out Swamp 4 and Pandora in the banana grove, and filled her in on that adventure.

Erika and Alicia quickly stocked the Olympians' cage with food packets and whole bananas. The hungry micos tore into them.

"Who's the new two-legger?" asked Venus.

"That's Dr. Kay, the boss of the zoo. You're too young to know her but without Dr. Kay, we wouldn't even be here," said Hera. "At the zoo I heard the monkey keepers saying that she figured out that our species needs to live in pairs or family groups, not in large groups with a lot of males and a lot of females, like those other big ugly monkeys at the zoo."

Dr. Kay was indeed responsible for the remarkable success of zoo tamarins in the past 20 years, countering the male-dominated world of zoo directors and curators who thought that the social lives of all monkeys were pretty much like that of baboons. But adult female tamarins fought with other adult females, and adult males fought with other males. "Once placed in pairs, with just one adult female and one adult male, the fighting ends and infants are born," she wrote in a prestigious journal. Zoos everywhere followed her advice, and the population had grown from 40 to nearly 400. The increase was especially fast because golden lion tamarins typically have twins.

She had also found that fathers begin to carry infants when they are a few weeks old, and provide much of their first solid food. Most of the twins survive when the father helps the mother raise them in this way. Further, when the twins become juveniles and young adults, they also help to raise younger brothers and sisters. Pandora and Prometheus had carried and given food to Hera and Hercules, and all four were helping with Venus and Vesuvio.

"Dr. Kay had a lot to do with our coming here, too," said Hera. "She and Dr Cardoso cooperated to begin a conservation program for tamarins in the wild, and we're part of that."

"Well, that may all be true," said Dad, "but I'd be perfectly happy at the zoo. Besides, she may be brilliant, but she rubs me the wrong way."

"You *rubbed* with her?" exclaimed Prometheus.

"Can't you think about anything else?" said Mom. "It's just a two-legger expression."

Prometheus and until yesterday Pandora were indeed having a hard time thinking about anything but their social future. At 18 months of age, they were maturing into young adults. Pandora had already "found" a mate, and none too soon. Mom had recently been hissing and threatening Pandora at the food bowl, and there would have been a battle royal if Pandora had not been removed. Dad would soon try to evict Prometheus.

After about ten minutes of focused, wordless observation, Kay said: "I can see their progress on feeding, and their locomotion deficiencies. Let's get back to the field station and make a plan."

Chapter 17
Kay's Decisions

They ate lunch on the veranda. Peter squeezed and sweetened fresh passion fruit juice, and managed to find a few ice cubes in the little fridge.

"So, what are we waiting for with them?" Kay asked, pointing to Swamp 4 and Pandora.

"We need to find a section of forest with no other wild tamarins," said Peter. Ira added: "And we need to make sure that his wound heals."

"Today is Sunday. Let's plan on releasing them on Wednesday if he's OK. Can Carlos find a place in the next two days?" asked Kay, who had clearly reached a decision but was leaving enough space for disagreement.

"Ira, what's the plan for the Olympians?" asked Kay, moving to the next topic.

"I think their locomotion will improve in a month or so."

"Why do you say that?"

"I've been looking at the data. At first they were on the ground in 30% of our observations, on the wood frame and wire mesh in 65%, and on thick branches in 4%. But by yesterday they were spending about 25% on the ground, 50% on wood and wire, 20% on thick branches, and 5% on thin branches. They are making progress."

"Those differences could be random. You don't have much data yet, and if it is a real trend you don't know if it will continue."

"This is the same sort of behavior change that we saw when the micos started to eat from food packages rather than fixed food bowls," answered Ira.

Erika knew to stay out of the scientific conversation. Alicia, having been raised in a large family where disagreements were not openly aired, moved just her eyes to Kay, Peter, or Ira, whomever was speaking. "Stay close to the hurricane's eye," she was recalling.

Changing direction, Kay said: "Ira, we can't spare you from the zoo for another month. We need you to work with other zoos to get some younger gorillas and orangutans so we can get some reproduction going; we need babies. And, the board has accepted your plan for a tropical forest exhibit and you need to lead the planning team."

"Same for you, Erika," she went on. "We've been paying overtime for other keepers to cover for you in the monkey section, but money is tight."

"The zoo is totally behind our work here in Brazil but they are paying us for our work in Washington, so you need to get back. From what I see, Alicia will be able to cover things here. Peter's post-doctoral fellowship is good for another year, so he'll be here to keep an eye on things."

Alicia was overjoyed by Kay's vote of confidence, but more than a little worried by the responsibility. Ira, Erika, and Peter all nodded to express their confidence in this part of Kay's decision. But Ira and Erika, at least, were not happy about the timing.

"So let's plan to release the Olympians later this week. You two can stay for a week afterward to see how things go."

Ira said: "OK, we can monitor the micos and provide food and support after they are out of the cage. Alicia can continue after we leave."

"How long do you plan to feed them?" Kay asked.

"Until they are clearly able to find enough food for themselves, maybe months," said Ira.

"But if we feed them, they won't be motivated to move around and find food. They'll stay near the cage and wait for bananas," said Kay.

"If we are going to reintroduce monkeys to the wild, then we have to let them go," added Peter.

"But the process has to be gradual," said Ira, sensing that Kay and Peter had already discussed this.

"Ira, you are used to the total control and responsibility we have for animals in zoos, but this is different. You just have to let go. Stop playing God." said Kay, with a definite air of finality.

Peter brought out a bottle of the sugar-based, clear, high-octane alcohol known as *cachaça* ("kaSHAHsah"), so favored by Brazilians. He poured a shot into everybody's glass of passion fruit juice. This concoction is known as a *batida* ("baCHEEda"), which means "crash" in Portuguese. The first glass eased the tension. Ira, fearing for the monkeys, continued the conversation.

"So you want us to do a 'hard release'; food for just a day or two and then hands-off. If a monkey gets lost and separated from the group, we don't bring it back. If it gets sick or hurt, we don't take it to the vet. And if it's starving, we just take data?" asked Ira contentiously.

"We don't have the time or enough people to do a soft release," answered Peter, "and if we are ever going to reintroduce enough zoo-born monkeys to save this species here in the wild, we have to streamline the process."

The seriousness of the topic was no match for the power of the alcohol, and tempers began to flare. The "crash" was underway. Alicia decided to catch a ride to the highway with a passing ranger patrol, and then take the bus to town to spend the night with her family.

Finally, Ira said to Erika: "Let's head to the tent for a night." The peccary explosion didn't even startle them this time, and Erika wasn't even very concerned about mosquitoes in the tent.

Chapter 18

Honeymoon

Erika was in a rage. "I fell in love with you because you cared about animals. And now you're going to release these tamarins to the wild without any support. Their lives are in your hands. They trust you and depend on you, and you just caved in to a decision for a hard release. It'll be do or die for them, and I'm afraid it will be more 'die' than 'do'."

"But I made the case as strongly as I could, and you have to admit they have a point. Beside, Kay is my boss."

"No, ultimately you are responsible for what you do," said Erika, ending the conversation by rolling over in the sleeping bag with her back toward Ira and falling to sleep.

Ira's eyes opened at 5:30, just before dawn. His head hurt from the drinks, and yesterday's conversations ran through his mind. How would he dig himself out of this hole? The answer of course, as always, is to get up, face the day, and get on with it.

Erika struggled out of the tent a few minutes later, sad and sullen. She brushed her teeth and washed her face without even looking at Ira, who was taking two granola bars out of his backpack.

"I grabbed a thermos of coffee and two cups when we left the field station last night. It's still warm," he said handing her a cup.

She managed a weak smile, which he took as an opening.

"This is not personal you know. Kay and Peter believe in us, and they like us. They care about the monkeys and the success of this project just as much as we do, but they have a different perspective. We can't prove that our perspective is more realistic," said Ira.

"You scientists. I can't prove I'm right but I know I am. I *know* monkeys, and these monkeys are not ready to be released," answered Erika.

"If you have some new thoughts, I'll go back to them but otherwise there is no sense in rehashing old arguments. But I think we should add a new type of observation, which we'll call 'Fall': when a mico slips and loses its grip, even partially, while walking on natural vegetation, we'll score a 'Fall'. This will give us a way to express locomotion problems and measure improvements."

Ira and Erika made up with a morning kiss and a warm embrace.

"They're mouth sniffing again," said Hercules, "and they haven't even eaten that cookie bread yet. A long time too."

"Feed the monkeys," said Ira. "We have to get the microbus back to the field station. Somebody can drive us back here and we'll take data today."

Kay and Peter were having coffee as they pulled up at the field station. Peter said: "Good news. We may have a place to release Swamp 4 and Pandora. Alicia saw her brother last night. He works on a big ranch on the south edge of the reserve that has about 75 hectares of swamp and hilltop forest. The owner remembers when micos lived there, and he'd like to have them there again."

Swamp 4 and Pandora both recognized the little live traps that Alicia put in their cage, but they were so hungry for bananas that they went in and got caught.

"Uh-oh," said Pandora as the traps snapped shut. "Something is going to happen." Swamp 4 only chirped a contact call.

Sure enough, Alicia took the traps from the cage and put them in the bus. Carlos grabbed the nest log, and they all set off for the Rio Vermelho ranch.

"We have to drive all the way around," said Peter, "because there is no crossing over the river that divides the reserve from the ranch. Actually there is no *vehicle* crossing. The river is usually narrow, so micos can cross where the boughs of trees touch or where logs fall across."

They pulled up at an old house, built in the 300 year-old Portuguese colonial style. Once magnificent, the house was showing its age but was still impressive. Senhor Mauricio, the owner, met them as they pulled up. He was deeply tanned, in his mid-70s, thin as a nail and just as hard.

Alicia handled the introductions, and the housemaid brought out cups of thick sweet coffee. Carlos set off into the forest.

Peter explained the project in fluent Portuguese, and Mauricio nodded positively. He said he would like to have tamarins on his land. He asked if he could bring family and friends to see them, and Peter agreed, as long as they did not feed them.

Then Peter added: "You'll have to agree not to cut any trees in the forest, or allow hunting there, or allow your cows to graze in there."

Mauricio held out his hand and the two shook in agreement. Cups were drained and the six conservationists went to work.

Ira and Erika shooed the two micos into the nest log in the confines of the bus, and secured the mesh over the hole. Ira got his finger too close to the mesh of the trap, and Pandora bit him squarely through the nail of his index finger. "Ouch!" he grunted.

"Got him again," thought Pandora.

As the team walked through the forest, everybody stayed well away from Kay, who swung her machete with wild enthusiasm. There was really no need, since Carlos had already cut a fine path, just the size of a doorway.

Carlos gave directions on the two-way radio, and they found him high on the hillside under a magnificent tree. Carlos had chosen this tree because he believed that micos liked to survey their surroundings from the highest point. He was waiting when the team arrived with the nest log, wire, pliers, hammer, and a sack of bananas.

"This is a wonderful spot," said Kay. "Is that the reserve across the swamp down there?"

"Yes," answered Peter, "but we haven't surveyed for micos there yet."

Carlos climbed the tree, and as Peter handed the nest box up to him, Pandora said: "There's no cage here. Are they going to set us free?"

No answer from Swamp 4, but she did not really expect one. She was mostly thinking out loud now.

Carlos removed the mesh cover, and Swamp 4 was out and gone before Carlos' boots hit the ground. Alicia followed him with the radio receiver.

Pandora exited cautiously, but could hear Swamp 4 chirping softly, high in a nearby tree. She tried to join him, but climbing was hard for her. She detoured to find thick branches, got lost, and had to stop and listen for him. She tried to walk on some thinner branches, but kept slipping and falling.

"See the 'Falls'?" Ira whispered to Erika.

Finally, she got close enough to Swamp 4 to see that he was eating small purple fruits. She realized she was surrounded by them, and gave one a try. "Not bad. Juicy but a little sour," she said to herself. She crunched on a pit. She looked over at Swamp 4 to see if he was swallowing the pit or spitting it out. Definitely spitting it out, so she did too. She was just getting into a feeding groove when Swamp 4 sped off in a series of lightning-fast runs and jumps.

"Hey Swamfor, wait up," she called, mangling his name (she did not speak English as well as Hera). She struggled to follow, and caught up to him again. Her arms and legs were aching with exertion, and she was higher above the ground than she had ever been in her life, by far. Swamp 4 was now eating slightly larger brown fruits. She tried one. These had small seeds, and she copied Swamp 4 by swallowing them. This fruit was less juicy but sweeter.

Just as she started eating these, he took off again, this time going down a tree trunk and disappearing into a huge bromeliad plant. She followed, guided by a single loud chirp of the type made by a mico finding a tasty frog or insect. She looked down into the bowl formed by the spiky leaves, and saw a mass of spider webs, with water at the bottom. Swamp 4 was searching deliberately through the bowl. He grabbed for a cricket that escaped but flew up and hit her in the chin. Without thinking, she grabbed it, chirped, and bit its head off. Swamp 4 approached and she handed him the bug's body. He chomped it down noisily. "Good teamwork, Swamfor," she said.

Swamp 4 lapped up some water from the bottom of the bromeliad, and Pandora did likewise. He climbed out of the bromeliad and took off.

She followed, catching up to him as he chirped loudly at a small green snake. He grabbed the snake with blinding speed, bit off its head, and began to swallow it, with quick chewing motions. The snake disappeared into his mouth like a piece of spaghetti. He did not offer to share it, but she didn't care.

"I wish I could tell the family about *that*," she thought.

Swamp 4 then stretched out on a thick branch, inviting her to groom him. She complied. "He's OK," she thought. "I can learn a lot by watching him, and he seems to wait for me. I'd sure be in trouble without him."

Patters of rain grew into a downpour. Swamp 4 climbed to the very top of a large tree, where vines grew in a thick tangle. She followed, her climbing skills improving quickly. He disappeared into the vines. She followed and was surprised to find a dry spot. They sat side by side and fell asleep, contented.

The team below folded up the antenna of their radio receiver, stowed their note pads, and headed back to the bus. Ira's finger was really sore and the nail was turning purple.

Chapter 19
Baby Bump

"So what does Mauricio get for letting us work on his land?" asked Erika as the bus bounced toward the highway.

Alicia answered quickly: "He's rich and lives in Rio. He can afford to allow some forest to remain on his ranch. He really wants to see some of Brazil's lost plants and animals restored, and he'll get a lot of prestige by bringing his wealthy friends and business partners to see 'his' micos on weekends."

"That's a win-win," said Kay, "and the word will spread among some influential people."

After showers and lunch, the group sat in the shade of the veranda. Kay said: "Well we're ahead of schedule with Pandora and Swamp 4, thanks to Alicia's finding a good place to release them. Peter, can you and Alicia check on them for the next few days?" Peter nodded in agreement.

She went on: "We're set to release Olympians on Friday morning. Cardoso will be here; after all, reintroduction was his idea to begin with. And there will be media coverage - network TV crews and the two national newspapers."

Ira's chest tightened. "Don't you think that's risky, having lots of people tromping around in the forest, scaring the monkeys and getting in our way?"

"Remember, one of our goals is to make the public aware of the need to conserve the environment, and this is a golden opportunity. People will lap it up – a family of adorable monkeys coming home to Brazil."

Erika's eyes were riveted on Ira, but he knew the conversation was closed. "Erika and I will spend the next few days and nights at the cage, taking data, making sure the micos are well fed and healthy, and trimming trails. We'll pack enough food for ourselves and the monkeys, and you can drop us off. I'm going to radio Jorge and ask permission to make a small campfire so we can make coffee and heat up food."

An hour later, Alicia was driving them to the drop-off point. "Did Jorge OK the fire?" she asked.

"Yes, as long as we keep it small and well-contained."

Erika unconsciously rubbed a bump on her head, and then wondered where she had hit it.

Alicia said: "I can see the tension about the release. I want you two to know that I agree that the Olympians need some more time, and they will need lots of support when they leave the cage. But I don't have the expertise to join the discussion, so I'm keeping my mouth shut. I'll do the best I can to help."

"Thanks Alicia. That means a lot, and you're doing the right thing. Keep an eye on Pandora for us over the next few days, OK?"

Alicia helped Ira and Erika carry all the supplies to the tent. "I'll feed the micos and take some data while you're putting everything away." she said. "It's too bad we don't have an extra radio to leave here."

At 5 PM, Ira settled in to take data on the micos as they went into the nest log for the night. Alicia headed back to the bus. "See you at 9 on Friday."

Erika and Ira were now totally alone, which is what they wanted but it was nonetheless a little scary. The buzzing cicadas and madly chirping frogs reminded them that they were strangers in this place.

After the micos had settled in, Ira found enough dry wood to start a small fire, and produced a gallon jug of cheap Brazilian red table wine. "I asked Alicia to pick up some wine on her way back to the field station yesterday, and this is all they had at the gas station," he said, as he poured the wine into tin cups. "Cheers. This is our dream come true." They hugged and sipped: "We'll it's not merlot but it'll do," Erika said of the thin and overly sweet wine.

"I must have bumped my head somewhere," she added. "I've got a swollen sore spot up here."

They warmed up some beans and rice that Tina had packed, had another cup of wine, and prepared for bed. Once again Ira snagged a tent pole with his shorts as he entered the tent, admitting a swarm of mosquitoes and threatening to tip the whole thing over. "Can't you keep your butt down?" Erika said, exasperated.

It was only 8 PM, and they couldn't sleep. Erika's head hurt, and Ira was going over plans. Finally they dropped off.

A cougar's "caterwaul" starts as a loud, fearsome snarl that glides into a mournful moan, interspersed with raspy breaths. It woke them both, and they snapped up, wide-eyed.

"That's a mountain lion," said Ira, "and it's close. It's more interested in the peccaries than us, and it sounds like it's looking for a mate."

"Thanks Einstein, that's a big comfort." But the pain from the bump on her head overrode even the fears of a prowling mountain lion.

The night passed slowly. They slept fitfully. By dawn Erika, usually very tough, was hurting badly. "Can you look at my head? I don't think this is a bruise, and it really hurts."

"Sure, when the light is better. Let's wash up and take some data on the micos waking up. I'll put some water on for coffee."

He was immersed in data collection when Erika sat down on the bench beside him. Tears were welling in her eyes. She was sobbing and shaking with pain. Something *was* seriously wrong, and Ira's attention leapt from micos to Erika's head.

"Bend your head down and let me take a look." He gingerly parted her fine blond hair and found a reddened bump. "Looks like a spider bite."

Then, the bump *moved*!

"Crap," said Ira to himself. He carefully took Erika's pulse: 64 per minute. Then he counted the movements of the bump: 34 per minute. The movements could not be caused by blood flowing in her scalp.

Ira had taken a course at the Smithsonian Institution called "First Aid for Scientists Working in Remote Locations." He had learned how to temporarily patch puncture wounds in the chest, which the instructor said was the most common injury to field scientists, caused by falling on cut bamboo or tree saplings. He had learned how to temporarily stabilize broken limbs. He carried a fairly well stocked first aid kit. But he was stumped by a moving bump in a scalp.

"What is it?" Erika asked, grimacing in pain.

"Not sure, but it's not a bite. I'm thinking."

He looked carefully at the bump with a small magnifying glass, and then saw clearly the moving shape: a maggot!

Maggots are a stage in the life of a fly. A female fly lays her eggs, usually on a dead animal or feces. The eggs develop into creamy, wingless, inch-long creatures called larvae, which feed on the carcass. They keep feeding until they turn into adult flies. Erika probably had a scratch on her head from a thorn or branch, and a fly, in this case probably a botfly, laid an egg in the wound. A scab had formed over the egg, the wound healed, and the egg hatched into a larva, growing the whole time on a diet of *her flesh*. The rhythmic movements under the skin were made by the larva as it munched.

Erika was literally giving birth to a flesh-eating insect!

"I think you have an abscess," Ira said, sparing her the most gruesome part of the story.

"What can we do?" Erika asked. "I'm in agony."

"We can wait a day or two until it swells so much that it bursts open by itself. The pain will get worse, and there is a chance the infection could spread." Ira knew that the larva would ultimately eat its way out of Erika's skin.

"We can get you to a doctor but it's a two and a half-hour walk to the field station, and then at least another two hours to a clinic. More pain, made worse by the walking."

It would be 20 years before everybody working in the forest would be carrying cell phones. But now, Ira was thinking, they were only 120 kilometers from one of the biggest, most modern cities in the world but they might as well be on the moon. Going into the forest without a radio had been a huge mistake.

"Or, I could lance it right here. The outer skin on your scalp has hair follicles but not too many arteries and nerves. If the abscess is just beneath the outer skin, we should be able to open it without too much pain or bleeding." Since he could see the maggot so clearly, he was hopeful it was just beneath the outer layer of skin. If it weren't there, he'd have to stop.

"Do it," she said.

"Here, take two aspirin. That's all I've got for pain, except for some ointment that I'll put on later. Sit down on the bench."

He draped a towel over her shoulders, and wiped the area around the bump gently with alcohol wipes. He clipped her hair around the bump with the small scissors on his Swiss Army knife, took a single-edged razor blade from his kit, wiped it with alcohol, and gently shaved the area. Erika winced from the pain caused by even this slight pressure.

He picked a stick from the fire, blew on its end, and held first the blade and then a tweezers against the glowing wood. He laid the sterilized tools carefully on the towel on her shoulder, and wrapped them with alcohol wipes. He kissed her and wiped the tears from her eyes.

He wiped the baby bump with alcohol and squeezed some lidocaine ointment on it; this would kill some of the pain.

Show time. Ignoring the perspiration that stung his eyes and the mosquitoes that swarmed around them, he made a small cut in the bump. Erika yelped in pain, and the beast popped halfway out. He removed it with the tweezers, flung it away, and clamped an alcohol wipe on the cut. Another yelp.

A bird swooped down and snatched the bloody maggot from the ground. The maggot was now the munched.

"The pain is gone, all gone, just like that," Erika said, smiling up at Ira. He cleaned the area again, put on some antibiotic cream and a gauze pad. There wasn't much bleeding but lots of seepage came from the wound.

"Keep your hat on," Ira said, "and keep sitting up to minimize bleeding." As soon as the abscess had drained and the pressure had been relieved, the pain had gone away. "Now we just have to keep it clean and disinfected."

Chapter 20

The Not-So-Great Escape

The afternoon and the next few days were idyllic. Erika's head was healing quickly, with Ira cradling her and dressing her wound several times. The weather was sunny, with a slight breeze, which kept the mosquitoes away. Ira cleaned up Carlos' network of trails for 500 meters around the cage, to make it easier to follow the micos after they were released. He carried a jar, and caught crickets for the micos as he worked. He was hoping to see the huge boa again, but it did not show itself. He did find the cougar's claw marks in a tree trunk, visual advertisement of its presence, just 100 meters from their tent. For a while he just walked the trails slowly, taken in by the sheer beauty of the forest; he called this "tree-bathing", after a Japanese expression.

The micos played, and eagerly tackled any mystery food package that Erika was able to devise. "It's nice to have these two-leggers around all the time," said Dad. "I still don't like that papaya but the crickets are great."

Venus broke off a piece of vine and wrapped it around her neck, copying Dad's radiocollar. Soon Hercules, Venus and Vesuvio were also wearing "collars", just like Dad's. Mom and Prometheus felt it was too juvenile, and felt sure that Dad's collar was more than a decoration but of course they didn't know how.

Hercules observed Ira and Erika carefully: "There they go again - mouth sniffing."

Ira and Erika were happy and affectionate but they worked hard, taking pages of data, including falls and near falls when the monkeys were on natural vegetation.

On Thursday morning, Ira poured the last of the wine into a canteen, rinsed the empty wine bottle, filled it with clean water from the spring, and set it in the sun.

"Look," Ira said over breakfast. "The group as a whole has gone from 2.1 falls per hour to 1.1 in just a week, and most of the falls are by Dad. But, they are still spending 70% of their time on the ground and on wood and wire."

As dusk settled and they documented the group's entrance into the nest log, Ira said to Erika: "Well, tomorrow is the big day. I think we're ready, but I'm still not sure about the monkeys."

"I'm not ready," Erika grumbled. "We're having guests and media tomorrow, and I haven't showered or washed my hair in three days."

"Come over here and drop those grungy clothes," Ira said. Seven micos came out of the nest log and seven pairs of eyes watched Erika remove her "skin".

"There's those nursers......," said Prometheus, but he was cut off by Mom: "Don't say another word!"

Ira climbed into a low tree and began trickling water, warmed by the sun, from the wine bottle over Erika's head.

"Not only a shower, but a warm shower, the first in weeks," she said gratefully. She luxuriated, soaping up and washing her hair. He smiled: "From this aerial view, I can see that your hair is even growing in but you'll probably want to keep wearing a hat for a while."

Ira used cold water from the spring for his shower. They both changed into their last clean sets of field clothes, and settled on the bench with tin cups of wine.

The show over, the micos snuck back to their nest log, unobserved.

Ira made grilled cheese sandwiches over an open fire. Despite his best effort to keep his butt down, he repeated the tent-tipping, mosquito-inviting entrance as they settled in for the night. Erika, resigned, just sprayed the tent with repellant. Ira wondered whether it was legal to kill mosquitoes in a biological reserve.

They rose at dawn and decided to skip early-morning data collection. Erika provided lots of mystery packets of cut fruits, and two bunches of small bananas for the micos. Ira made coffee, and warmed leftover cheese sandwiches.

"We want them to be as full as possible when we release them. It will take them some time to find food in the forest," she said.

"It's silly but I feel like a coach, and want to give the team a motivational talk before the big game," mused Ira.

Peter, Alicia, Kay and Carlos arrived at about 8AM, dressed in spotless, crisp field clothes. Kay sported a lovely purple silk neck scarf that did not look a bit out of place. Carlos went to the reserve gate to meet the visitors, and soon cars and vans were pulling up to the trailhead.

Informed by radio, Peter, Kay, and Ira went up to meet Dr. Cardoso. He was beaming, and walked the trail with the agility and strength of a young man. For nearly five decades he had explored the Amazon and Atlantic Coastal rainforests, and identified hundreds of new species of plants and animals. Golden lion tamarins were among his favorites, and in the 1960s he had appealed to Brazil's government leaders to create the Poço das Antas Reserve. Their support reflected his international stature as a scientist. But the reserve was not adequately protected, and Cardoso had documented the steady loss of forest to illegal cattle grazing and tree cutting. He also documented that this loss of habitat, combined with poaching tamarins for the local and international pet trade, had reduced their numbers to about 200 – they hung on by the slenderest of threads.

Cardoso knew that even with renewed protection, human management would be required if their numbers were to grow. New forest would have to be planted, and tamarins from zoos would have to be reintroduced. He and Dr. Kay had met at a scientific conference in the 1970s, and formed the collaboration that had led to this day, the very first reintroduction of zoo-born golden lion tamarins to the wild. (He had not yet heard the Pandora story).

Two crews from national TV stations clumsily hauled their cameras and sound equipment down the trail to the cage, slipping, swearing, and swatting mosquitoes. The newspaper reporters were less encumbered but just as uncomfortable in the steamy forest. The micos obliged them by clinging to the cage wire for dozens of pictures and unlimited minutes of filming.

Dr. Kay and Dr. Cardoso retold the story of their collaboration at least five times, and she added material on the global environmental crisis, animal extinctions, and the role of zoos in environmental conservation. She struggled with Portuguese, which made her more sincere and credible. Cardoso was fluent and suave. They made a great team, and would win many Brazilian hearts and minds as the story hit the news. Peter, in his excellent Portuguese, introduced the Olympia group and Ira and Erika, and told the story of the group's zoo origin, preparation and travel.

Off camera, Alicia gave Ira and Erika some really good news: "We've checked on Pandora and Swamp 4 several times in the past three days. They are staying together. His face is healing, and she seems to be able to keep up with him. I decided to count how many times I saw her lose her balance and fall or almost fall," she went on, "and there's a definite decrease." Ira looked at Erika, both appreciating just how smart this young woman was.

"Today's plan is simple," Peter told the group: "We are going to open the trap door on top of the cage. We expect the micos to leave the cage quickly, and move into the forest, staying together as a family. The adult male, the father, has a radio transmitter built into a neck collar, and we will be able to follow his signal. There is a network of trails around this cage, so we can move easily through the forest. We'll follow them until they find a sleeping place tonight."

Hera listened to all of this raptly, and translated for her family: "This is it. They are going to release us into the forest today. We'll be free!"

"I'm not leaving," said Dad. "Why should we go? We have food, a cozy nest log, and protection from that big snake."

"But it's still just like living in a zoo," protested Prometheus. "I'd like to be really free, and find a mate and start a family of my own."

Venus and Vesuvio struggled to find a nipple but Mom denied them. "You're too old for that now."

She went on: "We each have to make a choice now. I'm sticking with Dad. If you kids decide to go, be sure to keep an eye on your brothers and sisters."

Peter showed the gaggle of reporters and photographers the trail to the latrine, and invited them to get comfortable before the release. Their response, especially the grimace on the really cute evening news anchor, made it clear that they would be heading back to Rio as soon as possible.

At 9AM sharp, Carlos pulled on a rope that opened the trap door on the top of the cage. None of the micos even looked up. Ira and Erika took data on their behavior, and opening the door seemed to have no effect. Everybody waited, sweated and swatted. Actually, Peter never swatted mosquitoes because the sound and movement scared wild animals. Showing incredible self-control, he would firmly pinch each mosquito as it bit him.

At 9:48, Hera climbed up the cage mesh and, hanging upside down, crept to the trap door and eased herself over the sill. This would go down in science as the second reintroduction of a zoo-born tamarin (Pandora had been the first), although none of the conservationists dispelled the media folk's assumption that today's was the very first. The story had to be electrifying and uncompli-cated to get popular attention. Of course, if asked they would have told the whole Pandora truth.

Hera's twin brother Hercules was next to exit, at 10:01, rock-eting past Hera and climbing a thick tree that grew just at the side of the cage. He climbed until he came to its first big branch, where he stopped, looking down and all around.

"This is amazing," he called down to his family.

Venus and Vesuvio were clinging to Prometheus, and thus hitch-hiked into the wild as Prometheus exited and joined his younger brother a few minutes later. Hera climbed up to the branch too, and the kids all sat together, wide-eyed with excitement.

"Dad, Mom, you've got to see this."

Energized by freedom, Prometheus actually long-called. "I wonder if there are any other micos around?" he mused.

The scientists and the media folk were delighted with these developments, and lenses zoomed in for close-ups of the kids in the trees. None of them, of course, knew what the micos were saying to each other. The micos learned and used some English words, which they could use with each other, just like humans could pick up some tamarin calls. Peter and Alicia were excellent long-callers, at least to other humans' ears, but they didn't fool the monkeys.

The cute news anchor asked Dr. Kay: "What are they thinking?"

"We have no way to know scientifically," she answered, regretting her answer immediately. She was absolutely correct, but the TV audiences wanted something more endearing.

Mumbling about deadlines and the long drive back to Rio, the journalists began packing up and walking up the trail, looking forward to their air-conditioned, mosquito-free offices and studios (and bathrooms). Kay, Peter and Carlos left as well.

As they left, Ira asked: "Is it OK with you if we give them some bananas?"

"Sure, for a day or two," answered Kay.

Ira, Erika, and Alicia embraced in celebration, as the last sounds of vehicles faded with distance, and the tree frog calls and the barely-audible, continuous chorus of buzzing mosquitoes once again became the dominant sounds.

"Dad, that looks like fun," said Mom. "Let's go up and join them."

"No way," said Dad. "That's a long fall."

"Well, I'm going, just for a few minutes."

Venus and Vesuvio were especially happy to see her, but Mom once again spurned their attempts to nurse. She had decided that their infancy was officially over.

The group rested together. Mom was groomed by everybody. Hercules began a game of tag-and-wrestle with Venus and Vesuvio, running out and back on the branch and up and down on the trunk. Hercules disappeared around the far side of the trunk.

"Wow, look at this." He had found a tree hole. Tree holes are formed when a branch breaks off at the trunk, and rainwater seeps into and softens the center of the trunk. Sometimes, woodpeckers excavate big holes too.

Mom peered down. "Don't just charge in there," she warned. "Who knows what's living in there?"

Hercules peered in, and entered cautiously. Venus and Vesuvio charged in after him, and they were lucky this time. The hole was empty.

Hera and Prometheus even joined the game, and the five ran up and down the tree and in and out of the hole for two hours.

"Not much stress here," Ira observed.

Mom rejoined Dad in the cage, and the others followed. They were hungry, and tore into the bananas.

"That was so cool," said Hercules.

"What are you going to do if the two-leggers stop giving us bananas?" Dad asked him.

Late in the afternoon, Prometheus climbed out of the cage, up to the newly discovered tree hole. As dusk settled, he climbed in. Alicia asked: "Is he going to sleep there tonight, by himself?"

"Let's see."

In the last minute of failing light, Prometheus changed his mind — maybe lost his nerve — and ran down to join the family in the nest log in the cage.

Carlos picked up the three weary scientists and they joined Drs.

Peter, Cardoso and Kay at the field station. Peter had taken Kay and Cardoso to visit the translocated Swamp group, across from the field station in the afternoon, and found the group healthy and together. They actually had a territorial dispute with a neighboring group, mostly calling, chasing, and arch-walking, and seemed to have successfully carved out a territory.

Peter had bought a young pig from an itinerant herder who sometimes grazed his flock at the edge of the reserve. It was running with juices and a spicy rub as it roasted over an open fire, and beer, wine, and passion fruit *batidas* were already flowing.

Ira and Erika showered, changed, and joined the celebration, reminding each other to stay close to the eye and not to drink too much. In the old Brazilian style, the men carried sheath knives and carved the grilled meat directly off the spitted pig. They gallantly filled plates for the women before taking some for themselves. Dr. Kay and Erika both, independently, swore silently that they would never again attend a Brazilian barbeque without their own sheath knife.

Chapter 21

The Taste of Freedom

Carlos took Erika, Alicia, and Ira to the Olympia group at dawn, returned to the field station, and brought Dr. Kay and Peter at 8. Dr. Cardoso had returned to Rio after last night's supper, high on the heady combination of success, self-fulfillment, good colleagueship, and good food.

The team of scientists was woefully underworked on day 2. *Nothing* remarkable happened. The Olympians simply repeated their behavior of yesterday afternoon, from dawn to dusk. They did go a few meters higher in the big tree, but that was it. Clearly their expectations about life in the wild were not the same as Kay's and Peter's. Ira and Erika were satisfied, because things were still under control.

Dr. Kay paced impatiently, waiting for the micos to move into the forest. Without discussing it with anybody else, she hung some bananas about 10 meters from the cage to lure them out. She drank coffee that they had brought in a thermos, ate pistachio nuts that she had brought from the States, and even smoked a cigarette.

Finally, just after noon, she said: "Peter, let's take down the cage."

"Are you kidding?" asked Ira, already sensing that she was not. "They need some more time. They are beginning to leave the cage on their own."

"They use the same tree, over and over," Kay responded. "It's not even one meter from the cage. They are using only the trunk and the thick branches. They've not hunted for the frogs and crickets that are surely hiding in dead leaves on the narrow branches. They've not gone to the very top of the tree where there are fruits growing in the sunlight. They go back to the cage to eat and sleep."

"They are gaining strength and agility and confidence. They'll start to move when they are ready," said Ira.

Erika, Alicia, Carlos, and even Peter watched this discussion without participating.

"They won't move until they have to," said Kay, "and now they have no reason. When we take down the cage, they'll have a reason."

"Now who's playing God?" Ira thought, but wisely decided not to say.

"I'm going to drive back to the field station for lunch, and then go to the highway to make some calls," Kay said. "I'll be back at 2. In the meantime, I'd appreciate everybody helping Carlos to remove the mesh." With that, Kay walked off. End of discussion.

"Dad, explain this she-rubs-me-the-wrong-way thing," said Prometheus. "Is there a right way and a wrong way to rub?"

Carlos climbed to the top of the cage and began prying up the nails that fastened the wire to the frame. He was careful to save all of the nails. Within an hour he was handing rolls of mesh down to the others. The whole top of the cage was open.

Then he took off the door, and began to remove the mesh from the sides. Erika and Ira continued to collect data on the group's behavior, which was easy because they stayed in the nest log, frightened by the ruckus. Peter and Alicia carried the rolls of wire up to the trailhead.

Kay returned at 2, as promised. "Look at this," she said, waving a copy of Saturday's *O Globo* national newspaper. There, on the front page of the Arts and Leisure section of the weekend edition were pictures of Hera leaving the cage ("The first monkey ever to be reintroduced to the wild", the article said), and the five youngsters up in the tree. There were also pictures of Drs. Cardoso and Kay, with lots of quotes.

Ira was a bit put out to see his and Erika's names buried near the bottom of the article, but said: "This is fantastic. You sure succeeded in getting the message out."

"They should have put it on the front, front page, with the real news," Kay said testily, "not in the third section as if this were some sort of movie premiere."

"OK," she went on, "Where do we stand here? I saw the wire stacked by the road."

"Only two sides left to take off," said Peter.

"That's good for now. Let's stop the racket, step back, and see what they do. I brought some meat pies and Cokes for lunch for everybody."

They moved up the trail and ate hungrily. Peter wished he had some hot sauce. Ira produced a bottle of the fiery sauce from the last of their food supplies at the tent.

About an hour later, Mom came out of the nest log as usual but without her typical caution. She climbed up the one of the remaining mesh sides, walked on the top wood beam of the cage to what used to be its rear side, and jumped to the rock face behind it. Without looking back, she began to climb up the cliff, jumping from ledge to ledge, sometimes even climbing on small trees that had managed to take root in the rocks.

"Mom, wait!" called the kids but she moved up as steadily as the little spring-fed waterfall tumbled down.

"Where on Earth is she headed?" said Erika.

"She looks disoriented to me," said Ira.

"She's been reintroduced," said Kay.

Peter and Carlos tried to follow but the cliff was too steep and slippery to climb safely.

Mom stayed on the ground, but climbed up the entire cliff, higher than she had been in the tree, and disappeared from sight.

"Any higher, and she'll go over the top into the old quarry," said Peter, "and that ain't great tamarin habitat. Carlos, let's drive around to the quarry and see if we can find her."

The five kids rushed up their big tree and called for Mom to turn back. Prometheus long-called and long-called, but there was no reply.

"I'm scared," said Vesuvio.

"Stick with us and you'll be OK," answered Hera, but the truth was she was scared too. The two infants climbed on to Prometheus, who tolerated their extra weight.

"Dad, are you OK?" Hera yelled down.

"Yes, but I can't believe Mom took off like that. It's not like her at all." He was on the ground, working his way around the two sides of still-attached standing wire mesh. A cricket jumped in front of him, and he caught it. Ira made a note.

With that, Dad became a cricket-catching machine, hopping along on the ground and catching the insects. Venus and Vesuvio came to the ground and begged for some crickets. Dad willingly shared, but otherwise seemed oblivious to his family.

Dad kept moving away from the cage. Venus and Vesuvio looked at him, and then at Prometheus, Hercules, and Hera, who were resting up in the tree. They climbed up to their brothers and sister.

As the evening approached, Dad, now full with crickets, looked for a water bowl. He was thirsty and tired. He looked for the nest log but was several hundred meters away. He could hear Prometheus' occasional long calls, but could not figure out how to move toward him. Mosquitoes buzzed around him, biting him on his face. He panicked.

Thoughts and visions of bowls of fruit and water, and Mom and the rest of his family whirled through his brain.

"Whinerbugs......thirsty........Mom........sleepy." Then he saw a hole in the ground. He had no idea that it had been made by an armadillo, a small, long-clawed, insect-eating animal. He was looking at an armadillo burrow, and was too exhausted and inexperienced to recognize that the fresh spider web over the entrance indicated that the hole had not been used lately. He charged in, and fell asleep instantly.

"I lost Dad's signal," said Alicia. Should I go look for him?

"Sure", said Kay, "but keep your radio on."

Peter and Carlos returned soon thereafter, with no news of Mom. "There are very few trees in the quarry but we still couldn't see her. We walked all around the edge, but she's just disappeared."

Prometheus was long-calling but there was no reply from Mom or Dad. "We'd better get to the nest log," Prometheus said to his younger brothers and sisters.

"Not much more we can do here," said Kay. "Call Alicia in, and let's get back to the field station."

After welcome showers and a change of clothes, the group gathered on the veranda for a beer.

There was little to celebrate. Mom and Dad were both missing, and Ira and Erika were angry and concerned that Kay had so suddenly ordered the cage torn down.

Kay began: "Let's dismantle the rest of the cage and pull the nest log in the morning. I've changed my flight to midnight tonight. Jorge is going to pick me up in a few minutes and take me to the airport."

"Ira, you and Erika can return to Washington next Friday. I've already confirmed your flights. Alicia will stay on to monitor the Olympians, and help Peter with the fieldwork. We have enough funding to hire an assistant to work with Alicia for a few months."

Ira thought: "At the rate we're going we won't need her, much less an assistant, for more than a few days."

Jorge's Land Cruiser pulled up outside. The good-byes were stiff but respectful. The mood was dark, the wine tasted bitter, and the beans went down like cardboard.

As she cleared the plates, Tina asked if she and John Wayne could visit tomorrow to see the micos in the forest. JW's look of happy anticipation helped lift everybody's spirits, and the entire group agreed to leave at dawn for the cage, or at least what used to be the cage.

Chapter 22

Tight Squeeze

After eating breakfast and packing lunch, the team piled into the microbus for the trip to what they were now calling the "release site"; it was no longer "the cage".

"Well, we've lost two of seven," said Ira.

"We can't be sure they're dead though," said Alicia.

"Dad may have found a hole to settle in, and that would block the signal," said Peter.

"We have to be optimistic, of course," said Ira, "but if a mico disappears and is not seen again, we have to count it as 'lost', as surely as if it had died."

The now five-mico family was waiting for food near the nest log. On Kay's orders, the team gave them only one small banana each, making sure that each animal got its share.

"The nights are cool, especially at this time of year," said Peter. "Last night it was only 13 degrees Centigrade. Micos need a shot of sugar first thing in the morning to get their metabolism going. Then they can hunt for insects and other animals."

"That's about 55 degrees Fahrenheit," Ira calculated, mainly for his own understanding.

"No signal from Dad", said Alicia.

"Carlos and I will drive around to the quarry and look again for Mom," said Peter.

John Wayne was giggling and pointing at the micos as they scraped the banana peels clean. Prometheus led the family up "their" tree, but this time they climbed to the very top. Soon, seeds began to rain down on the observers.

"They must have found some fruit," said Ira, thinking that maybe Kay's strategy had been right.

Dad was not doing as well. He had crawled out of the armadillo hole, cold and thirsty. He had heard the microbus arrive, and began to walk unsteadily in the direction of the sound. When he came to an obstruction, like a big fallen log, he'd reverse direction to find a detour, rather than just hopping up and over. "I wish I had some water and fruit," he said to himself. "Even papaya would be good now." It was his last thought.

Back at the "release site", John Wayne said: "Mommy, I have to make pee-pee."

Alicia said to Tina: "You can take him to the latrine, which is about 50 meters down that trail. Do you want me to come with you?"

"No, we can find it." Tina took JW's hand and set off for the latrine, while Ira, Erika, and Alicia collected data. Now they had to use binoculars because the micos were so high in the tree, feeding at the very top. Many of their observations were "?", meaning they could not be sure exactly what each tamarin was doing. Their necks ached with the strain of looking straight up; they would soon learn to back away 20 meters when trying to watch micos in the treetops.

Alicia, who was wearing earphones to monitor the radiocollar signal, jumped up and said, with a big smile: "I've got Dad's signal!"

She picked up the antenna and quickly triangulated on the signal. "He's near the latrine, I think. I'll go find him."

She picked up her machete and ran for the latrine trail. "Tina, I'm coming. Do you see a mico?"

Alicia saw JW, standing at the edge of the latrine, gleefully watching the golden arc coming from his little penis. Tina held him steadily by the shoulders.

The signal got louder and louder as Alicia approached the latrine. "Dad must be right here!" she thought.

She would remember the next seconds as a single frame in a

movie, with thoughts and actions fused into an instant. She saw the huge boa, its arrowhead shaped head raised and ready to strike at JW. She saw the barely-visible bulge in its body. She screamed at Tina, who jumped backward. Alicia pushed JW into the latrine, just as the monster struck. Its weight fell across her feet. JW and Tina were screaming. Ira and Erika were running toward her on the trail. She raised her machete to kill the snake, but paused. The snake slithered off hurriedly, having to settle for the appetizer, Dad, and not the main course, little JW.

Ira and Erika picked JW from the pit, an indescribable mess. Better than having the life squeezed out of him in the coils of a huge constrictor (though they might have been able to kill the snake and extract the boy from its grip).

JW never saw the snake. "Why did you push me in there?" he said angrily at Alicia.

"Sorry, I thought it would be a funny joke," she replied, her coffee-colored skin bleached with fear.

"I don't like you anymore," said JW.

"She's really a nice lady," said Tina, but JW was having none of it.

The five of them walked back to the release site, all eyes on the ground looking for the snake. Tina cleaned up JW and washed his clothes as best she could in the little waterfall.

As their hearts slowed, the four adults hugged and Tina tried to express her gratitude to Alicia. "If we ever have a girl, I'll name her after you."

"Words can't describe what you just did, Alicia," said Ira. "Your quick action kept JW from being seriously injured or killed."

Alicia, ever modest, could not think of anything to say. She would have bad dreams for weeks.

"So why didn't you kill the snake?" asked Erika.

"There just didn't seem to be a reason," said Alicia. "It was running away."

"But it's out there, and might attack again," said Erika.

"It won't try to take an adult person — too big," said Ira. "A boa doesn't get that big in this forest without steering around people for years, but a 40-pound child was just too irresistible."

The micos came down to their low branch, and began to groom and snooze in a ray of sun. Prometheus long-called periodically, in a plaintive attempt to locate Mom and Dad. He was unaware that this was to have unintended consequences. The team was just too hyped to take any more data.

They heard the microbus arrive. Peter and Carlos walked quickly down the trail. "We didn't find her," Carlos said.

"Well, Alicia found Dad, and there is no question that he's dead. We just have to wait a few days to collect his remains and retrieve the collar."

"Carlos, please take us home," said Tina. "JW has made a bit of a mess of himself and needs a real bath." Despite the first washing, JW smelled awful.

"So how do we start explaining the morning to these guys?" asked Ira, but then the three women began to laugh hysterically. Peter and Carlos just stood there, clueless.

"Daddy, Alicia pushed me into the poo poo hole," lamented JW.

Chapter 23
New Neighbors

Carlos returned two hours later, gave Alicia a hug, and spoke softly to her in Portuguese.

Ira and Erika had filled Peter in on the morning's events. Peter's responses were typically no-nonsense: "Alicia is a hero." "Let's track the snake until it defecates, retrieve the collar, and put it on Prometheus." "Now, let's take out the nest log."

The mico family watched with alarm as Peter and Ira unwired their little home and carried it to the microbus.

"The two-leggers are taking our sleep box. Where are we going to sleep?" asked Hercules.

"Let's check out the hole in this tree again, and see if it's big enough for the five of us," answered Prometheus.

They climbed slowly down to the hole, headfirst. Ira noted that some primates, like gorillas and chimpanzees, always climb down trees feet-first. People and woodpeckers too. Tamarins, like squirrels, usually came down headfirst. "That would make a good research project," he thought.

Prometheus entered the hole, then Venus and Vesuvio, then Hera, and finally Hercules. He had to squeeze in. "This will do for now, but we'll have to find someplace else as the twins get bigger."

The long calls came suddenly, from about 200 meters away. The family poured out of the hole.

"Mom, Dad?" asked Venus, hopefully.

"No, that's not them," said Prometheus. He began calling in return, and headed straight for the intruders, a wild family. Hera and Hercules followed, driven by some unfamiliar but strong urges.

They too were long-calling. The youngest twins were forgotten at the hole.

Prometheus, Hera, and Hercules were struggling to get to the intruders. They fell repeatedly, and finally just began to run on the ground. They were unaware of Dad's fate and had not yet learned that the ground was a dangerous place for a tamarin.

The intruders, with their fluid runs and jumps, closed in quickly. They chased and arch-walked vigorously at the three young adults, but there was little contact and no biting. Ira, Erika, Peter, and Alicia caught up, and each began to take notes intently.

Ira said: "Alicia, you take Prometheus, Peter take Hera, I'll take Herc. Erika, you go back and watch the kids." His idea was good but the assignments would prove to be wrong.

The encounter lasted for about 10 minutes, and the intruders disappeared as quickly as they had come. The chases had driven Prometheus and Hera back toward "their" tree, but Hercules had become disoriented and headed in the other direction. Peter, with his considerable field experience, might have been able to follow him, but Ira could not. Hercules evaporated into the forest. There would be ample room in the nest hole that night.

"Wow, where did they come from?" asked Prometheus as Venus and Vesuvio jumped on his back and Hera caught up breathlessly.

"They must have heard you long-calling, and came to check us out and chase us," answered Hera.

"Will they come back?" asked Vesuvio.

"I kind of hope so," said Prometheus. "During the chaos I saw a real cutie, about my age." Hera began to groom a scratch on Prometheus' shoulder.

"Don't even think about leaving me with these two," said Hera. "Where's Herc?"

"No idea," answered Prometheus. Their family had shrunk to four.

The conversation on the ground was similar. "Wow, where did

they come from?" asked Alicia.

"Don't know," said Peter, "but they probably were drawn in by the Olympia long calls. It was a pretty typical group encounter. Lots of chasing and chattering, probably trying to establish a territory. But we think the adults might also be checking out potential mates during these contacts."

"Where's Ira?" asked Erika. On cue, Ira stumbled into the clearing. His shirt was torn, and he had a scratch on his cheek.

"Lost him," he reported.

"Did you hear that?" asked Hera. "Do we dare long-call to help Herc find us?"

"I'm too tired for another fight," answered Prometheus. "Let's go up and get some fruit."

The rain began about 5 PM. Carlos had brought lunches and coffee for the team but they had not had time to eat them.

Ira said: "I think Erika and I should sleep here in the tent tonight, to see if Herc comes back, and to be able to follow the group as soon as they wake up."

"OK, we'll bring breakfast in the morning," said Alicia, as she, Peter, and Carlos set off up the trail. "By the way, I tuned in on Dad's radio. The boa is in the swamp; bad news for the peccaries."

"Sorry, I should have asked you before volunteering to stay here tonight," Ira said to Erika after the others had left.

"I wouldn't want to be anyplace else," she replied. "This has been quite a day."

The now-four-mico family came down (headfirst) to their nest hole and climbed in, grateful for the security and warmth that it offered. There was no sign of Hercules.

Ira rigged a tarp to cover their little bench and table, and Erika set out the ham and cheese sandwiches and cookies that Tina had packed.

"No chance of a fire tonight," said Ira. They ate without speaking, and then sat on the little bench, holding hands. Both were thinking whether Mom and Hercules would survive the cold and rainy night, what effect Kay's decisions had on the events of the last days, and, most awfully, how Dad died. This was a time for silent "what-ifs".

Ira said: "Don't say it. There will be plenty of time to talk." He wrapped his arm around Erika.

The night was far from silent. The rain triggered a tree frog chorus, backed by the different tones and rhythms of drops, drips, plops, runnels, and trickles of rain. There is no such thing as a "steady rain" in a forest. Darkness made it easier to listen.

Predictably, Ira's pants got caught on the tent as he entered, admitting mosquitoes and some rain. Erika was prepared for the former, and sprayed the tent with repellent. By midnight, their ground cloth was submerged and water began to soak into their sleeping bags. All in all, it was a miserable night.

Chapter 24

Keep An Eye On Your Brothers and Sisters

Ira and Erika got up at dawn. They were wet, their sleeping bag was wet, and their clothes were wet. This would not have been a good advertisement for REI or L.L. Bean. The micos got up a little later. They were warm, and their hair was dry and fluffy. At least it stopped raining.

As Erika and Ira drank the dregs of cold coffee from the thermos, the micos tore into the sweet juicy fruits at the top of "their" tree. Hera spotted a dead, rolled-up leaf. Remembering Erika's mystery packages, she stuck her hand into one end ("MM" for micromanipulation, Ira scored). She lost her balance momentarily ("Near Fall", Ira scored), righted herself, and probed some more. She felt the clammy frog skin, and instinct took over. She clamped down hard, pulled out her hand, and bit the head off the struggling frog. The "chirp" came out of her mouth involuntarily, and Venus and Vesuvio rushed to her, rasping for a share. Each got a bite. Since Hera was the focal animal, Ira captured the whole sequence.

Hera did not direct the young twins' attention to the leaf, as a human might have. But the youngsters saw the leaf and connected it in their minds with "frog". They were learning without a true teacher, although they were modeling their behavior on Hera's. A famous primatologist was later to compare this to the way apprentices learn to make sushi from a master.

All four micos (and Pandora over on the Rio Vermelho ranch) were also learning another important lesson, each from his or her own independent experience: If you try to walk on slender branches, don't hold on to the *same* branch with hands and feet. Grab onto two or three *different* branches to distribute your weight, and the branches won't give way and sag. Same for landing after a jump. They could never have learned this in a zoo, because there were not many slender branches in their cages, and no need to use them if there were. This newly learned skill was now allowing them to get to the sweet fruits that grew *in the slender branches* at the top of the tree. They would also be better runners and chasers if they ever met another tamarin group, and they could avoid going to the ground. This lesson came easily to Venus and Vesuvio because they had been too young to really move around independently in their family's zoo cage, and thus had never learned to walk on two-by-fours. They didn't need to "unlearn" anything. It took a little more practice for Prometheus and Hera to get it. Was Hercules learning it also?

Peter, Carlos and Alicia showed up at 7, with fresh coffee, bread, honey, and cheese, and some dry clothes. They took over the data collection while Ira and Erika went up to the minibus to change and eat.

When they returned to the clearing, everybody was gone! Erika said calmly: "Let's just sit here and listen. They'll tell us where they are."

A few minutes later, Prometheus' long call pierced the morning mist. "West," said Ira, "about 100 meters." They set out, only then noticing the freshly cut branches along the narrow trail that Carlos had cut with his machete.

They caught up with Peter, Carlos and Alicia a few minutes later. Ira's and Erika's walking through the forest was also improving.

"They're moving better," said Peter, meaning the micos, not Ira and Erika. "They're not plastic monkeys anymore."

Alicia added: "They're staying together, and micromanipulating a lot. They've actually caught a few frogs and insects, and found some more fruit. I can see that your training is paying off."

Prometheus was long-calling, actually hoping the other group (and the cutie) would show up. He was also hoping that Hercules or Mom might appear too. But he was feeling stronger and more confident, and was honoring his mother's wish that the family would watch out for each other.

Peter said: "Carlos, Alicia, and I have to check on our wild mico groups, and the Swamp group. Can you two stay with these guys?"

"We'll try. We've got water and sandwiches. Can we borrow some repellant?" The mosquitoes were out in force. Ira and Erika were slapping; Peter was pinching.

Peter said: "We'll pick you up at 4. Jorge is dropping off a candidate for our new assistant job. We have to interview him." Alicia and Erika noticed the "*him*".

The sound of the microbus had just receded when "the Intruder group" (actually, Ira and Erika didn't know if it was the same group, but Prometheus knew at once that it was) appeared. Ira counted six or seven, as they charged in and began to chase the Olympians. Prometheus was ready, more skilled in the trees, and more than a little interested by the "cutie." He began to long-call and chutter angrily. His hair was erect, and he was arch-walking impressively. As he charged into the intruders, Hera, and even Venus and Vesuvio, followed. The intruders began to retreat. Despite superiority in numbers, they were apparently impressed with the Olympians' confidence and new sense of ownership of the territory. They climbed to the very top of a steep hill, with the Olys in pursuit. Ira and Erika struggled to hack a path through the undergrowth, and were sweating and breathing hard from exertion.

Ira was determined not to lose another mico in the forest, and he had learned to stop and listen for a few seconds to locate them. They all topped the hill and began to climb down the other side. Ira could glimpse pasture below, signaling that they were approaching the reserve's border. Again, the intruder group slipped away. Ira and Erika caught up with the Olys and were delighted to see all four micos.

Breaking their rule against eating and drinking in front of the tamarins, Ira and Erika drank deeply from their canteens.

"That was so impressive," Ira observed. "These guys really stuck up for themselves, stayed together, and defended their turf."

"Now what?" said Erika.

"We'll follow them back to their nest hole, taking data the whole way. This is an important moment."

But the micos, physically unhurt, just sat in a scrubby tree at the edge of the pasture, looking confused and uncertain. There would be no fruit or water here. The leadership that Prometheus had shown minutes ago had evaporated.

They did not move much in the next hour. They walked a few meters north, then east, then south, and then north again, retracing their steps, over and over.

"If I had to guess, they're lost," said Ira. "We know we have to go east, uphill and then down, following our trail, to get back, but they seem to be clueless." Then, it hit him: "Zoo-born tamarins, having lived in cages, have never learned to plot a route or follow a trail through an unfamiliar area; they don't know anything about wayfinding."

"OK, but do we leave them here?" asked Erika.

"Well, we can't catch them, so how do we get them back to the hole?" Ira asked.

"Watch," said Erika, the clever zookeeper, remembering the simple trick used in every zoo to get animals to move to a different area.

She pulled out two bananas, gave one to Ira, walked a meter uphill, peeled the banana, and held it out.

"Don't let them get more than a tiny bite. They have to be hungry for this to work."

Sure enough, Vesuvio approached her for a lick, and Hera moved toward Ira. Erika and Ira walked another few meters uphill, and the hungry micos followed for a nibble.

It took one and a half tedious hours to get the micos close enough to "their" tree to be able to get there on their own. Erika gave them each a banana. It was 3:45, and Ira and Erika had to get to the trailhead. The micos climbed to the top of the tree and began to eat fruit. The "Pied Piper Rescue Technique" had been invented.

"I knew how to get back," said Prometheus. "I was just resting. Did you see that girl?"

Venus said quietly to Vesuvio, between mouthfuls: "I was hoping Mom was with them. Did you see any sign of her?"

"No, and I miss her a lot."

"Well, Prometheus and Hera are taking good care of us. They share frogs, and if we follow them we find fruit and insects. I'm not really even hungry."

"We have to remember to groom them a lot."

Chapter 25
William Joins The Team

William was a dark-skinned Brazilian, slender and tall. His hands were too big for his frame, his smile too big for his face, and his teeth too big for his smile. He exuded quiet strength, warmth, and optimism, without a trace of arrogance. He seemed not to be aware of how handsome and charming he was (Erika noticed immediately). Alicia's face was unreadable; she had learned in her young life to be wary of first impressions.

Peter introduced William to Ira and Erika as they came into the field station.

"Nice to meet you William. Would you mind if we get cleaned up, and then we can talk?" Ira asked.

"Of course," William answered shyly.

Peter began the conversation a few minutes later, as the group assembled on the veranda. "William has a degree in botany, with a special interest in forest management."

Alicia swallowed at the "degree" word; she had graduated from high school with very high grades, but her family did not have enough money to send her to college.

"A plant person. What have you been doing since you graduated?" asked Ira.

"I've been working with the government, studying satellite photos of the Amazon," William answered.

"Satellite photos?" Ira asked. "Aren't they just for military intelligence?" (This was only 1984, and it would be 20 years before it would be possible for just anybody to bring up a satellite photo of anywhere on Earth on a smart phone or laptop. Indeed, cell phones and laptops had not even been invented yet.)

"Mainly military intelligence, and people are surprised to find that Brazil is a world leader in satellite imagery. The world's super powers are always knocking at our door, and sometimes sneaking through it, to get the technology", William answered, in very good English.

He went on: "Who knows how the intelligence people use our photos, but we can also use them to look for forest loss in the Amazon. Each year, about 4% is cut and burned for farmers to grow crops and raise cows. Your fast food restaurants and super markets are big customers for Brazilian beef and orange juice."

"So why do you want to work with us?" asked Peter.

"First, I want to do some boots-on-the-ground conservation," he answered. "It's one thing to sit in an air conditioned office in front of a computer and collect information that's useful for conservation, but I want to be on the front lines, and actually *do* something for conservation."

"You said 'first'; what else?"

William smiled shyly. That smile clinched this interview, and would win William many supporters in his lifetime. "I love plants and trees," he said, "but I've always loved animals too, since I was a little boy. I read about Jane Goodall and her research with chimpanzees, and Dian Fossey's studies of gorillas, and I want to do that kind of field work."

"But those are big, spectacular apes, living in the heart of Africa," said Ira.

"Yes, but golden lion tamarins are the heart of Brazil. They don't live in any other country in the whole world. And they are so human-like, living in families with everybody helping to raise the babies. They're like my family." (Alicia warmed to this observation; micos reminded her of her family too.)

"How much field experience have you had?" asked Ira.

"Just some weekend hiking." Alicia relaxed a bit with this revelation.

"Let's have some supper and get some sleep," said Peter. "We'll head out early in the morning."

"Let's sleep here tonight," Erika said quietly to Ira. "Less travel back and forth. I'll also whip up a banana bread for dessert."

Everybody noticed that William ate a huge amount of beans and sausage, wondering how he stayed so thin. He devoured two thick slices of banana bread, but everybody else did too. Surprisingly, Erika had noticed, with all of the bananas in Brazil, nobody baked banana bread.

Everybody also noticed that William cleared his own dishes and silverware from the table, and took up station at the sink to wash all of the dishes and pots and pans. This was the custom at the field station, but many visitors were too insensitive or shy to take the lead. William's large-family upbringing was evident, and showed a good sense of teamwork.

The whole team left at dawn for the Olympia release site. William was dressed in jeans and a neatly pressed white shirt. Carlos loaned him a pair of rubber boots. He stood out from the others, in their well-worn field clothes and hiking boots.

"This will be interesting," Ira whispered to Erika. "Have you noticed how Peter likes to put newcomers through a rigorous first day in the forest? Remember how he pushed us with the Swamp group rescue? He tests everybody quickly, and lets them discover for themselves if they really have the right stuff for this kind of work."

The Olympians were already at the top of "their" tree, eating fruit.

Ira asked Alicia to begin to take data on their behavior, and to introduce William to the protocol for data collection.

He then briefed Peter on the Pied Piper rescue of the previous day.

"So you fed them bananas," said Peter, after hearing the story.

"Small amounts, as a tool to lead them back to a familiar area. They were clearly lost, and probably would have died of starvation or exposure if we had not led them back," Ira explained.

"Isn't that a soft release?" asked Peter. "What do you think Kay would say?"

"Peter, I get your and Kay's point that soft releases take a lot of time and field people that we may not have. But what is the sense of doing hard releases, no matter how efficient, if the animals are going to die?"

"And," Ira continued, "I personally can't stand by and take data on how long it takes for a monkey to die of starvation."

"Point taken," said Peter. "Sometimes our concern for the welfare of animals conflicts with our conservation goals."

"Next time, we'll do a better job of preparing the tamarins, with more emphasis on locomotion on natural vegetation. Maybe then they will survive a hard release," said Ira.

"Maybe it would be good to rearrange the vegetation in their zoo cages every few days," Peter suggested, "so they learn to plan and use new pathways."

"Exactly," said Ira, sensing that he and Peter at least were moving closer on the right technique for reintroduction.

Prometheus' long call was returned, this time from the south, and the Olympians were off, running and jumping.

"Look at them go," said Peter.

"There was no trail leading in the direction the micos were heading, so Peter led, clearing a small path with his machete. To Peter, a path through the forest should be a low, narrow doorway, just big enough for a human to squeeze through. Alicia and William followed, collecting data as best they could, and Erika and Ira brought up the rear. It was straight uphill, with lots of mud and thorns. They all started to sweat and breathe heavily, happy to stop for a moment to listen for the calls of the now-invisible micos.

They crested the hill, and headed down toward the swamp.

"Watch where you're walking," said Alicia. "I didn't bring the receiver and antenna, so we don't know where the boa is."

"Should've killed the thing," thought Erika.

The two groups of micos met with the usual melee of chasing, chattering, arch-walking and nipping. Several monkeys lost their grips and fell, one at least 8 meters.

"Hi," said Prometheus shyly, as he and the attractive young female stopped within a meter of each other. For a moment they were oblivious to the chaos, and just stared at each other. Prometheus' heart raced, but just then Vesuvio cried out in pain. The big-brother part of Prometheus took over the Romeo part, and he raced away to rescue Vesuvio. The little guy had fallen into the base of a palm tree and been stuck by some large spines. By the time Prometheus had helped him get back on his feet, the encounter was over. The intruders slipped away again.

"We have to trap those wild intruders and put one or two collars on them," said Peter, "and we better get a collar on Prometheus pretty quickly."

The Olympians rested a bit, and then began the repetitive pacing, back and forth on the same branches, that Ira and Erika had seen yesterday.

"Lost again," said Ira. "Get out some bananas." Erika was already peeling one.

"Can I have the notebook?" William asked Alicia. "Vesuvio was my focal animal, and I managed to get ten good observations on him during the encounter. I wrote them on my hand."

Erika, Ira, and Peter gave each other knowing looks. Few observers can keep up with observations during a group encounter, let alone on their first day. William's shirt and jeans were still spotless, and he had barely broken a sweat.

Peter said: "William and I will leave you to visit some wild groups. Carlos will pick you three up at 4, and we'll meet at the field station."

Chapter 26
Stung

This time it took only 55 minutes to entice the Olympians back to familiar ground. Micos and observers seemed more skilled at the Pied Piper routine, and the micos seemed to spot the nest hole from farther away, and navigate to it more expertly.

Alicia, Ira, and Erika relaxed and drank from their canteens. The micos stretched out on a thick horizontal branch for some warm sun, grooming, and snoozing: Venus and Vesuvio did most of the grooming.

"So, what's your opinion of William?" Ira asked Alicia and Erika as the three observers calmly took data, lying on their backs on the ground with their heads propped on their backpacks (another good way to watch monkeys in trees).

"For somebody without much field experience, he gets around pretty well in the forest," said Erika. "I don't think he's got a big ego; he'll be a good team player."

"He'll catch on to data collection pretty quick too," added Alicia. "But he probably wouldn't stay with the project very long; he's ambitious."

"It would be cool if he could get us some satellite images of the reserve and the surrounding ranches," said Ira. "We could look for patches of forest where we could reintroduce tamarins." (Brazilian intelligence nixed this idea; it would be two decades before aerial views would be officially available to project personnel.) "If not, he could at least introduce us to some of the new technology that's sure to come."

"She didn't talk to me but we sure locked gazes," reported

Prometheus. "She'll be joining us before long."

"Whaaat?" said Hera, Venus and Vesuvio simultaneously.

"How would that work?" asked Hera. "Will you kick me out?"

"And what about us? Would she become our mom?"

"I don't know," said Prometheus, truthfully. He then headed up the tree to eat fruit; the others followed, weighted with a whole new source of stress in an already stressful week.

A light rain began at 3, and the micos came down to their warm, dry hole.

Prometheus entered first, followed by Hera. A second later, Prometheus exploded out of the hole. "Ouch, ouch!" he cried, swatting and flailing furiously. "Stingerbugs!"

Venus and Vesuvio, in a moment of childish fear, jumped on Prometheus' back, and they too were stung a few times by swarming bees. Prometheus, with the youngsters on his back, ran for their lives. He stopped about 50 meters away. The bees had dropped the chase. The three micos rubbed and scratched furiously at their bee stings, and felt dizzy and light-headed.

"Those stingerbugs hurt!" said Vesuvio. "Why are they stinging us?"

"I think they took over our new home," answered Prometheus, "and they're not going to let us share it."

"Where's Hera?" asked Venus.

"Where's Hera?" asked Erika. "Did she come out?"

Hera's face appeared at the hole's entrance. She was surrounded by buzzing bees. Slowly and unsteadily, she climbed out, and then fell 8 meters to the ground. She didn't move.

"Wait until the bees calm down," said Ira. "Those look like African killer bees, and it looks like they've taken over the micos' hole as their new hive. Let's move back."

The bees retreated from Hera's motionless body in a minute. Ira walked in quickly but without making a disturbance, and picked her up.

"No pulse," said Ira as he returned to Erika and Alicia. Maybe we could save her if we had an epi-pen, but I think she's gone. Look how swollen her body is."

Alicia took the body gently, and listened for a heartbeat. A tear formed in Alicia's eye but she wiped it away before it could roll down her cheek.

"Let's get to the trailhead," said Ira.

"Where are the two-leggers taking Hera?" whined Vesuvio.

"I think the stingerbugs made her very sick," offered Prometheus.

Alerted by radio, Peter had already converted the dining room table to an examination table, and had assembled what medical supplies he had. Alicia laid Hera on the newspaper, and they listened for heart sounds with a stethoscope.

"Nothing!" said Peter. "I'm sorry."

"Too bad that the first mico you get to see close up is dead," Peter said to William. "Weigh her," he instructed.

William tenderly laid Hera on the scale. "442 grams"

"She weighed 445 when we shipped her, and she looks like she gained 20 in the cage in the last few weeks," said Erika.

"Wouldn't you expect them to lose some weight when first reintroduced?" asked Peter.

"Especially when we don't feed them," thought Ira.

"Confirm tattoo," Peter said, in his usual business-like manner.

William looked quizzically at Peter.

"Each mico has an individual number tattooed inside its right thigh, for permanent identification," said Alicia. "Let's look."

"1447," she reported.

"That's really her," said Erika.

Peter began to examine the body. "No cuts, or broken bones that I can see. The body is very swollen. And look at these red spots — can they be stings?" (A week later, when Hera was professionally autopsied, they would prove to be bee stings.)

"Let's count them," said Ira.

About an hour later, Ira and Peter compared their counts.

Ira: "132."

Peter: "131. Close enough. That much venom in a body weighing less than a pound would be instantly fatal. She just couldn't get away."

They preserved Hera's body in a jar of formalin until they could bring her to Rio to the national primate laboratory for a professional autopsy.

Ira confessed that Hera was his favorite because of her curiosity. He held his emotion back, but said: "Well, that's four lost out of eight, all in only five days. Not a great outcome."

"Wouldn't you expect most of the losses at the beginning?" asked Peter.

"The bright side is that we still have four of eight, and Mom and Hercules could even be alive," said Ira, landing quickly on his feet. "Let's clean up and have supper. I'd like to sleep at the tent tonight and try to trap the Olympians early in the morning. We need to get a collar on Prometheus."

"Uh, I need to catch the bus back to Rio tonight," said William shyly. "Will you call me with your decision?"

A split second of eye contact and nods from the others prompted Peter: "You're hired. When can you start?"

"Now?" asked William, smiling, "and thank you." His clothes were still spotless, but Peter made a note to issue him some field clothes.

Erika and Ira headed back to the tent after supper. The pigs exploded, and Erika wondered about the boa, especially when she visited the latrine.

"I wonder where Prometheus and the kids are sleeping," said Ira.

"We'll see in the morning," said Erika, as she crawled fluidly into the tent. Ira caught his pants on the tent again. Erika thought he was doing it on purpose now. He wasn't.

Chapter 27

Can Animals Have Stepmothers?

Erika and Ira sat near the tent at dawn, sipping thermos coffee from tin cups. They scanned the area, waiting for the micos to wake up, hopefully nearby.

A few minutes later they heard the softest of peeps, a contact call, from the top of a medium-sized tree, about 30 meters away.

Erika scanned with her binoculars, and Ira prepared to write down her observations.

"I see them – it's Prometheus," she said with relief. "Vesuvio, and there's Venus. They're all safe. They must have been sleeping under a vine tangle near the top of the tree. They look warm and fluffy. Who is our first focal animal today?"

Before Ira could answer, Erika whispered loudly: "Wait, there's another mico there. Mom? Hercules? No, there's no mark on the tail. It's a stranger."

Prometheus said "Good morning" to the stranger but of course drew no verbal response.

"Can she talk?" Vesuvio quietly asked Venus.

"Not two-legger talk, or else she's just really quiet."

"What happens now?" he asked his sister.

"Well, big brother is not long-calling this morning. Maybe he found what he was looking for."

"I hope the two-leggers bring Hera back," said Vesuvio.

"Don't count on it," Venus answered. "Let's eat."

Erika began to dictate observations to Ira. She started with the new mico, who was staying very close to Prometheus while the group ate fruit.

"I got a good look at its back end," Erika reported, "and there are no testicles. Must be a female." (Male and female golden lion tamarins are about the same size and the same color. The only way to tell them apart from a distance is by the presence or absence of testicles.)

"I wonder if she left the Intruder group to join up with Prometheus," mused Ira.

"What shall we call her?" Erika asked.

"Olympia Nine, O9," Ira answered. "Let's not use any more human names. When I held Hera yesterday, it was like losing a friend. A name just invites too much emotional connection."

Erika was not at all sure about this, but there would be time for discussion later. "O9, 12 meters, less than 2, Eat, Prometheus, uhh O4......," she dictated to Ira.

They collected two rounds of data on all four micos. All they did was eat. Then, at about 10 AM, they settled down to rest and groom. All three micos groomed Prometheus, O9 from the head end and Venus and Vesuvio from the tail end. So far, O9 seemed to tolerate the two youngsters.

"Should we set out the traps so we can put a collar on Prometheus?" asked Ira.

"Let's not risk upsetting this new family just yet," suggested Erika.

"OK, let's get the bus back to the field station and report in," said Ira. "We only have three days before we have to leave. I'd like to see Pandora again."

Chapter 28

Why the Red River is Red

After lunch, Ira said: "Alicia, we'll drop you off at the Olympians so you can follow the 'new family'. Take the radio receiver and see if you can get a signal from the boa, but don't walk in on it; we can do a visual later. Erika, William, and I are going to see Pandora and Swamp 4."

After dropping Alicia off, the three drove west out of the reserve, south on the highway, and then back to the east to Senhor Mauricio's Rio Vermelho (Red River) ranch. The ranch was bordered on the north by the São João ("Sow Joe-OW") River, and on the south by the Red River. The São João was also the south border of the reserve. Both rivers ran from the mountains in the west to the Atlantic Ocean. The river water started out clear and sparkling in the highlands, but got progressively muddier as it flowed through the lowland forests and swamps.

The ranch's entrance road snaked around low hills, some blanketed in orange groves and others dotted with cattle. For a while they drove along the São João, and then within sight of the Red. Ira was struck by the color difference. The São João was caramel-colored, but the Red, despite being only about about two kilometers away, had a distinctively clay-red hue.

Senhor Mauricio, and a boy of about 11 came out of the house as the vehicle approached.

"This is my grandson Sergio," said Mauricio.

"And this is William, our newest field assistant," said Ira.

"Where's that young woman —what's her name?" Mauricio asked.

"Alicia," answered Erika.

"That's it, Alicia. A widower like me doesn't get to see too many attractive girls out here."

Mauricio's cook appeared with glasses of freshly squeezed orange juice, just in time to distract Erika from a twinge of jealousy.

"Would you like a shot of *cachaça* in your juice?" Mauricio asked.

"No thanks, we're here to check on your monkeys," said Ira.

"Can Sergio go along?"

"Sure. William is going to try to locate their signal." Ira read the two collars' frequencies to William, and gave him a chance to set up the antenna and receiver, and try to find the monkeys.

Looking at Sergio, who was learning English in school, Ira said: "Each mico has a collar with a small, battery-powered radio that transmits a beep that tells us where the monkey is. If we can find the beep, we can triangulate on the mico. Otherwise, we probably couldn't find them."

"I've got Swamp 4," reported William proudly. He handed the headset to Sergio and said: "Here, listen."

"I can hear it," said Sergio, "but how do we find the mico?"

"Move the antenna from side to side, back and forth, and stop where the signal is loudest. That's the direction we walk."

Ira let William take the lead (he was wearing a brand new field shirt, pants, and boots). It would take a little longer to find the monkeys, and maybe a bit more walking, but William needed the practice.

"Check Pandora's signal," asked Ira. "Let's hope it's near Swamp 4's. That will mean they're still together."

"Already did; they are together, or at least near each other." Erika smiled.

They found the micos in 35 minutes, at the top of a hill from which they could look over at the reserve to the north, on the other side of the São João, and over the Rio Vermelho Ranch to the south, as it stretched to the Red river. Wilderness on one side;

cows, oranges, and people on the other. In between, two micos and an island of forest.

"There they are!" said William proudly.

"Good work," said Ira.

"There's our two-leggers!" said Pandora, momentarily forgetting that Swamp 4 could not understand. She liked life with her new partner, but missed her family and the swarm of two-leggers that were always around.

Sergio was fascinated, and completely taken with William, who shared everything he had learned about golden lion tamarins over the next 15 minutes.

This day, Swamp 4 and Pandora had begun to enlist the support of the next generation of Brazilians for environmental conservation. Sergio was apt to be an opinion leader, since he came from a wealthy and respected land-owning family and was already a distinguished student.

Sergio had also found a new hero in William, and the two would become good friends.

"They look great!" said Erika. "Their weight is good, their hair is dark blond and fluffy, and they seem bonded. Look at them devour that fruit. I wish we could weigh them here." William made a mental note of the last comment.

"How long is their pregnancy?" asked William.

"I like the way you think, William," said Ira. "125 days. Even if she were pregnant, she wouldn't be showing yet." Sergio blushed.

Pandora began to groom Swamp 4, wondering if Erika was going to put out a few bananas. She missed bananas, and had been eyeing some banana trees at the base of the hill, near the ranch house. Swamp 4 was too frightened of people to go there with her.

When they returned to the house, Sergio excitedly reported every detail to his waiting grandfather. When he was finished, Ira, trying out some newly acquired Portuguese, asked Mauricio: "How does the Red River get its color? From clay?"

Mauricio's expression changed suddenly. His eyes focused at a point in the distance, and he grew serious. He motioned for everybody to sit, and put his arm around Sergio.

"What I am going to tell you must stay in the wax of your ears," said Mauricio gravely. (William had to translate "stay in the wax of your ears".)

"One day, probably around 1920 or 1925, when I was about Sergio's age, my father told me to saddle my horse and get my hunting rifle. I was excited, thinking we were going to the swamp to hunt peccaries. But we rode south instead," he continued, "toward the Red River."

"When we approached the riverbank, we saw two small clay huts, some straggly gardens, and worn clothes drying on makeshift lines. A dozen nearly naked children, a few skinny chickens, and four dogs were running around. Smoke curled from cooking fires inside the huts."

"Two women, one pregnant, came out of the huts. Two men, fishing on the riverbank, dropped their poles and began to run."

"My father drew his rifle from its scabbard, and shot each man once. They fell, and rolled down the riverbank. Then he shot three dogs, and told me to shoot the fourth. I did."

"He told the women that he would come back tomorrow, and that he would shoot them and their children if they were still there."

"Imagine the impression this made on me; I was speechless. My father explained that our ranch had been given to our family over two hundred years earlier by the Portuguese king. Our ancestors had farmed sugar and coffee, at times using slaves, and made a vast fortune. Many times, over the centuries, he explained, people tried to take our land. There was no police department, no border markings, and no registered deeds. You had to defend your land yourself. By common law, if squatters settled on your land for a year and 'developed' it, they would have a claim to it. You had to run them off, forcefully if necessary."

"My father said he had warned these squatters twice but they had not moved. We rode out the next day, and the place was abandoned. But every few years, we had to deal with new invasions."

Done with his story, Mauricio looked Ira straight in the eye: "To answer your question, the Red River is colored forever with the blood of squatters and their dogs."

"I'll tell Alicia you were asking for her," said Ira.

Chapter 29

DOA

There was little conversation on the way home. Ira and Erika had been stunned by Senhor Mauricio's story.

"I've heard such stories," said William. William wanted to talk about Pandora and Swamp 4, but Erika and Ira had had enough for the day, or so they thought.

As they passed through Senhor Paulo's ranch on their way back into the reserve, they were flagged down by a ranch-hand carrying a bundle in a newspaper. He was speaking in excited Portuguese. William translated.

"One of the dogs that lives on the ranch brought home a mico and dropped it, dead, on the porch of the house. The man swears he had nothing to do with the mico's death."

They unrolled the newspaper and saw the lifeless body, with a black ring at the base of its tail, and another at the tip: $1 + 5 = 6$. It was O6, Hercules.

"How did he get all the way over here?" Ira asked. He noted that Herc was very thin, and bore the welts made by ticks, before they abandoned the lifeless, cooling body. He also saw what looked like shallow bite marks on his neck and back.

"Better get him back and get a good look," Ira said, rewrapping the body.

At the field station, Peter joined them at the hastily converted dining room table. William had already weighed the body, and reported: "Tattoo number 1448, 392 grams."

Wow, that's light," said Erika. "He weighed 478 at shipment, and he's really skinny. Probably had not found much to eat." Indeed, the formal autopsy at the primate center would later find that he had only a few small pieces of vine in his stomach, no formed feces in his large intestine, and no body fat.

"He disappeared on Sunday, and managed to travel about 5 kilometers, across the whole reserve before running out of gas on the ranch on Wednesday," said Peter.

"How do we know the dog didn't kill him?" asked William.

"We don't, for certain, but notice that there are no bruises around the bite marks," said Ira. "If he had been alive when the dog got him, there would have been some bruising and bleeding around the bites."

"So the dog was a scavenger, not a predator in this case?" asked William.

"Looks like it," said Erika. For the second time in two days, Erika preserved one of their precious tamarins in a bottle of formalin.

"We better go and pick up Alicia," said Ira. "It's after 5. Let's hope she has better news."

She did, on two counts. "Our young lovers are staying close together and doing all the right things. She is tolerating Venus and Vesuvio. They all just climbed into a vine tangle for the night."

"I also have a fix on Dad's radio collar. Do we have time to retrieve it?" she added.

They got a jar from the car, and walked gingerly in the direction of the collar. Erika kept thinking that she and Alicia only weighed a little more than 100 pounds each, probably not much more than an adult peccary.

There was no sign of the boa, but they did find a very large pile of stinking boa poop. "Must be quite fresh," Ira observed. "Not even many flies yet. Actually, it may be vomit rather than poop."

Using sticks and "gloves" of leaves (the field workers would later carry latex gloves), they loaded the slimy, reeking mess into the jar, noting the radio, and some teeth and golden hairs as they did.

"We'll have to strain this through water, over and over, and recover the radio and parts of any animals that the boa ate in the past week."

"Before supper?" asked Alicia.

They decided to hold the poop/vomit wash for the next morning. They took showers and enjoyed some cool bottles of beer, and beans and chicken for supper.

"This poor chicken must have died from old age," said William.

"Well, it's been a crazy day," said Ira. "Two of our disappearances are both confirmed deaths now, but we have no new losses. Four of eight are still alive and adapting well to the wild."

"And," Erika said, "two of our captive-born micos are now paired up, with an opportunity to reproduce in the future. That should boost the numbers, and help to mix wild and captive genes."

"Good job, congratulations," said Peter, toasting with a glass of Brahma beer.

After supper, Erika suggested that she and Ira sleep in the tent. They packed some food and coffee for the morning, which would be their last in the field on this trip. Ira also stashed a bottle of nice red wine for sitting in front of the fire this evening.

Chapter 30

Parting

Ira and Erika set out the traps on a low branch in the morning, but Prometheus and his family paid no attention. They were finding enough food, and didn't really need bananas.

Erika repositioned the traps and peeled the bananas used for bait. "Let's take a walk and leave them alone for a while," she said. They went tree-bathing for half an hour, and when they returned all four micos were in traps. Venus and Vesuvio had managed to ride into the trap on Prometheus. They were too big to be carried anymore, and the three of them in one trap looked laughable.

"Let's head back and get these guys processed," said Ira. "I hope Alicia and William have cleaned up the collar."

"Things were just settling down," said Prometheus. "Where are the two-leggers taking us now?"

The assistants had indeed cleaned and sterilized Dad's collar, and they had rinsed and strained the rest of the snake's gift to science. They had begun the tedious task of separating out Dad's remains, but there wasn't much to put in the third bottle of formalin. They also found traces of a capybara, a large semi-aquatic rodent.

The processing went smoothly, though it was a bit tricky to separate Prometheus, Venus, and Vesuvio for their injections.

Prometheus had lost 8 percent of his body weight, compared to when he had been shipped to Brazil. The two youngsters had gained weight, but they were still growing. All three were in good condition.

"Should we put Dad's collar on Prometheus or O9?" asked Peter.

"Can't we spare another collar so we can have one on each? I'll order some new collars as soon as I get back to work on Monday," said Ira.

Aware of the importance of being able to track this family, Peter agreed.

O9 weighed 535 grams, and was given dye rings at the three-quarters mark and the tip of her tail.

"I get it," said William, "4 + 5 = 9."

"She hasn't reproduced, and seems to be about Prometheus' age," said Erika. "They make a good pair."

The micos were put in traps and moved to the veranda to recover.

"We leave in the morning," said Ira, "so we should do some planning."

They reconfirmed that William and Alicia would work together to follow and take data on the Olympia group, and Swamp 4 and Pandora. They would not provide any food, except to lead the Olympians back if they got lost, which was becoming less likely by the day. The micos were learning their territory, and O9 already knew the area. Alicia would call Ira in Washington once a week to report, from the one phone at the corner bakery in her small hometown. Alicia and William would be paid the equivalent of $50 US dollars a week, plus room and food at the field station, and their field clothes.

They also agreed that Ira would write a report of the Olympia reintroduction, and begin to plan for a second reintroduction next year.

After hugs all around, Carlos took Alicia to the highway so she could catch a bus home for a few days off. Ira and Erika began to pack for their trip home. He found an unopened bag of tortilla chips and a can of cheese sauce in his suitcase, and Tina supplied some hamburger so Erika could make nachos. The Brazilians devoured this novel meal, and made them promise to bring more chips when they came back.

In the morning, William, Ira and Erika gave the Olympia group, now awake and peeping softly, some bananas. They checked the radio transmitters and carried the traps to the bus.

"Wait," said William. "It's not going to rain, so can I take the scale with us? I have an idea for weighing tamarins in the field."

Ira and Erika were perplexed but they agreed.

They released the micos at the exact spot at which they had been trapped.

"Everybody OK?" asked Prometheus. "Let's stay together now."

"That sticker with the sleepy juice hurt almost as much as the stingerbugs," said Vesuvio.

"Get over it. You're fine now."

"You two look very nice with your new collars," said Venus.

The four micos climbed up a tree for a rest, and William began to set up the scale. It was a battery-operated digital scale, with a small platform on top. He placed it securely on a fallen log, and cleared all of the bushes and limbs away. Then he tied a string from one small tree to another, and tied a piece of banana in the middle of the string, directly over the scale.

"What is that new two-legger doing now?" asked Prometheus. "Is this some kind of trap?"

Vesuvio, ever hungry for a banana, went down to grab the banana. There were no limbs leading to the banana, so he walked out on the fallen log. William pulled on one end of the string and raised the banana over the scale. Vesuvio jumped on the scale and reached for the fruit, getting a small handful. Then William tightened the string more, and Vesuvio had to stand on his hind feet and reach up to get it.

"Watch the scale with your binoculars," said William to Erika and Ira.

The numbers jumped around as Vesuvio struggled for the banana, which William kept just out of reach. The little guy stopped reaching and stood on all fours on the scale for a few seconds.

Erika called out, excitedly: "268 grams!"

They repeated the game a few times, and got several weights that differed by a gram or two. The average agreed with the weight taken earlier at the field station when Vesuvio had been sedated. William had devised a way to weigh micos in the field, without having to trap them!

"Fantastic," said Ira. "We can have a hands-off stream of data on body condition and on growth."

"We might even be able to tell if a female is pregnant," said Erika. "They gain between 40 and 50 grams during pregnancy."

William and Erika took data on the Olympians while Ira packed up the tent and camping supplies. William and Alicia, like most Brazilians, saw no reason to sleep in the rainforest at night. They would start work early in the morning and stop late at night, but they wanted their showers and dry beds.

Erika and Ira had a last look at the micos (hopefully just the last for *this* trip), headed back to the field station, showered, and said goodbyes. Tina shared the news that she was pregnant. Carlos beamed, and John Wayne declared that he would have a sister.

"Thanks for everything Peter. We could not have done this without you," said Ira, hugging his colleague and now friend.

"I'll be back in Washington in April, and we'll make the plan for round two," Peter answered.

Erika and Ira boarded the bus on the highway for the terrifying ride to Rio, and were checked into the Hotel Gloria at 6 PM.

Chapter 31

Erika's Ultimatum

The Gloria had lost some of its five-star splendor since it had been built in 1922, but it was still clean, and safe, and had wonderful views of the two most famous Rio landmarks, Sugarloaf Mountain and the huge statue of Christ that lords (or looms, depending on one's religious outlook) over the city. Ira had asked for a room at the rear of the hotel to have a view of the sunset over the mountains.

They unpacked, showered, and dressed in something other than field shirts. Erika wore a light dress. They went into the streets of the surrounding Flamengo district (not as trendy but less pricey than the better known Copacabana and Ipanema) and found a pizza restaurant. Pizza was Ira's favorite food, and he was missing it. But pizza making was in its infancy in Rio at the time; theirs came with fried eggs as a topping. They were disappointed, but the Chianti was good.

It was already dark when they got back to the room. They sat on the tiny balcony, taking in the sparkling lights of the city as they stretched to the west and then rose on the mountainsides.

Erika broke the mood: "Tomorrow we go home. There's no good time to say this so I'm going to say it now. I love you, and I took the job in Washington to be near you. I know you love me but I don't really know *how* you love me, what *kind of* love you have for me. And if I don't know, then our friends and colleagues don't know."

Ira understood. His ex-wife and some of his friends thought Erika was a *fling*, part of a mid-life crisis.

"Wait here," he said.

He went into the narrow streets of Flamengo to an all-night, outdoor crafts market, or "hippie fair" as it was called locally. He bought a hand-made wooden ring and a single rose, and then stopped to buy a bottle of champagne.

Back in the room, he knelt on one knee, offered Erika the rose, and asked: "Will you marry me?"

"Yes," she said, with tears of happiness. He slipped the ring on her finger, stood, and kissed her deeply. They celebrated with the bottle of bubbly, watching the blinking lights and deepening darkness from the balcony. Michael Jackson's music video *Beat It*, which was taking Brazil by storm at the time, was playing inside on the TV.

In the morning they had coffee sent to the room, and worked out and took eucalyptus-scented saunas in the hotel gym. Then they headed for the Flamengo beach. Despite his recent engagement, Ira could not help but notice the slender young Brazilian women in their tiny bikinis. He and Erika were amused as the girls constantly tugged and readjusted the 10 square inches of cloth, to make sure that no part of their body that was not meant to be seen could be seen. The skimpiness of the bikinis and the intense modesty just seemed contradictory.

Erika redirected his attention. They selected a freshly caught fish, and had it crisply fried at a stand on the beach. They picked the sweet white flesh and crackly skin off the bones with their fingers, and washed it down with a really cold Antarctica beer. They sunned and swam, taking care not to get burned; three weeks in the forest had left their bodies white.

They bought a few souvenirs, went back to the hotel, showered, packed, and headed to the airport for the 11 PM Pan American Airlines flight back to the States. Their trip to Brazil had fallen in November and December, the warm rainy summer in South America. In Washington, the North American winter had set in.

Chapter 32

Back On The Job

They arrived in Washington on Saturday afternoon. During the flight they had agreed that Ira would give up his apartment and move into Erika's small house in a Maryland suburb. They did not set a wedding date.

A Nor'easter had dropped 20 inches of snow on Washington on Friday, and the city was digging out. Ira and Erika had no parkas, hats, or gloves, and they had left their boots and raingear at the field station. They walked to and from the Metro subway stations in sandals, and were shockingly cold when they got home.

On Sunday, Ira went to his office to catch up on correspondence. He passed the American bison (commonly called "buffalos"), snow still piled on their backs, kept from melting by the thick layer of insulating hair; warm inside, cold outside. He marveled at Nature's original version of the fiber-filled parka he was now wearing.

There were a few visitors enjoying the winter beauty of the park, but the offices were deserted. There was a new computer at his desk but he had no idea how to use it. Dad and papaya, Ira and computers; What is it about adult males and novelty?

He called Kay at home to let her know they were back, and brought her up to speed on the current status of the tamarins in Brazil. He also told her about his and Erika's engagement in Flamengo. Kay told him that the Zoo's new director was on the job and eager to meet Ira. She also said that she had resumed her work as a scientist. They agreed to meet the next day.

Ira began to draft a brief preliminary report on the reintroduction, using pen on paper. He decided to use the less formal first-person plural, active voice ("We reintroduced eight zoo-born golden lion tamarins....") rather than the more formal third-person passive (Eight golden lion tamarins were reintroduced...."). While science guided his thinking, this was not a scientific paper. It would be a report to donors, his Smithsonian colleagues, Brazilian officials and scientists for whom English was not a first language, reporters, and the general public.

"On December 3, 1984, we released the first captive-born golden lion tamarin (*Leontopithecus rosalia*) into the Atlantic Coastal Rainforest of Brazil. We reintroduced seven more on 7 December."

The report continued: "The first, a female known as O3, was re-introduced with a wild-born male that was expelled from his group (the 'Swamp' group) after they were rescued from an unprotected forest that was being cut down. The other seven were released as a family group, known as the 'Olympia' group. They were: O1 (adult breeding female), O2 (adult breeding male), O4 (subadult male), O5 (juvenile female), O6 (juvenile male), (O7, weanling infant fe-male), and O8 (weanling infant male). O3 and her wild mate were released on a private ranch; the Olympia group was released in the Poço das Antas Biological Reserve."

"We had kept the eight golden lion tamarins (GLTs) of the Olympia group at the Smithsonian National Zoo for six months, before they were flown to Brazil. We trained them at the zoo to find food that was placed at random locations, hidden inside rolled leaves, at unpredictable times of the day. We had placed these foods so the GLTs would have to run, jump, and hang, and thus to develop physical strength and agility. We had observed their responses to predator models (providing real predators was not allowable at the Zoo)."

"Zoo veterinarians had certified the GLTs' health, and kept them in quarantine at the Zoo for one month before shipment to Brazil. After their arrival in Brazil, we held them in a large forest cage for ten days so they could acclimate to the release site. We continued their training and health monitoring in this cage."

"Our data show that these tamarins had progressed in finding and eating spatially scattered foods, hidden foods, and whole foods. Their health and condition was excellent at the time of release. However, we had failed to anticipate two major deficiencies: the ability to walk, run, and jump on slender, flexible branches; and the ability to find their way through unfamiliar environments. These deficiencies in locomotion and wayfinding hindered the GLTs' ability to find food and return to a familiar sleeping site. They spent too much time on the ground, which brought them into contact with predators. They seemed inattentive to potential danger, and were slow to express territorial ownership of the release area."

"O3, being paired with a wild male, appeared to model her behavior on his, and thus learned quickly to find natural food, locomote, and wayfind. She is still alive and thriving, 12 days after reintroduction."

"O1, the Olympia adult breeding female, became disoriented and ran from the release site shortly after she was reintroduced. She has not been seen again, and is presumed dead. O2, the adult breeding male, was eaten by a boa constrictor two days after reintroduction. O5, the juvenile female, was killed four days after release by African killer bees that had taken over the group's sleeping hole. O6, the juvenile male, became lost and disoriented after a territorial encounter with a wild tamarin group, and starved to death after travelling the entire length of the reserve; his body was recovered five days after release after it was scavenged by a domestic dog."

"O4, the subadult male, and the infants O7 and O8 are still alive, ten days after reintroduction. O4 seems to have paired with a young wild female, and they seem to be caring for the infants."

"Thus, nearly two weeks after reintroduction, four of these captive-born reintroduced tamarins are alive, and four have been lost."

"The reintroductions had full support of Brazilian wildlife

authorities and leading Brazilian primatologists. Two major newspapers and two national TV networks covered the work. Two dedicated and capable young Brazilians continue to monitor the survivors, using radiotelemetry. The reintroduction is part of a larger study of the behavior and ecology of wild GLTs being conducted by Dr. Peter Madison, a Smithsonian post-doctoral scientist."

"Thoughts on Future Reintroduction"

"There is a continuing need to supplement the wild GLT population by reintroduction of captive-born animals. Because the reserve may already have as many GLTs as it can support, we may have to do future reintroductions in forest fragments on private farms and ranches, rather than in the reserve itself. This will require an effort to identify suitable release areas and gain the confidence and cooperation of private land owners."

"We may find that survivorship is higher if we pair a captive-born GLT with a wild mate, rather than reintroduce a group of all-captive-born individuals. The wild-born individual helps the captive-born learn behaviors that are critical to survival by providing a model."

"It is clear that we will have to address locomotion and wayfinding in pre-release training. We will have to replace sturdy climbing frames in the GLTs' cages with naturalistic branches, with many small diameter twigs. Further, we will have to completely rearrange these branches every day or two, so the GLTs will learn to navigate through unfamiliar spaces. We will have to observe and record the ways in which GLTs learn to use and find their way through natural vegetation. We will also continue training in food-finding, and perhaps in vigilance to possible threats."

"We are still undecided about the amount of time GLTs should remain in their forest cage in Brazil before they are released, and how much food they should be given, for how long, after they are released. Too much time in the cage, and too much post-release feeding are labor-intensive and thus more expensive, and may reduce the incentive for the GLTs to actually search for food. But releasing them too soon, and discontinuing feeding shortly after release may not allow enough time for them to learn what is necessary to survive in the wild. At present, there is not enough scientific evidence to favor a "soft" or "hard" release."

"We will be applying for funding and time off from our Washington-based duties to do a second reintroduction in 1985, and for writing papers about the reintroduction for publication in scientific journals."

Ira would give the report to the secretary in the morning for typing and copying, but first he wanted to show it to Erika. He drove gingerly to her house on still-icy roads, and was greeted at the door by Freya, her huge female German Shepherd. Erika had trained Freya for obedience and protection, using German commands. Freya had not fully accepted Ira, and was not yet aware that Ira would be moving in.

"Would you like to stay for supper?" Erika asked. "I've made some good German goulash."

"Can't resist," said Ira, "but I can't stay late. I have to get home and start packing so I can be out of the apartment by the end of the month."

"That's good for me too," she said, "since tomorrow is my first day back at work. Would you take Freya for her evening walk while I heat up the food?"

Freya was ambivalent. She always wanted a walk but since she was trained in German and Ira didn't know the commands, he had to walk her on a leash. The park was full of late day dog walkers and cross-country skiers. Ira could enjoy the dog's world because the yellow and brown smell messages, normally detectable only by dogs, could easily be seen by humans on the snow. Freya joyfully contributed to the dog conversations and enjoyed the cold and snowy outing.

Like most scientists, Ira knew that dogs and monkeys and many other animals could communicate emotions, wants, and warnings with sounds, smells, and body postures. But there was no scientific evidence that they could hold complicated conversations, with "what-ifs" and discussions about memories or plans. Despite his scientific belief, Ira was trying to talk with Freya anyway. "When I move in to your house, I'll take you for long walks every night." "Does she let you sleep on the bed?" Freya pricked up her ears and wagged her tail but showed no sign of understanding. "I have to improve my German," Ira thought.

At supper Ira said: "I've drafted a preliminary report on the reintroduction. Before I circulate it, I'd like your feedback. Do you think you could read it by lunch tomorrow?"

"Great," she said.

"It's not typed yet but it's readable."

Chapter 33
Another Ultimatum

Ira sat down expectantly for lunch in Erika's tiny office in the Zoo's monkey section. "Well, what did you think?"

"It's a great report, but there's one big problem. It's the 'we are still undecided' part, about hard or soft release. Maybe you are still undecided, but I am definitely not. There may not be enough *scientific* evidence," she continued, "but I *know* that the tamarins need more time to acclimate and need a lot more support after they are released. They need food, plenty of it, for weeks. They need water bowls. They need to have a familiar sleeping box or nest log for as long as they want to use it. More of them have to have radio collars, so we can find them if they get lost. We need to clearly commit to returning them to the release site and their family if they get lost, even if we have to trap them and carry them back. We need to be better prepared to provide medical care if they get hurt."

"Look," she continued firmly, "I work with these monkeys every day. I *know* what they want and need and feel. I'll never have your scientific expertise but you're too....... disconnected."

She continued: "I loved every part of the work in Brazil, and working together there is a memory we will always treasure. I don't blame you for any of the outcomes. We just didn't know. But now we do know, or at least *I* do."

"There's no good time to say this so I'm going to say it now," she said.

"Uh-oh," Ira thought. "I heard that line before. She sure has a way with ultimatums."

"Ethically, I can not participate in another reintroduction unless there is a commitment to a "soft" release, with lots of post-release support."

"But the GLTs will be much better prepared next time, after training on locomotion and wayfinding," Ira responded.

"That's true, but it's not enough," Erika countered. "I've got to get back to work. Will you come to dinner – leftover goulash?"

Chapter 34
Vote Of Confidence

"Come in and sit down," said Dr. Kennedy Warren, the National Zoo's new director. "Have you had lunch? Would you like some coffee?" he asked cordially, extending his hand.

"Coffee would be wonderful," Ira said. "It's very nice to meet you Dr. Warren. Welcome to the zoo. I'm new here too. It's a great institution."

"Call me Ken," he said. "Tell me all about Brazil."

Kennedy Warren was himself a tropical biologist, an expert in coral biology and reef conservation. He had been heading an oceanographic institute when he was tapped to run the zoo. He held a doctorate in ecology and was an author of dozens of scientific papers and books. His interests went well beyond corals and the oceans, and he had a boundless curiosity for all animals and plants. He also relished good music, literature, wine and food.

Ira recounted the three weeks in Brazil, following the script of his report, not yet revised to include Erika's "suggestions".

"That sounds terrific," said Ken. "You *must* plan a second reintroduction. This is too important to stop now."

"Well, I'm not really satisfied with a 50% loss rate in the first two weeks," said Ira. "The Bronx Zoo reintroduced zoo-born bison in 1907, and all of them survived for a long time."

"Really, 1907?" asked Ken.

"Yes, it's the first scientifically described animal reintroduction," answered Ira.

"Well, bison must be easier. They just have to stick their head down and munch grass. Tamarins have a lot more to learn."

"Thanks for your confidence," said Ira. "I'll have a written report on your desk in a week, after it's been reviewed by Dr. Kay and Dr. Peter. Can we talk more about the next reintroduction then?"

"Ah, Dr. Kay," said Ken with a smile. "What a piece of work. She did a great job as acting director, and said she wanted only to get back to her research. But she calls every day to tell me how to run the zoo."

"Sounds familiar," said Ira. "But I'm back on the curator of primates job here now. What would you like me to tackle first?"

"Our ape collection needs to be shaken up. Two elderly gorillas that have never reproduced, and three lazy, overweight orangutans do not meet our visitors' expectations. We need to liven things up in the ape house."

"I'm a member of the gorilla and orangutan management groups that coordinate the efforts of American zoos for these species," said Ira. "We have a good building, nice yards, great vets and nutritionists, and good keepers. I'm sure the management groups would be willing to send us some young animals. And Dr. Lisa is fully supportive of putting the apes on diets, to improve their health. The keepers will resist because they like to give the apes treats, but they'll come around."

"Speaking of keepers," said Ken, "I understand that Erika Hedstrom worked with you in Brazil. How did she do?"

"She's enormously knowledgeable and hard-working, and cares deeply about animal welfare," said Ira. "If we continue with reintroductions, I hope she will be able to help. But I have to be honest, she's more than just a colleague – we're recently engaged."

"Wonderful, congratulations!" said Ken. "We'll have to be careful to separate the work and personal life."

"I've got another task for you, Ira," Ken continued. "I know that you worked on a tropical rainforest exhibit at another zoo, before you came here, and I hear it's terrific. But as a tropical biologist, I want to *immerse* our visitors in a setting with real trees and uncaged animals. The board and I have read your proposal for an Amazon exhibit, and I think we can bring this off. Would you head the design team?"

"I'd be honored."

"Great. I'll be looking for your reintroduction report, and a concept paper on the Amazon exhibit. Not much will be happening over the Christmas and New Year holidays. Let's meet in early January."

Chapter 35

Hard Returns

"Well, that went well," Ira thought as he walked through the zoo, back to his office. The day's sunshine had finally melted the snow from the bisons' backs. He smiled, recalling the conversation about bison reintroduction.

The office was humming with the work and collegueship of the zoo's other curators. Ira was happy to be back, and they were happy to see him. The secretary followed Ira into his office and said: "Sit down. I'm going to give you a computer lesson. Thirty minutes now will save us all enormous amounts of time later."

After his lesson, Ira laboriously typed his report onto a floppy disk. He was a poor typist but he was able to use the machine, with one major exception. As he would with the electric typewriter, he hit "Return" at the end of every line. The secretary would later have to remove dozens of hard returns from the report.

He struggled with the post-release management paragraph. He respected Erika's knowledge and opinions, but he also respected Kay's and Peter's. He could request funding for extra time for field assistants to support the micos for months after the release; that was not a big issue. The big issue was whether all the post-release support would actually slow the micos adaptation to the wild. But they would never adapt if they were dead. "Slow" is better than "never". Better to err on the safe side, with a "soft" release with lots of support.

He edited the key paragraph, making the changes in italics so Erika could pick them out quickly.

"*There is still some uncertainty* about the amount of time GLTs should remain in their forest cage in Brazil before they are released, and how much food they should be given, for how long, after they are released. Too much time in the cage, and too much post-release feeding are labor-intensive and thus more expensive, and may reduce the incentive for the GLTs to actually search for food. But releasing them too soon, and discontinuing feeding shortly after release, may not allow enough time for them to learn what is necessary to survive in the wild. *Although we lack conclusive scientific evidence, we feel that a 'soft' release is safer than a 'hard' release. We will provide extra food, water, and a sleeping box after release for as long as the GLTs return to them. Every adult over 500 grams will carry a radio collar. We will rescue and return tamarins that get lost, and provide medical care to injured or ill individuals."*

He saved the file, printed off the report, and made copies for Erika and Kay (e-mail was not yet available).

At 5 PM, he met Kay at the bar across the street from the zoo's main entrance.

"I am so happy to be back at the research department, working with scientists and animals every day," Kay said. "I've begun a long-term study of the zoo's giant pandas, and will be going to China next week to explore collaborations on panda conservation in the wild."

"That's incredible. We need your vision and leadership for our zoo's science," said Ira. "I know you also want to hire some molecular geneticists and reproductive biologists; both fields will be important in the future."

"I just have to convince Ken," she answered. "He's not the quickest learner."

Ira, tactfully ignoring the opening to gossip about Ken, told her about his meeting with him, and then slid the copy of the reintroduction report over to her. "Have a look at this tonight and let me know what you think."

Kay started reading at once. Both sipped their Amstels as she read.

"Two major newspapers and two national TV networks covered the work *prominently*", she grunted.

"How are we going to find all of these private ranches?" she asked, without expecting a reply.

"I really like your new pre-release preparation ideas."

"Thanks, but you and Peter came up with some of that too," Ira said.

"What is this stuff about a soft release?" she exploded. "You don't have any funding yet for another reintroduction, let alone the extra money for the assistants and the radio collars for a soft release."

"I'm sure we'll get the funding," Ira replied.

"You're just playing God, refusing to give up control, keeping them as plastic monkeys!" she spluttered.

"With the new training technique, I think they'll adjust very fast, and we won't need to support them for long," said Ira, trying to stay calm. "We might as well err on the safe side."

"What do Peter and Erika think?" she asked.

"Erika thinks a soft release is essential. I think Peter, and Alicia, are leaning toward more post-release support as well. Once I get your input, I'll send the report to them for their comments."

"At least come up with some guidelines for deciding when and how fast to reduce the support. Also, could we move the extra food farther from the sleeping site each day, to motivate them to move into the forest?"

"Great ideas!" said Ira. "Kay, would you agree to be the co-author of this report and on any scientific papers we write?" He was definitely staying close to the hurricane's eye.

"I just assumed we would," she said coolly. They drained their beers and went their separate ways in the cold evening.

Freya was waiting expectantly when Ira walked in, and watched him vigilantly as he hugged and kissed Erika. The paths in the park were free of ice and snow, and the three of them took a jog in the last light of day. Freya was happy to be off the leash, and followed Erika's commands perfectly. Back at the house, Ira sneaked a bit of goulash into Freya's supper.

"Here's the revised paragraph on post-release support," Ira said. "I think you'll be satisfied. Kay agrees, as long as we add some criteria for gradually decreasing support."

Chapter 36

Monkeys In The Kitchen

Ira airmailed copies of the report to Peter and Alicia the next morning, and ordered radio collars with the last of the funds in his reintroduction grant. He made morning rounds of the ape house, checking in with the keepers and carefully observing each of the apes. He had some brief meetings, and was starting to identify the right folks for the Amazon exhibit planning team. He wrote some letters to the chairpersons of the gorilla and orangutan management groups (using the new computer, with no hard returns), and asked for time at the February meetings to make the case for getting some younger apes for the National Zoo.

Finally, after lunch, he was able to think more about the 1985 reintroduction. He was pleased that he had apparently gotten support for a "soft" release from Dr. Kay. She was no longer his boss, but he respected her opinion and valued her backing. Erika was happy too. But Ira really believed that the key to successful reintroduction of golden lion tamarins was *pre-release* training, and he now knew how to design a training program. He needed to keep the tamarins at the zoo in a large cage, maybe even one of the outdoor bird aviaries. Otherwise, despite rearranging all of the branches in the cage, their wayfinding skills would never be challenged.

He walked down the hall to the bird curator's office, and asked if he might be able to use an aviary in the spring and summer of 1985.

"Sorry," she said, "but I can't spare the space. Ken has asked me to put more birds on exhibit."

The cage that was reserved for the tamarins was large compared to the cages usually assigned for small monkeys, but not nearly large enough to challenge and sharpen wayfinding skills. It was about as big as the kitchen in Erika's suburban house.

"You want to put monkeys in my kitchen?" Erika asked as Ira chatted about the dilemma while seasoning the hamburgers he would later grill on the deck, despite the cold. (He reserved a few pinches of unseasoned meat to add to Freya's supper.)

"No, no, I was just using the kitchen as an example of the size of the cage we have for training the tamarins."

"I do work at the zoo, you know," she teased. "I am familiar with cage #34."

"Of course. I'm just a bit distracted."

"Cage 34 will be big enough," Erika said. Besides, with the green light for intensive post-release support, pre-release training will not be so important."

"I don't think so," replied Ira. "Pre-release training will be more important than ever. If they don't know that they have to eventually look for food, and if they are not skilled in walking and climbing on thin branches, they won't ever bother to move away from the nest log, or box, or whatever we use. Kay's idea about their not bothering to move into the forest because they don't need to will then really be correct. They'll just stay around and eat your bananas."

"Come on out on the deck while I light the grill," he suggested. Freya wagged, sensing an opportunity to check out the back yard again. The night was clear and frosty.

"Not quite a campfire in the forest," Erika said, warming her hands over the grill, "but this is OK. I see your point. Maybe it's a matter of emphasis. I think post-release support is more important than pre-release training, while you think the training is more important. We can't lose if we do both."

"I just wish I had a bigger cage for the training," said Ira.

Ira settled into bed first. Erika was still brushing her teeth. He felt a wet nose in his back, and moved a bit toward the center.

Ninety pounds of grateful warmth curled up against his back with a grateful sigh.

"*Raus!*" she commanded, as she came into the bedroom.

For a split second Ira was unsure who was being ordered out of bed. Freya knew, and trotted off to her own bed with resignation.

"I can't believe it. You don't want to give a hungry monkey a banana but you'll sleep with a dog."

Chapter 37

Plan '85

After the holidays, Ira got the reintroduction report back from Peter, with "well done!" handwritten at the top. He also penned a comment next to the part about reintroducing captive-born tamarins paired with wild-borns: " Ira, there is no doubt that 'survivorship' would higher if we pair a captive-born GLT with a wild mate, like Pandora and Swamp Four, rather than reintroduce a group of all-captive-born individuals. But we need to develop techniques to reintroduce groups of all CBs. Suppose there were a disaster that wiped out the entire wild tamarin population – a big forest fire or a disease for example – and there were no WBs left alive?"

"Good point," thought Ira, and he rewrote the paragraph. This was quick and easy with the computer; Ira was starting to like this papaya. He also added that they could now weigh the monkeys in the field, and thus would tie the amount of extra food to the micos' weights; more food if they were losing weight. There was no response to the report from Alicia, so Ira printed off final copies. He sent the original to the Frankfurt Zoo in Germany, which had provided funding for the 1984 reintroduction, and requested $28,000 for 1985. His budgets included salaries for Alicia and William for a full year, four months of preparation of the tamarins at the National Zoo, shipping, vet costs, lots of extra food, and enough radio collars for six micos. He did not have to include funds for buying the monkeys, which was fortunate because they were priceless. The monkeys would be contributed free of charge by the zoos participating in the breeding program.

He sent copies of the final report and the grant proposal to

Ken, Kay, Peter, and Erika, and to the zoo's public affairs office. It was time to get some publicity and boost public awareness and support for the work.

He met with Dr. John, a colleague at the zoo and the chair of the committee that managed all of the golden lion tamarins in American zoos and research laboratories. Dr. John was a genetics expert, and knew the pedigrees of every golden lion tamarin living in captivity anywhere in the world. He ran a "dating service", selecting a male from Zoo X, and a female from Zoo Y, to start a new group at Zoo Z. His main criterion, after age, was that they be as distantly related from each other as possible; no kissing cousins allowed.

"John, we need a family group for the 1985 reintroduction. Six, perhaps eight individuals." Ira felt like he was ordering furniture.

"I was thinking you'd need some monkeys," answered John. "I've got a great group that is living now at the Brookfield Zoo in Chicago. They've been living in that large habitat in the Tropic World building. They are not closely related to any of the animals in the Olympia group."

"That is a large space," said Ira, "but it has only concrete trees with just a few large-diameter branches. They'll probably need training in getting around on natural trees."

"There are now six in this Brookfield group," John went on, "and the way they reproduce I wouldn't be surprised there are more coming."

"That would be good," Ira responded. "We are intrigued that the two infants of the Olympia group were able to survive, while their parents did not. Maybe youngsters have some sort of an advantage."

"I'll tell the Brookfield folks to put the group into pre-shipment quarantine, and set a shipping date," said John. "We should probably get them sometime around March."

Alicia called the following Friday, as she had each Friday since early December. Pandora and Swamp Four, now living on the Rio Vermelho ranch for six weeks, were ranging widely and staying together. Bees had taken over their nest log but the micos were finding other good sleeping places. Pandora had begun raiding Senhor Mauricio's banana grove, and he was not happy. But Sergio was pushing his grandfather to share some bananas with the micos, and it was really easy to watch them so close to the house. Most important, the pair was ranging down to the shore of the São João river, and had traded long calls with micos in the reserve, on the other shore. There was a place where a big tree had fallen across the river, providing a bridge. She was predicting that one or the other group would cross the river soon. William had been able to weigh Pandora every week (her weight was steady) but Swamp Four was having none of William's scale game.

Prometheus (O4, Ira reminded her), and O9, his young wild-born mate, were still together and Venus and Vesuvio (Ira gave up reminding her not to use names – it was hopeless) were following along. It was the dry season (though it still rained several times a week), and there was less fruit in the forest. They were eating crickets and frogs, but the two youngsters were not gaining weight. "Can I give them some bananas?" Alicia asked.

"In the morning, until they start gaining weight again," said Ira.

Otherwise, the Olympia group was doing fine, having encounters with a neighboring group once or twice a week. Peter was trying to trap, mark and collar the neighbors.

Alicia provided the exact weights in grams for each of the animals they had weighed during the week, and exact distances that each of the groups had traveled on the days Alicia and William had followed them. She was carefully storing the behavioral data under her bed at home. "There have been very few "Falls" lately," she added.

"How's William doing?"

"Fine," said Alicia.

"Why didn't you comment on the report?" asked Ira.

"Because it's fine," she replied.

Ira knew that Alicia did not waste words; these short responses did not indicate any dissatisfaction, but he wished she were more expressive. Of course, over the phone, he could not see her flashing smile and sparkling eyes.

"We've got a group for the next reintroduction, and I've applied for funding. If all goes well, we should be bringing them to Brazil in early September, after we train them here at the Zoo all summer," reported Ira. "If the grant comes through, you and William can continue working, and we can even give you a raise."

"Thank you," she said gratefully.

"Now you have to find a place to release the group. Please discuss this with Peter and William, and let me know your ideas next week."

"OK."

"Anything you need?"

"Peter needs radios," she said.

"I've ordered them and I'll send them as soon as they come in."

"I've got to go," she said, "There are people waiting to use the phone." (The phone, the only one in Alicia's tiny hometown, was in the corner bakery/bar, and there was usually a line of callers on Friday afternoon.)

"*Ciao!*"

"Ciao, boss," she said.

Ira typed up the conversation, as a record and as a way of keeping Kay, Erika, Ken, Jorge, and others informed.

He drove home in a fine, driving snow, anticipating a nice winter weekend. "Home" was now Erika's house. She had helped him move his few belongings, mostly books, clothes, and tools, after Christmas. Erika and Freya were training Ira about the rules of the house, although the two of *them* did not always have the same idea of when and what Freya should eat, where she should sleep, and how often she should be walked.

Chapter 38

Squirrel Bridge

Ira was idling at a busy intersection, the wait made longer by cars sliding on accumulating ice as they tried to get through the green light. He watched a squirrel hurry over the intersection on a telephone wire, digging up a stored nut on one side and carrying it to the other. Crossing the street on the pavement would mean certain death, and staying on one side apparently meant no nuts. Ira watched the squirrel make three trips before he was finally able to drive through the intersection. A thought began to gnaw at him.

Erika and Freya were waiting at home, and the three set off for the park. Freya sat at street corners, heeled, and ran freely, all on Erika's German commands. Ira practiced, and Freya's understanding of his German seemed to improve.

"Soon you'll be able to walk her without a leash," Erika said.

"When are you going to tell me the command for 'attack'?" Ira asked.

"A girl's got to have a few secrets," Erika said impishly.

Changing the subject, Ira asked: "When a squirrel crosses a street on a telephone wire, or a monkey crosses a river on a fallen tree, why don't they fall off?"

"Because they are built for it. They have claws and nails for gripping, and the strength to climb."

"Obviously they can't fly across like a bird or a bee, but why doesn't the squirrel cross on the ground, or the monkey swim across?"

"Because they'd die. Where are you going with this?"

"So they are *restricted* to the wire and the tree. They have *no other choice*, if they want to cross. Even though they are literally free, they are restricted.

"So is Freya. She could run away but she stays with us," said Erika.

"Exactly! She stays with us because she likes us, and she knows she'll have a good meal and a warm bed tonight." (Of course the details of the meal and the bed were yet to be determined.)

"But she's trained," said Erika.

"Sure," said Ira, "but I'm not and I stay around too."

"I'm working on the training part," Erika said. "Remember to take your boots off in the mud room, before you come into the house."

The conversation turned to lighter matters. Maybe they could do some cross-country skiing tomorrow if the snow continued.

But the restriction-despite-freedom idea was growing like a maggot in Ira's brain.

Chapter 39

"What Have You Been Drinking?"

Ira, Erika, and Freya were curled up on the couch, enjoying a Sunday afternoon cup of French-pressed coffee. Freya was zonked after two days of cross-country skiing through the park and over the golf course. Ira was trying to watch a football game, in which neither Freya nor Erika had any interest.

"Tell me more about this squirrel bridge idea," asked Erika.

Ira turned off the TV; the game was decided anyway. "Think about the outside yards for the zoo's apes, lions, and tigers. Why don't the apes and big cats escape?"

"Because there are moats and tall walls that they can't jump over."

"Exactly," said Ira. "They are prevented from escaping by their own physical limitations. They *can't* jump out."

"Yes, OK.....," she commented.

"But the squirrel could jump down from the wire, and the tamarin could jump into the river. They are not physically limited but they *choose* not to jump."

"Of course; they know it would be suicidal," she said, growing impatient.

"So the squirrel on the wire bridge and the monkey on the log bridge are in a *psychological* cage, confined by fear. But there are other kinds of psychological cages. Why don't I go to Pittsburgh this afternoon? I have a credit card, and could be at the airport in an hour. But I don't want to go. I have you, and the prospect of a good meal and a warm bed. And I have to be at work in the morning. I could go to Pittsburgh but I *choose* not to go because I like it here and I am afraid of losing my job if I don't show up in the morning. I am in a sort of psychological cage!"

"So," Erika said, "you're describing a form of soft reintroduction. If you provide a group of GLTs with a nest log, lots of food, water, and each other, they'll be in a sort of a cage, even if there is no physical cage of wood and mesh."

"That's part of it," said Ira.

"But Mom and Dad ran away," Erika said.

"Yes, but we were not providing a lot of food, and we freaked them out by starting to dismantle the cage. And, if they had been trained in locomotion and wayfinding they might have come back. If they had had radio collars, we could have found them and brought them back."

"OK, said Erika, "you are describing the "soft" release that we've all agreed to use next year. Why the 'psychological cage' idea?"

"Because I want to use it here at the zoo for training. Cage 34 is too small. I want to release the Brookfield group in the woods in the middle of the zoo, in a psychological cage," Ira said, beaming.

"You mean you want to set the monkeys *free* in the zoo?"

"Not free, but in a psychological cage."

"What have you been drinking?" Erika said.

Chapter 40

"What Have You Been Drinking?" (2)

"What have you been drinking?" Ken asked Ira when they met the following Wednesday. Ken was smiling and his tone was light.

Ira had written up his idea on Monday and sent it to Ken for approval. He wanted to quarantine the Brookfield group at the zoo for a month, and then, at the end of April when the weather was warm, he wanted to release them in the Beaver Valley area in the heart of the zoo. Beaver Valley was two acres of tall oak, beech and maple trees, surrounded by animal yards, pools and buildings. This setting would provide enough naturalistic space for a realistic and effective pre-release training program.

"I'm not really a zoo guy yet," Ken went on, "but it seems to me that our job is to keep animals in our cages and yards, not set them free in the heart of Washington, D.C."

"Well, as I've written in the proposal, they would not really be free; they'd be in a psychological cage."

"Ira, it's a great theory but they would still be free."

"OK, but they can't hurt anybody, and at least four of them will have radio collars and we can find them if they do make a run for it."

"I don't have the expertise to fairly evaluate your idea Ira, so I'm going to call a meeting of all the major stakeholders: Dr. Lisa to speak to medical issues, the entire curator staff, our education director, our publics affairs person, Dr. Kay to speak to the research and conservation value, and zoo security. Send them all a copy of your proposal and we'll meet next week."

"I understand."

"If you can reach consensus, fine. If not, I'll listen to the whole discussion and will make a decision," said Ken. "I think you might get hosed pretty good."

Chapter 41

"What Have You Been Drinking?" (3)

The group met in Ken's conference room on the following Wednesday.

Ken began: "Thanks everybody for taking the time to discuss Ira's unusual proposal. I hope we can reach a consensus and guide Ira's thinking about how best to prepare golden lion tamarins here at the zoo for later reintroduction to the wild in Brazil. This is important work, central to the Smithsonian mission for 'the increase and diffusion of knowledge'. Who would like to start?"

Kay jumped in: "I'd like to echo what Ken said about the importance of this work. This is one of the most timely and credible conservation projects being conducted by any zoo, anywhere."

"But Kay," said the small mammal curator, "You are hardly objective, being one of the architects of the program. More important, we've got a zoo to run here in Washington, and Ira's proposal would make our work much harder this summer."

"Be specific; how would it complicate our work?" asked Ken.

"First, we'll be chasing monkeys all over the park trying to catch them, and they might even climb over the outer fence and escape into the neighborhood."

"OK, security is an issue. Ira, how do you respond?"

Ira stayed very calm: "You've read my thinking about the psychological cage. I know it's a new idea, but remember what happens when we try to catch an animal that has accidentally escaped from its cage?"

"It usually tries to get back into its home enclosure," mumbled several of the curators.

"Exactly. Escaped animals are scared, and want to get back into their cages," said Ira. "But even if these tamarins do run out of Beaver Valley, we'll have radio collars on them. We can find them, trap them, and bring them back."

"Oh, and who is going to do that?" asked the small mammal curator. "You're talking about a 24/7 operation. We don't have the staff to be running after monkeys day and night."

"Well, night is not the issue; they sleep at night. I propose that we recruit a group of volunteers, like the ones that Kay uses to collect panda data. They can keep an eye on the GLTs all day, and call us if they are straying out of Beaver Valley."

The education director said: "Our volunteers are truly wonderful; dedicated and conscientious, but it takes a lot of work to train, schedule and supervise them."

"OK," said Ken, jotting on an easel: "Let's add staffing to security on the list of problems. What else?"

"Diseases," said the bird curator. "They will be in contact with the zoo's wild birds, squirrels, and insects, which can all carry disease."

"Think about it," said Dr. Lisa. "All of those animals can squeeze through cage mesh or under fences as it is now. They feed from the same bowls as the birds and the monkeys in the collection. There is no new threat on the disease front."

The bird curator immediately wished she had thought a bit longer before speaking.

"Predators," said the curator of lions, tigers and bears. "There are hawks and foxes in the park, and they could take a tamarin."

"True," said Ira but we think these tamarins know instinctively how to recognize and avoid many predators. If they don't, better to find out here than in Brazil."

"Great," said the media director. "How am I going to explain 'predation at the zoo approved by zoo staff' to local reporters?"

"Explain it honestly," said Ira. "Predation is part of life for tamarins and many other animals. If we are going to reintroduce GLTs, we have to talk about predation. And, don't forget that we feed live mice and baby chicks to our snakes and some of our birds."

"But that's different. It's not approved predation on an animal in our zoo collection. You know, Ira, when I first read your proposal I said to myself: 'What has he been drinking?' You seem to be unaware of the possibility for really negative publicity from this. I'm thinking about the 'bloody visual': an escaped tamarin run over by a car outside our front gate on Connecticut Avenue."

Ira smiled: "You're not the first to read about this idea and think I've been hitting the tequila. But there's also the potential for some really *positive* publicity in this. Many of our visitors are uncomfortable about keeping animals in cages, and seeing zoo animals running around in what appears to be complete freedom will be very popular."

Ken: "We'll list publicity as a plus and a minus. Nobody has spoken about the key issue for Ira, and that's the small size of Cage 34, and his goal of having a larger, more naturalistic space for training the GLTs. Does anybody question that purpose?"

When there was no response, Ken added 'more effective prerelease training' to the list of positives.

"How will we get the nest box up into the trees, and then get food and water up there?" asked the small mammal curator.

"Great question," said Ira, wishing that Erika had been invited to the meeting. "We've designed a pulley system that will haul the box 20 feet up into the trees, and a spring-loaded door for the box that we can open and close from the ground so we can trap them if we have to, in the box at night when they are sleeping. We can also haul up food and water on pulleys."

Then the small mammal curator dropped a bomb: The Animal Welfare Act, which regulates the way that we manage mammals in zoos, requires that we provide 'safe and effective containment for the security of the animals and the safety of staff and public', and that we 'assure continuous availability of fresh and nutritious food'. I don't think the federal inspectors will approve the free-ranging tamarin idea."

Dr. Lisa: "I've already notified the inspectors and two of them are coming out next week to meet with Ira and me to review the proposal."

An hour had flown past. Ken asked: "More comments?"

The education officer dropped another bomb, this one a good bomb in Ira's opinion: "If this works the way Ira predicts, our visitors will have an unforgettable experience at the zoo this summer. They will be face-to-face with 'free' zoo animals, and will really learn about the role of zoos in conservation."

"OK," said Ken. "To summarize, minuses first: standards of animal security could be compromised, there will be an extra staffing burden, and there could be some negative publicity. On the positive side, Ira's reintroduction training will be better, there could be positive publicity, and there would be strong educational value. Logistics and disease potential seem not to be problems."

He paused to allow any further comments. There were none.

Ken continued: "Dr. Lisa, please include me in the meeting with the federal inspectors. I'll make a final decision when we hear what they have to say."

Chapter 42
Team Building

Ira and Erika picked up the Brookfield group at the airport in March, and drove them back to the National Zoo's animal hospital for a month-long medical quarantine. Erika had been assigned to care for them, which would give her a chance to learn about the six monkeys and their personalities.

The meeting with the federal inspectors in February had been productive. They approved what they named "the free-ranging tamarin exhibit" as long as all of the family members weighing more than 500 grams were given radio collars, fresh food and water were provided twice daily, and there would be a trained observer to watch and follow them from the time the monkeys woke up and left the nest box to the time when they went to sleep. The inspectors agreed that these observers could be trained volunteers, as long as they carried two-way radios, and Ira was around to back them up if there were a problem.

After the meeting, Ken approved the exhibit for the summer of 1985. He told Ira that as a newcomer to the zoo profession he had been surprised that the way animals were kept and shown in zoos had not changed much over the past 75 years, and the profession needed to be more innovative. He had added "innovation" to the list of positives for the free-ranging tamarin exhibit. There was a bit of grumbling from the curators when Ken announced his decision, but most saw the value of the idea and were willing to give it a try.

Ken asked the education director to recruit volunteer observers. She enlisted 42 people, including a retired army colonel, a congressional staff member, a well-known sculptor, an emergency room nurse, and a few soccer moms. Most of the others were seniors. They shared a common passion for animals and a fiery interest in wanting to make the world a better place for them. Ira and Erika led them through 16 hours of training over eight weeks, at the end of which they were well versed in tamarin biology and behavior, and knew how to observe monkeys and use radio telemetry. They signed up for two- and even four-hour shifts between 6 AM and 8 PM, seven days a week, from early May to late August.

On the second Friday afternoon in March, Alicia told Ira over the phone that she and William had weighed Pandora (whose taste for bananas persisted), and she had gained 20 grams in one month. Was she pregnant, or just finding a lot of food? Ira told Alicia about the Brookfield group. He was delighted to hear that she was talking with the young owner of the Santa Helena ranch about releasing micos on his property. The ranch had several hundred hectares of forest, some quite old with large trees, and was surrounded on three sides by other ranches and farms with forested hilltops. The owner, Senhor Nelson, was well educated and enthusiastic about nature conservation.

That evening, Erika was eager to tell Ira about her impressions of the Brookfield group, and Ira was eager to tell her about Pandora. "The mother's name is 'Emily'," Erika began. "She's 6 years old, and has already given birth three times. She's totally in charge, and more assertive and curious than Mom in the Olympia group. The father is 'Rufous', also six, and is stodgy and lazy, just like Dad had been. The oldest kid is 'Niko', who is two and a holy terror, into everything and always trying to escape from the cage. So far there is no aggression between him and Rufous but it's coming. 'Opie', a male, and 'Petie', a female are 1 year-old twins, with personalities like Niko's. The youngest is 'Sandy", a female, just 2 months old, still nursing and being carried by everybody in the family."

"How is their running and climbing?" asked Ira.

"Hard to say, because the quarantine cage only has a climbing structure made of 2 X 4s," said Erika. "But their appetite is good and they play and groom a lot. They also like their wooden nest box, and actually slide the door shut at night by themselves; I don't know how they learned to do that."

"Have you given them any whole fruits or mystery packages?"

"Not yet. Dr. Lisa wants to keep their diet simple and constant during quarantine. We've been giving them a new product: canned tamarin food. It's like dog food (Freya's ears pricked up), but it's got all of the stuff a tamarin needs."

"Do they like it?" asked Ira.

"They eat it in the morning when they're hungry, but they gobble up their fruit in the afternoon. They are also micromanipulating in every crack or crevice. I haven't seen a cockroach in the cage in a week."

"Any health problems?"

"None so far. Dr Lisa is going to anesthetize them soon for a good check-up. Should we dye their tails and put on collars now? Except for Sandy, they all already have tattoos; we'll tattoo Sandy during the check-up. I'll also make sure all of the tattoos have been recorded correctly."

"Double check the sexes too," suggested Ira, "I'm suspicious about a female named Petie. It wouldn't be the first time that somebody got a sex wrong."

"We also have to check Emily's teeth," said Erika. "I think she has a broken canine tooth."

"I'll bring the radios and receiver to the hospital on Monday. Probably just three?"

"Opie and Petie are probably still under 500, so just three."

"I'd love to see them," said Ira.

"No visitors until quarantine is over, even during the check-up. I have to change my uniform and boots each time I go into the quarantine area," said Erika, "and I have to wear a surgical mask while I'm with them."

"Where were Emily and Rufous born?" asked Ira.

"Emily was born at Brookfield, and Rufous at Monkey Forest, a small privately-owned zoo in Florida. He's directly descended from GLTs brought in from Brazil in the 1960s, and has some rare genes."

"We have to describe the Brookfield group to the volunteers in next week's training session, so they can begin to learn about them and memorize them," Ira thought out loud. "Should we use their names, or the less emotional 'B1, B2, et cetera?"

"Honey, we want emotional attachment at this point," said Erika. "The volunteers will be more involved, and names will make it easier to get the zoo visitors to relate to the monkeys, our program, and conservation in general."

"True, but we want the volunteers to be objective observers. And, it will be less painful if we lose a monkey to an accident or illness if he's called 'B4' rather than 'Opie'."

"That's a chance we have to take," said Erika.

"You're right. I just wish the names weren't so dorky."

Chapter 43
Males Can Innovate

It was an unusually warm late-March Saturday in Washington. Ira and Erika invited Dr. Kay and her boyfriend, and Dr. Peter and his wife over for a barbeque. Peter was back in D.C. for several weeks. Naturally tamarins dominated the conversation, as Peter brought everybody up to date on his work in Brazil, and Ira and Erika talked about the Brookfield group and the new free-ranging exhibit.

"What preparations should we make in Brazil for the Brookfield group?" asked Peter, as the group sat on the deck enjoying the spring warmth. "Do you want a big cage on the Santa Helena ranch?"

"No, we'll use the psychological cage idea. But we'll need the small cage at the field station to hold the group while they recover from the trip, and get used to a new nest log" said Ira. "We'll just catch them in their nest one morning, and move it to the ranch."

"Those logs are so heavy," said Peter.

Ira, who was sitting back-to-back with Peter on the plastic cooler full of beer, said: "We could use their wooden box from the zoo, but it would deteriorate so quickly in the forest. We need something light and weather-proof."

"I need another beer," said Peter, standing up.

Ira got up and Peter opened the cooler. The thought hit them simultaneously. A plastic picnic cooler!

Ira got his tools, and they went to work. The beer was moved inside to the refrigerator. They cut an entrance hole in the top of the cooler, to the exact size and shape of the hole in the original Swamp group's nest tree (Ira had drawn it in his journal). Then they put a hook on the back, attached a rope, and lifted it into a tree. "Perfect!"

Erika was impressed. "I'll sterilize it and ask Dr. Lisa if we can put it into their cage. We'll have to build the spring-loaded door to cover the hole. In the meantime, they can get used to it and saturate it with their group smell. Then we'll take out the wooden box."

"We can actually ship it with the monkeys to Brazil," said Ira.

"Not with the monkeys in it," said Kay.

"No, it would get too hot. And, the regulations require the type of kennel cages that we used last year," said Ira.

By the following Tuesday, the Brookfield group was using their new box eagerly. "The bright blue and white colors are obnoxious," said Erika, "but it's easy to clean."

Actually, cleaning a tamarin nest box is easy since they don't poop or pee inside.

In early April, Ira, Erika, and a few keepers selected a tree for the nest box in Beaver Valley. The zoo's graphics department was printing signs with the names and marks of the monkeys, so the visitors could identify them. Ira noticed that there were really tall trees – oaks, maples, beeches – and small shrubs and bushes, but there were few medium-sized trees. The middle layer of the forest, well developed in a tropical forest, was missing. Using the zoo's bucket truck, workers strung thick ropes in a web, extending 25 feet out from the nest tree, to make a middle layer. They also installed ropes and pulleys so food and water bowls could be pulled up to the 'front door' of the box.

The leaves flushed out in mid-April in a preview of the summer lushness and beauty. Squirrels scampered, and a red-tailed hawk decided to make her nest nearby. This was troubling, but the rats and mice that called the zoo home seemed to be a plentiful and right-sized food source for the hawk and her babies. Ira mapped the area, and made a grid so the observers could record the tamarins' location every 30 minutes. These locations would become a record of their favorite locations, and would show any expansion in the area they used.

Erika had been right about Emily's tooth. She had broken an

upper canine, the long tooth used to pierce insects and frogs. Dr. Lisa contacted a human dentist, who did a beautiful small-scale root canal on an anesthetized Emily. Petie indeed turned out to be a female, all of the tattoos had been recorded correctly, everybody got tail marks, and Emily, Rufous and Niko got brand new radio collars. All of the animals were declared healthy, although blood was drawn from each for lab analysis.

That night, after the animals had recovered from anesthesia and had explored their new marks and collars, there was a family conversation.

"What are these black rings on our tails?" asked Petie.

"Each of us has a different pattern," observed Opie.

"I wish I had a necklace," complained Petie. "The two-leggers wear them a lot and now you have them."

"It's not a man thing," said Niko, "but watch what I can do." He grabbed the tip of the four-inch wire antenna that protruded from the collar, and stuck it into a crevice where the cage's concrete floor met the block wall. "I can get it farther in then my finger." He probed a bit with the antenna, and sure enough out scurried a roach.

"Hey, that's mine," he said as Emily chewed the head off the insect with a potato chip-like crunch.

The volunteer observers were later to see Niko again use his antenna as a probing tool. It was the first time tool use by a tamarin had ever been documented.

But the tamarins' language would probably never be documented. Very few scientists even thought that animals could communicate like humans. And, while their words sounded the same *to the tamarins* as human words, and had the same meaning, humans could not hear them. If scientists ever did discover that tamarins spoke English, they would be able trace the origin to one of the micos that was imported to the U.S from Brazil in the early 1960's. That genius was a young female, who took to her zookeepers eagerly. She learned their language in her U.S. zoo, and her babies learned from her, and so on, until many of the tamarins in zoos could speak some English. She was Emily's (and Mom's) great-great grandmother, so the Brookfield and Olympia groups were talkers. Rufous didn't learn until he was paired up with Emily, and he still didn't speak well.

Ira anxiously opened the letter from Frankfurt zoo on a beautiful April morning. He didn't have to read too far: "Dear Ira, We are happy to inform you......."They had agreed to fully fund the proposal. The zoo's director, whom Ira had met twice at conferences, provided extra funds for radio collars, noting that some of the losses in 1984 could have been prevented if the animals had been collared. But he also pointed out that a 50% survival rate was above average for the reintroductions he had read about, and congratulated the team on its work.

Ira quickly called Ken, Kay, Erika and Dr. Lisa. They scheduled the release into Beaver Valley for early May, provided the weather was warm.

Chapter 44

Breakout

Erika snuck quietly into the quarantine section at 5 AM, slipped into the tamarins' cage, and snapped the door on the cooler nest box shut.

"Oh, not again," said Rufous sleepily. This was the way the group had been caught for physical exams, and that had been stressful.

"It's way too early for the two-leggers to be doing examinations, and none of us is sick or hurt," said Emily. "Am I right? Are we all feeling OK?"

"Whoa, they're taking the whole box off the wall."

"I can see some trees and daylight through the drain holes in the box," said Niko. "We're outside!"

"Not another silverbird trip, I hope."

Moments later, the box made a sickening, swinging ascent along the trunk of the nest tree in Beaver Valley. Workers in the bucket truck fastened the box to the tree. Erika pullied up bowls of canned tamarin diet and fresh fruit, and a bowl of water, tying them off right in front of the cooler nest box, and close to some thick branches that grew from nearby trees.

Down below on a nearby zoo path, Ira and a cluster of curious curators and keepers waited nervously, sipping coffee. Even Ken had gotten up early to watch. The first two volunteers stood by with clipboards, the radio receiver, and a two-way radio. There were no reporters or TV crews; the zoo's publicity director did not want coverage of what she still believed would be a "bloody visual."

"All set?" asked Ira. "Radios working?" The volunteers, fiddling and turning dials and adjusting headphones, nodded affirmatively.

"OK, open the box Erika."

She pulled on another of the bunch of ropes that now dangled around the tree, and the cooler box door opened with a snap.

"There is no mesh out there," said Emily to her family. "We're not in a cage. There's just trees and ropes."

Rufous elbowed her from the entrance hole. "So now what are we going to do? We are very high off the ground."

Emily pushed Rufous aside, and once again took in the view. "There's nice food and water right here by the door."

"Let's see," said Niko.

For the next 90 minutes, the observers below saw only a succession of faces peering out of the cooler box. They tried to identify the tamarins but couldn't really be sure who was looking at the moment. Even Sandy got a glimpse, but none of the observers could tell who was carrying her.

Ken, the curators and keepers began to drift away to their morning work, feeling that the release was less exciting than they had expected. Ira, on the other hand, was elated at the progress because it was consistent with the psychological cage idea: the tamarins could run away but they didn't.

Finally, Emily hopped out to the nearest branch, grabbed a piece of banana, and hopped right back in. Sandy begged for the food and she gave it to her, necessitating another trip outside.

"What's it like?" asked Opie.

"Your father is right – it's really high up. But I'm hungry and we need to feed Sandy, so you better give it a try."

By late morning all of the tamarins except Rufous had jumped out onto a branch, grabbed some food, and come back in.

"We don't usually eat in the box," chided Mom, "and this place is already getting messy. No more eating in the box."

Erika changed the food and water bowls at 1 PM, and weighed the leftovers. By subtracting the weight of the leftovers from the weight she had originally put in the bowls, she could estimate how much the group had eaten (minus a bit that they had dropped or that birds had stolen). Even Rufous had finally come out for lunch. Opie and Petie had jumped momentarily onto some ropes, but they hadn't yet risked a play chase. None of the tamarins had ventured more than two feet from the entrance to the cooler, but they did stay out longer to eat. They all obeyed their mom.

So it went for the rest of the first day, and the second and third days as well. Out, eat some food, in, out, eat some food, and so on. They all drank, pooped and peed. Freya got shortened walks on these days, since Ira and Erika had to be at the zoo before 6 AM to see the family wake up, and stay until they settled down for the night, after 6 PM.

Day 4 was very different. It started typically, with Erika hauling up fresh food and water at 6:30, and the family emerging from the cooler to eat. Emily was first, Rufous last. Niko carried Sandy, who ate a bit of banana though she was still nursing on Emily. Petie and Opie scarfed up a lot of canned food and fruits, and then began to play, for the first time in Beaver Valley. They chased and wrestled, first on the thick trunk of the nest tree. Then they ventured out on some sturdy branches and the ropes.

When they were 10 feet from the cooler, farther than any of the tamarins had gone, Emily cautioned them: "Get back here you two."

But the youngsters were delirious with the fun and exercise after spending days in the cooler. Soon they were 25 feet away. They could no longer hear Emily's commands.

Opie lost his balance on a swaying rope, and went upside down under the rope, still holding on.

"Near Fall," thought Ira.

Petie was not so dexterous. She slipped, and fell 20 feet to the ground. She landed on all fours, momentarily stunned.

Opie called down: "Are you OK? I didn't mean to push you off."

"Mom, dad, Petie fell," Opie called, but they could not hear him. He couldn't even see the blue and white cooler any more, and he panicked. He ran, in the wrong direction.

He stumbled on a clump of leaves, and fell to a slender branch that sunk sickeningly under his weight. He tried to jump to a thicker branch, missed, and fell to the ground.

Erika had found Petie and was leading her back to the nest tree with a banana. Ira told the two volunteers on duty to stay with the rest of the family, and set out to locate Opie.

Opie had climbed into some low shrubs, shook off the effects of the fall, and kept going. He followed the contour of the valley uphill, and after about 15 minutes got to the edge of the forest. There was a big pond and lots of ducks and geese; he had reached the zoo's bird house. Opie was missing, and Ira had lost him.

Ira called for some keeper help on his two-way radio. He hated to admit that the psychological cage had failed to hold Opie, but he needed more eyes and ears to find the lost monkey. Ira could hear the family long-calling down in the valley, and assumed that Opie could too. But Opie had crawled under a boardwalk that circled the pond, and huddled there in fear. The quacking of 900 ducks was deafening.

Ira and many of his colleagues searched the area, and actually walked right over Opie on the boardwalk several times. There were a few unspoken "I told you so's."

The publicity director made no effort to hide her doom and gloom, and waited for the first call from a reporter (local radio and TV stations scanned the zoo's radio frequencies, and would soon learn of the "escape").

The Brookfield family, with Petie reunited, settled down for a noontime nap in their cooler nest. The search for Opie was called off, but Ira continued to look for him. Ira was sad at the prospect of losing a tamarin, and embarrassed at this early failure of his psychological cage idea. Opie's breakout reminded him of Mom's and Hercules' panicked runs last year in Brazil. Mom had freaked when they began tearing down the cage. Hercules got lost after a scary encounter with the wild neighbors, and Opie had panicked and run after Petie's fall. Ira wished he had broken the 500-gram rule and put a radio collar on Opie, but it was too late for those regrets. On the positive side, the rest of the family was still in the "cage", and Ira had learned that day that tamarins could fall 25 feet to the ground and survive unhurt.

Chapter 45

Press Restart

"Well, at least we got Petie back." said Erika.

"Thanks to good post-release support," said Ira. "But I'm stumped about why some tamarins just run away. They panic, and run away."

"Shouldn't we expect some panicky moments from cage-raised monkeys that suddenly find themselves in the forest?" she asked.

"I guess," Ira said. "I'll have to modify the psychological cage idea, and of course we'll always need good post-release support."

"Let's hope that none of the others runs away, or you'll have to drop the whole idea."

"Back to cage #34?" Ira said. "I'm going to make one more loop up the hillside to the bird house and back before we go home."

He began the climb with heavy legs and heavy heart. The last rays of the sun were lighting up the tops of the tallest trees, while darkness crept into the lower part of the valley. It would be chilly tonight. He tried a pitiful imitation of a long call, and called Opie by name.

Ducks floated on the pond, some with bills tucked under wings, others munching on the last of the day's floating wildfowl chow. A few rested on shore, before taking to the pond to avoid the foxes and raccoons that stalked the area at night. Ira was looking down at a particularly beautiful teal, when the golden tail flopped out from under the boardwalk. It didn't register at first, until Ira saw the black rings. Opie was right here, literally under his nose.

"Erika from Ira," he barked over the radio. "I found him, under the boardwalk in front of the bird house. Bring a live trap and some bananas."

"10-4," she responded.

Moments later a zoo police car, red lights flashing, dropped Erika off at the pond.

"Need some help Doc?" asked the officer. "I heard your radio call, and gave her a lift."

"Thanks. Can you stand by for a few minutes?"

Erika quietly set two live traps with bananas, and crept close to Opie with a peeled one. It was too late in the day for him to eat. He would not be led or trapped tonight.

"How about trying to net him?" Erika asked.

"He might get scared and run again, and we could lose him in the dark."

Opie wrapped his arms around a 4X4 post of the boardwalk, laid his head against it, closed his eyes, and went to sleep, right there on the ground.

"Well, I guess I'm staying here tonight," Ira told Erika and the officer. "Maybe you could go to my office, grab the lunch I never ate today, and bring it up for my supper. A jacket and flashlight would be great too."

The officer took Erika to Ira's office and brought the food back to the boardwalk. Ira had found a bench and moved it to the shore of the pond so he could watch Opie.

"I'll bring you breakfast in the morning," said Erika, foregoing a good night kiss in front of the officer.

The officer said: "I'm on 'til 6AM. I'll check on you a few times and listen for any radio calls."

The night passed slowly. Ira watched a great horned owl drop on a prowling rat and fly off with it. Raccoons, deer, foxes, opossums, and cats passed through, but Opie slept soundly and unharmed. The officer stopped by twice, each time with a cup of steaming coffee.

Ira must have nodded off, and was awakened at dawn by Erika's footsteps on the boardwalk. Erika climbed down and kissed him.

"I brought a net. Let's just grab him while he's still sleeping."

With that, Opie opened his eyes. "Where am I?" he thought. Erika put down her coffee, and showed him the banana. He completely ignored her, preferring the piece in the trap instead. The loud "snap" of the closing trap scattered some awakening ducks.

"Thank goodness," said Ira.

"Now, how do we reunite him with the family?" asked Erika. "They're 20 feet up in the box, and he'll be in the trap down below."

"He'll be happy to be back in his cage," said Ira with confidence. "He'll run right up the nest tree trunk to the cooler box."

"Let's hope you're right," she said.

He was. Erika held the open trap against the trunk of the nest tree. Opie looked up, saw the box, and chirped softly. The family tumbled out of the box, all chirping excitedly. "It's Opie!" He scurried up the trunk for a happy reunion. Erika gave them fresh food and water, and they all ate hungrily.

Ira noticed that each of the monkeys peed and pooped within seconds of coming out of the cooler box. He stored this observation away, realizing that with proper timing and accurate placement of cups, he could collect samples from tamarins in the forest.

Ira and Erika enjoyed the coffee and granola bars that she had brought.

"Freya is really peeved," said Erika.

"I'll make it up to her when this settles down."

"*If* it settles down."

"Those candy crackers look good," thought Emily, "Better than this stuff from the can."

Chapter 46

Summer In The Woods

From the fifth day on, no more tamarins got lost. The family slowly expanded its range, and by the end of May they were regularly traveling 50 feet in all directions from the cooler box, and returning. They got steadier on the swinging ropes, and even used some narrow flexible branches.

Niko arch-walked and screeched at a squirrel as they both fed on maple seeds, high up in the tree. The volunteers thought that the tamarins were also eating insects, but this could not be confirmed.

One morning, zoo visitors saw Ira, Erika, and the volunteers looking up into the trees with binoculars, and followed their gaze to the tamarins.

"Look, there are monkeys loose in the trees! Did those monkeys escape?"

"No, we put them there."

"Why don't they run away?"

"Because they have their home, food, and family."

"That's the coolest. Why are you doing this?"

"To help them learn what they need to know to live in the wild. We'll be taking them to Brazil in September."

There would be thousands of variations on this conversation during the next four months. More than 1,000,000 zoo visitors would see the tamarins in their free-ranging exhibit. People came to the zoo intending to see giant pandas, great apes and big cats, but for those who happened to see them, the free-ranging tamarins were the highlight of their visit. The volunteers turned into educators as well as monkey observers, and would tell the reintroduction story hundreds of times. Some of the volunteers were resistant to this role; they were animal people first and foremost! The zoo's education director would become ecstatic with the exhibit's impact. Ken would talk quietly with potential donors about the zoo's new era of innovation.

The family ventured farther and farther from the box, staying within the valley. Niko and Emily usually led these expeditions; Rufous always trailed, complaining the whole time: "We've got everything we need at the box. Why do we need to go anywhere?"

In late June, they reached the end of Beaver Valley, and looked across a broad sidewalk toward the small mammal house and the outdoor bison yard. At that moment, the zoo's permanent group of golden lion tamarins, living in cage #34 at the rear of the small mammal house, made some long calls.

"Wow, let's go!" said Niko, who ran across the sidewalk on the ground. The volunteers radioed Ira and Erika frantically for help, and tried to keep the zoo visitors away from the tamarins. Niko, Emily, Petie and Opie arrived at cage #34 shortly afterward, and a battle royal ensued. Each group was astounded at the presence of the other. There was arch walking and screaming, but the cage mesh prevented any serious damage. The Brookfield family seemed to tire of the encounter after 30 minutes, and scrambled up to the roof of the building. There, in the clay roof tiles, they found an abundance of insects and spiders, which they ate hungrily. Rufous and Sandy, who was on Rufous' back, watched from the other side of the walkway.

Finally, the raiders crossed back to the woods, joined Rufous and Sandy, and the family navigated dead-on back to the nest box.

Ira was elated. "They got really excited," he later reported to Ken, "and could have gotten lost. But at least some of them now have a mental map of the area, and they could find their way home. Their psychological cage just got bigger, but it's still escape-proof."

"So what happened with Opie when he got lost at the bird house?" asked Ken.

"It was too soon after the release, and he hadn't developed a map of the area. He got scared, ran away, and didn't know how to get back. Now, after a month of gradually enlarging their range, they all know their way."

It's not that the tamarins didn't panic occasionally. One day a secret service helicopter flew low over the zoo. Fly-overs in Washington D.C. are rare because of presidential security, and the family mistakenly interpreted the silhouetted 'copter as a giant hawk. Instinctively, they dropped to the ground to escape, and then scattered in all directions. But within minutes they were long-calling and reassembling at the nest tree, because they now knew how to navigate through the forest.

During the summer, a graduate student began to study the navigational skills of the Brookfield family. During the day, he would observe their favorite rope and branch pathways through the trees. Then, after the family went to sleep at night, he cut the branches and tied the ropes in different directions.

"Whoa," called Niko as the group charged back to their enemies at the small mammal house. "Our pathway is gone. It's too far to jump. We need to find another way."

The young scientist documented how the family discovered detours, and more important, who led the group around the gap. Emily and Niko were the most common re-routers. Rufous, carrying Sandy, was a reliable follower.

For her part, Sandy was beginning to get around more on her own. She stayed close to her big brothers and sister. Like Venus and Vesuvio in Brazil, she had never walked on 2X4s in a real zoo cage, so locomoting in the trees of Beaver Valley was a piece of cake for her.

The graduate student suggested that a rope be put up over the sidewalk to connect the Valley forest to the small mammal house. There was no way to stop the family's charges, so it would be wise to keep them off the ground. The rope was quickly strung up, and the tamarins used it at once. When the tamarins crossed on the rope, Ira was reminded of the squirrel that started all of this.

One day, Niko, Petie, and Opie went from the small mammal house to the bison yard on an insect hunt. Opie jumped from a fence to a big shaggy stone, actually a bison lying on the ground. Opie was unaware that the thing was even alive. Ira thought this would have been a great picture, since, as he had told Ken, bison born in New York's Bronx Zoo had been the first zoo animals ever to be reintroduced to the wild, and had helped save this great North American animal from extinction.

By the end of summer, visits to the group in cage #34 had become a recreational diversion. Niko was attracted by a young female who lived in the cage, and she groomed and licked him through the mesh. He sometimes groomed her.

"I wish I could go with you," she said. "Please come back to see me."

He did, but this would be a passing summer romance. Niko would be leaving soon.

The Brookfield family's locomotion and navigation improved greatly over the summer. They covered the Valley from end to end, and went high into the trees to catch and eat cicadas that came out in late July. The graduate student's experiments help them learn about detours. There would be no ropes in Brazil, and the tree species would be different. The bugs would be different, and they would hide in different places. But the family was getting the general idea about getting around in the woods, and searching for food rather than just waiting for it. They found a fruiting mulberry tree that they visited every day for two weeks. They felt rain and wind for the first times in their lives, and endured mosquitoes. These were definitely not "plastic monkeys".

Even the publicity director became a fan of the free-ranging monkeys. She coined the term "boot camp" for the exhibit, and it stuck despite Ira's stodgy disapproval.

They also learned some bad habits. Emily learned how to cadge food from the visitors. Opie loved popcorn, and Sandy favored small bits of hot dogs. The family even learned how to graze on leftovers in trashcans. Rufous developed a taste for soda pop. They all spent too much time on the ground looking for these snacks. The volunteers now added crowd control to their work. They asked visitors to finish their food and drinks before walking through Beaver Valley, and intervened when somebody insisted on slipping some food to the begging monkeys. Trashcans with secure lids were installed. Ira found it interesting that the tamarins were never seen to sample any of the many mushrooms that grew on the valley floor.

"Mmmmm, look at that cold bite fruit," said Petie, referring to a popsicle.

"Our two-legger watchers will shoo you away if you try to beg for some," said Rufous.

"I'm starting to not like those watchers," said Petie.

There was also good news from Brazil during the summer.

"Pandora had twins!" Alicia reported breathlessly in a late-July Friday phone call. "She's carrying them and we've definitely seen them nurse. Swamp 4 is staying really close."

"That's terrific," said Ira. "What do you want to name them?"

"I've been reading up on Greek mythology," replied Alicia. "Pandora has a bad reputation, not anything like our sweet Pandora."

"So, what do we name her babies?"

"Of course it depends on their sexes, but William and I suggest Aphrodite and Hermes if they are a male and female."

"What would Swamp 4 think? I doubt he's into mythology," kidded Ira. "And a tamarin leg isn't long enough for an 'Aphrodite' tattoo. How about Red River 1 and 2, RR1 and RR2?"

"OK, boss," she agreed. The infants would prove to be a female and male, and two months later they were tattooed RR1 and RR2, but to William and Alicia they would always be Aphrodite and Hermes.

"Oh, and Tina's really showing now. She's about eight months along."

Looking for Handouts in Beaver Valley
Smithsonian's National Zoo photo by Jessie Cohen

"I hope John Wayne gets a sister," chuckled Ira.

Erika, Ira, and Freya celebrated the baby boom that night with a long walk in the park, a bottle of Chianti, and a good pizza. Freya passed on the wine but gladly gobbled the usually forbidden piece of bacon pizza. Freya had finally forgiven Ira now that she was getting her two daily walks.

Chapter 47

Virus

The zoo's records keeper applied for the international permits to ship the Brookfield family out of the United States and into Brazil. She also made flight arrangements for the tamarins. Ira and Erika were scheduled to be on the same flight, leaving on the first Sunday in October.

A 30-day pre-shipment quarantine was required for the monkeys, so Erika snapped the cooler box door shut on the Tuesday after Labor Day, and the tamarins were taken from their summer paradise and returned to their small boring indoor cage in the quarantine section.

Over the summer there had been more than 22,000 reports, many urgent and breathless, from visitors to zoo staff about escaped monkeys in the zoo. The staff was happy to see an end to this. Volunteers had recorded 435 pages of data on the behavior and ranging of the Brookfield group, including 96 "Falls" caused by overflying helicopters. The volunteers were worn out by two-hour shifts of trudging after the tamarins, answering questions from visitors, and breaking up illicit feedings. The young female tamarin in the cage #34 group was heartbroken at the sudden disappearance of her summer crush.

"Why are we back in here?" asked a disappointed Niko, but nobody in his family had an answer.

"If we listen to the two-leggers talk, maybe we'll find out," said Emily.

"But the little blond one talks to us in a different language," said Petie. "I can't understand a word."

The family was caught in the box five days before shipment, and once again taken from their cage and anesthetized for a complete physical examination. The whole family had gained weight over the summer; Emily was almost 800 grams.

"She's way too fat," said Dr. Lisa. Emily was sleeping so she didn't hear the insult. She also didn't hear Ira's reply: "Don't worry – she'll lose it in Brazil."

Emily, Rufous and Niko got new radio collars with fresh batteries. Opie and Petie had gone over 500 grams, so they got collars too.

"They look excellent," said Dr. Lisa when they were done. "I'll do the certificate of health as soon as I see the blood results."

On Friday, Ira got a call from Dr. Lisa: "Can you come to the hospital right away? We have a problem."

Dr. Richardson, the zoo's internationally famous expert on animal diseases, was also in Dr. Lisa's office when Ira arrived.

Dr. Richardson began: "I want to apologize in advance. We made a major mistake, but there is still time to correct it. When we collected blood from the Brookfield family last April, we did routine lab examinations, and they were all normal. But I also sent samples away to be screened for viruses. That took several weeks, and when the report came back it got buried on my desk and I didn't see it until this morning."

"So......?" asked Ira.

"It's a complicated story. Bear with me. As you know, there have been about twelve cases in American zoos in the past few years where entire golden lion tamarin families have died suddenly. They all suddenly stop eating, get sluggish, have seizures, and almost all of them die within a few days. There is no successful treatment. It's a form of viral hepatitis."

"I've read about it," said Ira, "but we've never seen it here."

"No, and none of the Brookfield animals has hepatitis or any other type of disease," assured Dr. Lisa.

"What's the problem then?"

"Rufous was exposed to the disease at the zoo in Florida where he lived previously, before being sent to Brookfield. He's one of the few survivors of an outbreak," said Dr. Richardson, in a calm and clinical voice.

"But he's fine now," said Ira.

"Yes, but he's carrying the *antibody* to the disease, a bodily clue that he once caught the disease and fought it off," said Dr. Richardson.

"We've all had mumps. We recover, and then carry the mumps antibodies for our whole lives," said Dr. Lisa, "even though we will never get mumps again."

"So, Rufous will never get hepatitis again," reasoned Ira.

"That's the problem," said Dr. Richardson. "The hepatitis virus is a type of virus that can remain, inactive, in the body for years and then sometimes cause a relapse of the same disease or even a different disease."

Richardson's social skills lagged behind his indisputable medical competence. Meetings like this made him nervous. He was speaking without looking at Ira, preferring instead to diligently clean his fingernails with a 6-inch buck knife.

Ira tried not to be distracted. "You're saying 'can' and 'sometimes'. How likely is this to happen?"

"We are just learning about this family of viruses, but it's clear that they don't really go away. It's possible we would be shipping a virus if we shipped him."

(dig…scrape…wipe…dig….)

"You're suggesting that we not send Rufous to Brazil?"

"That's one option. We need to decide, before Sunday."

Dr. Lisa said that she could sign the health certificate saying that Rufous was disease-free, but she would be uncomfortable knowing that he was carrying the hepatitis antibody, and maybe the live virus.

"What's the worst that could happen?" asked Ira.

"He could get another bout of hepatitis, or another viral disease, that could kill the whole family and even spread through the entire wild population. Even other species could be infected," said Dr. Richardson. "He could be eaten, and the virus hidden in his body could sicken the predator or a scavenger. The disease has not been reported in animals in Brazil, so there would be no immunity – zilch. The chances are small but the effects would be disastrous. Whole species could be wiped out."

"So, you're suggesting that I remove the breeding male - the father - of this family, two days before shipment!" said Ira, his mind racing to the consequences of changed paperwork, fighting in the group as Niko tried to take over, and social instability at a crucial point in the reintroduction process.

"We are so sorry to hit you with this now," said Dr. Richardson, "but this is too big to ignore."

"Can I sleep on it," asked Ira, "and tell you in the morning?"

"Sure." The knife flipped shut. Meeting over.

Chapter 48

Breakup

"We'd have to ship Niko separately, and find a different place to reintroduce him," said Erika that evening as they discussed the situation. "Otherwise he and Emily will fight or mate, and either would be bad."

"For sure," said Ira. "I think the paperwork issue can be resolved. An extra animal would be a problem, but one less should be OK."

"I don't think Rufous would be an especially good reintroduction candidate anyway," added Erika. "He's not nearly as agile and active as the others, and he resists change."

"Would we try to find a new male for Emily in Brazil?" thought Ira aloud.

They sipped their wine quietly for a few seconds, and then Ira said: "You know, the inconvenience and disruption are nothing compared to the risk to the Brazilian ecosystem. We just can't take that risk. Agree?"

"Of course," she said. "On Sunday morning I'll crate Sandy with Emily, Niko by himself, Opie with Petie, and leave Rufous behind."

"I'll call Dr. Lisa, and Kay."

Kay was furious. "This is bull, she said. How can you let the vets push you around?"

"Can we meet for bagels in the morning?" asked Ira. "I've had a long day."

They met the next morning in a deli known for really good New York-style bagels. Kay was quick to begin: "You should have invited me to the meeting. Richardson was just trying to throw his weight around, and maybe get a flashy publication out of the situation."

"I didn't have a chance to call you about the meeting, and I really think Richardson was trying to be constructive. They screwed up by not catching this earlier and giving us a chance to find a new male, but this really is a 'better late than never' situation. And Lisa was really trying to do the right thing, while respecting Richardson's and my situations."

"Well, I guess it's a done deal," sighed Kay.

"Seriously, Kay, you know this is the right decision. We'll get some blowback from the Brazilians about risk, but in the end it's the right call."

"Was it your decision to make?"

"Good question, and it raises a bigger issue. Last year you and I had some awful conflict over management of the reintroduction. You know how much I respect you and your scientific accomplishments, and I hope you know how fond of you I am. I often think there was a mix-up at a hospital, and you're really my sister. But those discussions last year turned into nasty arguments. Sometimes I thought you were arguing just for the fun of it."

"Recreational conflict," Kay chuckled, "I love it."

"Seriously, I'm not talking about who was right or wrong, but I am talking about who is taking the most professional responsibility. When it comes to the actual reintroduction, that's me. And if I have the responsibility, I need to have the authority to make the decisions. Of course I want to know what you, Erika, and Peter think, but in the end I need to make the calls. And this year, that means free-ranging training and intensive post-release management." Ira took a deep breath, expecting a furious response.

"OK," she said, and exploded into laughter. They hugged.

"I'm probably not even going to be in Brazil in the next few months," she said. "I'm going to China for a big meeting on giant panda reproduction and conservation. They're even talking about reintroducing pandas, which is a crazy idea at this point."

"You've just about saved golden lion tamarins as a species, and

now you'll do the same for pandas," Ira said. He was privately thinking of the Chinese scientists and students who would soon feel the
brunt of Hurricane Kay.

"Have a wonderful trip."

"You too."

Ira went to his office and called the bakery in Alicia's hometown. He left a message with the owner, in his best Portuguese, for
Alicia to have two cages ready at the field station by Monday morning. Somehow, he knew, the word would get to her.

Then he went home to pack. A new radio receiver and antenna,
and 20 radio collars took up most of his luggage space. Two large
bags of nacho chips were carefully wrapped in clothing. There were
Mag-Lites for everybody. At the time Mag-Lites were the only really waterproof flashlights and they are still among the best today.
A big bag of Mr. Goodbars got stuck into another corner; Brazil
was producing much of the best raw cocoa in the world but many
young Brazilians preferred American milk chocolate. A dozen plastic bottles of high-octane military-grade mosquito repellant went
in, carefully wrapped in several plastic bags. So did a jar of mixed
spices for seasoning tacos. Erika packed some cute outfits for John
Wayne and baby-to-be, and a pair of hot jeans for Alicia. Ira had a
digital pocket calculator for William.

Freya moped anxiously nearby, knowing full well the meaning
of suitcases being packed. But Erika's friend and colleague would be
staying at the house and doting on Freya. She would be well cared
for and spoiled rotten in the next few weeks.

Chapter 49

Rufous Retires

The Brookfield family was roused early on Sunday morning and allowed to "escape" into the quarantine area. Ira and Erika could not entirely escape the storm of poop and pee, and would both have to change shirts before the flight. The tamarins were skillfully caught in nets, and put into waiting sky kennels that had been bedded with soft hay and stuffed with grapes and quartered oranges. Erika scrubbed the cooler nest box, and everything was loaded into a waiting van.

"We're going outside again," said Niko. "I'm going to get to visit my honey today."

"Then why are we in these crates and not in our nest box?" asked Emily.

"Oh."

"What do you think, Rufous?"

"Ruf, where do you think we're going now?"

"Rufous?"

"Dad?"

"He's not here. They forgot him."

"Stop, wait!"

But the van drove out of the zoo and headed for the airport.

Emily was heartbroken. She knew now that they were going to be taken to another zoo, and that Rufous would not be going with them. She had been with him for four years, all of her adult life. He wasn't dynamic but he was sweet and caring, and a good father.

"Where's my daddy?" asked Sandy. "Did the two-leggers hurt him?"

"I don't think they'll hurt him, but I don't think we'll see him again," answered Emily with a heavy heart and sick stomach.

Rufous was devastated and confused. He was back in the zoo quarantine cage, alone, without his family or even a nest box, and nobody to discuss it with.

Emily was correct on both counts. The 'two-leggers' would not really hurt Rufous but he became a science project. He would be sent the next morning to a government communicable disease laboratory at Fort Dietrich, Maryland, and housed in a small cage with a male cotton-top tamarin that also carried hepatitis antibodies. He would be fed canned tamarin diet and be well cared for, but would spend the remaining five years of his life in boring high-security quarantine. He tried unsuccessfully to teach his cage mate some words, but for the most part, other than some occasional grooming, they ignored each other. To the disappointment of the lab's scientists, Rufous would not have another outbreak of hepatitis or any other viral disease. He would eventually die of pneumonia that his aging immune system could not fight off. But the scientists did indeed find live hepatitis virus in his tissues after he died. Rufous had been a walking time bomb.

Once in the air, Erika said: "I feel so bad for Rufous."

"Me too," said Ira. "This is one of those situations where there are no good options and we have to choose the 'least bad' one."

"Who actually made this decision?" she asked.

"I guess I did," said Ira, "but Dr. Lisa might not have signed the health certificate."

"What did Kay think?"

"She was angry at first, I think because she wasn't involved in the discussion. But she agrees, and I'm sure Peter would agree."

"Why didn't you involve Kay?"

"To be truthful, I didn't think of it. Things moved so quickly."

"Are you and Kay OK?"

"I think so. We had a frank discussion about last year's control struggles, and I told her that from now on I needed to make the decisions about reintroduction. She agreed, or at least didn't disagree."

"So now you just have me to argue with," said Erika, with a smile.

"I'm going to sleep," said Ira.

They landed in Brazil the next morning. There was the typical bureaucratic chaos and media frenzy. No mention was made to the media that the family now lacked a father.

Alicia was waiting with the microbus. "I finally got my driver's license, so now I can drive on the highway" she said proudly.

"You've got some precious cargo on board," Ira said.

But he needn't have worried. Alicia drove with the same effortless skill that she brought to all of her life's undertakings.

At the field station there were fond and noisy reunions with William, Carlos, Tina, John Wayne, and Peter. Carlos and Tina introduced their two-week old daughter, Alicia, who had just been christened. Her godmother Alicia beamed.

After just a few minutes, Emily, Sandy, Opie, and Petie, and their cooler nest box, were put into the cage at the field station that had been built last year for Pandora and Swamp 4. Niko was stashed in a smaller cage on the veranda, with a small wooden box. Erika and Alicia fed them and reassured them, in German and Portuguese respectively. They had no idea that the micos were having translation problems.

"Which one is the father?" asked Peter.

"That's a long story," said Ira. "Let's visit Pandora and Swamp 4, and I'll explain on the drive to the ranch." William gathered the radio receiver, antenna, machetes, and water while Erika and Ira changed into field clothes, and they all took off in the microbus.

When Ira had finished explaining about Rufous and the virus, Peter said: "Good call."

"Now we have to find mates for two micos, Emily and Niko," said William. "Maybe we can take the young female from the swamp group for Niko."

"Let's stop at headquarters and ask Jorge," said Peter. "Swamp 3 has already left the family but there are two younger female twins about Niko's age."

"Speaking of mates," said Alicia, "I need to tell you all about a sticky situation before we get to the Rio Vermelho ranch. When I go there to see the micos, I always check in with Senhor Mauricio and have a cup of coffee or a glass of juice with him. He's a wonderful man, and has asked me to marry him. I haven't given him an answer yet, but you may pick up some vibrations today."

The whine of the microbus engine was the only sound for about ten seconds. Everybody was speechless.

"We can talk about it later," Alicia said, looking directly at Erika, "but I didn't want you to be surprised."

Mauricio was waiting on the veranda with coffee and juice, having heard the microbus approach from a distance. He greeted Ira and Erika cordially, but his gaze was unmistakably fixed on Alicia.

William found Pandora's radio signal, and the team walked uphill to the old nest box, now inhabited by bees. Then they walked down to the river and found the family feeding high in a fig tree growing over the water. Hermes and Aphrodite, now four months old, were begging solid food from their parents with the obnoxious rasping begging call of infant micos.

"There's a spot up the river a bit where the river narrows, and the crowns of trees touch and form a bridge. I think they've actually crossed the São João into the reserve," said William.

"That's excellent. Hermes and Aphrodite will be able to look for mates there when their time comes," said Peter.

"And," said William, pausing for effect, "the Santa Helena ranch borders on this ranch. It's just across the Red River, on the other side of this ranch. When we reintroduce the Brookfield group there, this group and the Brookfield group might have contact. There will only be about 150 meters of pasture, and of the course the river, between them."

"That's a lot for a mico to cross," said Peter.

"For sure," answered William, "but maybe we could persuade Senhor Mauricio to let us plant trees to make a land bridge to connect the forests on the Rio Vermelho and Santa Helena ranches."

"Super idea," said Ira, "but we'll have to do some hiking to find the right place to build the bridge."

"I'm working on that with some of my former colleagues," said William with a wink.

"Would you like to visit the Santa Helena ranch now?" asked Alicia.

"I'm bushed from the trip," said Erika. Ira nodded in agreement.

"And I have to get out to check on a few wild groups yet this afternoon," said Peter. "One of these days we're going to hike through the reserve to the São João and begin to meet Pandora's neighbors. We've already trapped and collared the wild group near the quarry that Prometheus' mate came from."

On their way back to the field station they stopped at the reserve headquarters to see Jorge, and explain Niko's predicament.

"Sorry, but we can't take a mico out of the protected area," Jorge said. "I allowed you to take Swamp 4 because he was only in the reserve for one day before his father beat him up. But now the rest of the group has been there for nearly a year. Could you reintroduce Niko into the reserve?"

"Only if we're sure there's a group without an adult male," said Peter, "and even then it's unlikely an inexperienced zoo male like Niko could take over."

They gave Jorge a few Mr. Goodbars and a Mag-Lite, and headed for the field station.

That night, over Tina's delicious, garlicky beans and beer, the group continued to discuss options for their mateless micos. They made plans to visit the Santa Helena ranch the next morning, and Prometheus and the Olympia group in the afternoon. Alicia was looking to have some girl time with Erika to discuss her marriage proposal, but Erika fell asleep right after supper. It had been a long two days, with only a few hours of airplane sleep.

Chapter 50

Cathedral Santa Helena

The dirt road to the proposed Santa Helena release site did not pass close to the ranch house, so Ira and Erika did not get to meet the owner, Senhor Nelson. There was a locked gate at the entrance they were supposed to use, and Nelson had given William and Alicia a key. The road narrowed and darkened as they entered the tall dense forest. After about 500 meters the road became just a walking path. The two assistants had already carved out a small turnaround at the trailhead.

"It's another 500 meters up this trail," said William. "Please go first, Ira."

Walking face-first into a spider web is unpleasant for the walker and the spider. One minute the spider waits vigilantly in its sticky gossamer hunting stand, and the next minute it's plastered to a human head. When the spider is a dinner plate-sized giant orb-weaver, like the one that Ira was now trying to remove from his face, its eight legs stretch from ear-to-ear, chin-to-forehead, and pass through the human's eyebrows. Now the experience shifts from unpleasant to terrifying. It doesn't help to know that the spider is not poisonous, or to have walked into orb webs before, it's still terrifying. Ira rubbed and flicked but the web stuck like a thousand boogers. The web was so strong that it made a crackling sound when he pulled it off.

Ira had thought that William's invitation for him to lead the group into the forest on the narrow trail had been a gesture of respect. But the assistants knew that this forest was full of orb weavers, and if the light was not just right, you were bound to walk into a web. They were waiting like kids on Christmas morning for Ira to hit one, and were now enjoying his struggles. Ira and the spider finally emerged unharmed, though the spider had to weave a whole new web.

"Thanks a lot," said Ira.

They walked uphill and then down the other side. A stream rushed alongside the trail. Ira was now alert for orb-weaver webs, and they had to duck under a few. When they had descended into the valley they stood at the edge of a giant bowl, an amphitheater, of forest. These were the biggest trees that Ira had seen in Brazil. Many were over 30 meters tall. Little light penetrated the dense treetops, and the light that did get through traveled in tightly compressed beams, as if the bowl was lit by downlights in the branches. The air was chilly and damp. Bromeliads, moss, and lichens decorated the trees. There was a choir of the gurgling stream, calling frogs, chirping birds and whining mosquitoes. The steep architecture of the surrounding hills, the "dome" of soaring limbs of centuries-old trees, and the cool, dim, musty air struck Ira as Nature's model of a cathedral.

"What a beautiful place," said Erika. "I'm sure the micos will love it."

"We thought so too," said Alicia. "There's forest on the other sides of the hills, and it goes right down to the Red River to the north. We think there's about 238 hectares of forest, but most of it is drier and not as tall as this spot."

"I'm sure there were micos here at one time. I wonder why they disappeared," said Ira.

"Anyway, I think we'll have to release the Brookfield group soon, even without a mate for Emily," he continued. "They've been in a cage at the field station for two days; we can't keep them there forever, hoping that a male will turn up."

"We're ready if you and the micos are," said William, with Alicia's approval.

"Tomorrow morning?" asked Erika.

"OK, but let's head back to the field station and make sure we all agree to the plan for managing a soft release," said Ira.

Ira and Erika filled in the two assistants on the summer "boot camp" at the zoo on the drive back. The term "boot camp" prompted lots of page turning in their small Portuguese/English dictionaries. "Bison" was likewise unfamiliar, since there are no wild cattle in South America. William loved the description of Opie hunting for insects on the back of the reclining bison.

After lunch, Peter joined the four on the veranda of the field station.

Ira began: "We think this group learned a lot about finding food, moving on natural branches, and navigating during their three months of free-ranging at the zoo. These are not, to use Peter's term, 'plastic monkeys'."

"But we're not taking any chances, so we are going to do a soft release as well."

Erika continued: "We'll give them their familiar nest box, and we'll give them lots of food and water until we're sure they're finding enough on their own."

"How would we know?" asked Peter.

"By weighing the amount of food we gave them at the zoo, and subtracting what was left over, I was able to calculate how much they ate," answered Erika. "Each mico eats an average of about a quarter of a pound of food per day; 123.6 grams to be exact."

"If they begin eating less, they must be finding natural food," reasoned William.

"If they're not losing weight," said Alicia.

"Exactly," said Erika, "and that's where William's field weighing comes in. Are you still doing that?"

"Yes," said William, "and O9 has been gaining weight, but that's another story. If they're eating less of the food we give them, and not losing weight, they must be eating natural food."

"Exactly," said Erika.

"Why would the tamarins ever leave the area of the box and the food," asked Peter.

"We were all concerned about that last year," said Ira. "We'll start by putting the food just outside of the nest box. After three days, we'll move it 3 meters away, and after three more days we'll move the bowl 3 more meters away, each day in a different direction. If they don't find it, we'll move it back a little until they do."

"What if they get lost?" asked Alicia.

"We'll either lure them back with a banana, or trap them and bring them back."

"Does Kay agree with all of this?" asked Peter.

"I think so," said Ira, "but she's given me the OK to make the calls."

"I like the results-based management," said Peter. "You've got a clear plan to wean them off human support."

"The combination of the free-ranging experience before release, and the intensive support after release should really boost survival rates," said Ira.

Out in the banana grove, the Brookfield group members were also discussing their future.

"Why won't they let Niko be with us?" asked Opie.

"At least he's here," said Emily, avoiding what she knew to be the real answer: preventing mating between a mother and son. "I miss Rufous so much."

"It's warm and pretty here," said Petie, "but this is a small cage."

"I'm trying to figure out why we still have collars even though we're in a cage," said Emily.

"I don't have one," pouted Sandy.

"Here come the girl two-leggers with our afternoon food," said Opie.

Erika and Alicia, speaking affectionately to the micos in German and Portuguese respectively, distributed mystery packages, whole bananas, a papaya, and a mango in the cage. They put several of the small live traps, with doors wired open, in the cage to get the micos used to going in them.

"What's the stuff in the can?" asked William.

"Nutritionally complete tamarin food," said Erika. "We brought a whole case to get them started."

This was a new concept for Alicia and William, since not even canned dog food was available in Brazil at the time.

Niko long-called, probably wondering if he was going to get food too. His cage was too small for people to go in, so they just opened the door and put in a bowl of food and a fresh bowl of water. The plan was to move him to the larger cage in the banana grove after the rest of the family had been reintroduced.

Opie returned Niko's call, and suddenly new voices were heard from across the valley.

"Probably the Swamp group," said William.

Chapter 51

Unintended Consequences

After people and tamarins had eaten breakfast the next morning, Erika shooed the Brookfield group into their cooler box and fastened a piece of wire mesh over the entrance hole. Carlos unhooked the box and put it into the bus, and everybody but Tina, John Wayne, little Alicia, and Niko headed for the Santa Helena ranch. They were greeted by Senhor Nelson, and some of his family members and staff. Ira had not invited media this time. The spectators followed the bus on bicycles and horseback to the turnaround area at the trailhead. Dismounted, the procession headed for the cathedral. Carlos led, keenly locating spider webs and obliterating them with his machete. Ira carried the picnic cooler. Some of the field hands hoped it held cold sodas.

The release was a perfect replay of the first day in Beaver Valley. Emily came out first but did not go farther than 2 meters from the box. Opie, Petie, and Sandy followed and stayed close as well. They ate from Erika's bowls, played, rested, groomed, and ran in and out of the box. Nobody fell or ran away.

"I wish Niko and Rufous could be here," said Emily.

"Let's call to see if there are other tamarins here," said Opie.

"Let's just lay low for a while," cautioned Emily.

Opie long-called anyway. There was no response, but that didn't necessarily mean he was unheard.

Nelson's family and the ranch hands seemed to be impressed and happy, and Nelson was proud to be hosting the micos. They all left after an hour. Before leaving, Nelson invited the team to the house for refreshments, but they declined, explaining they'd have to stay until the tamarins went to sleep for the night.

Back at the field station, Tina went about her chores, stopping every once in a while to feed and change little Alicia. John Wayne played on the veranda. Niko, aware that his family was no longer in the banana grove, began to long-call for them from his cage on the veranda. They of course could not hear, but the Swamp group could. They finally could no longer ignore this intruder, who wouldn't shut up. The group moved downhill toward the house, crossed the swamp, and entered the banana grove. Niko and the Swampers were arch-walking, with the hair on their backs erect like an army of angry cats.

JW ran into the house. "Micos, micos," he told his mother but she didn't get the message, from her son or the monkeys themselves.

Erika and Alicia had asked Tina to feed Niko in the afternoon, and left his bowl in the refrigerator. Tina finally heard Niko calling at about 1 PM, and thought he might be hungry. She fetched the bowl, and she and JW headed for Niko's little cage on the veranda.

Animal care was not among Tina's many strengths. She just assumed that Niko would retreat when she opened the cage door. Instead he shot past her and headed for the banana grove where the Swamp group lingered. He was outnumbered but made a brave showing, despite being chased and nipped a few times. Tina went to the banana grove hoping to catch Niko. This frightened the Swamp group back across the valley. Niko of course assumed that his fearsome attack had caused the retreat.

Niko ignored Tina's invitations to return to his cage or to enter the larger cage. There were plenty of ripe bananas to eat here, and he was determined never to live in a cage again. He had reintroduced himself, into a protected biological reserve, with what was thought to be the last 150 individuals of his species living in the wild. He had also noticed one or two young females in the group he had chased away. Life was good.

Tina was mortified, and had no way of summoning help or

notifying anybody.

The team returned to the field station at 7:30 at night. The joy over the success of the release of the Brookfield group was quickly dampened by Tina's confession.

"It's OK," Ira reassured her. "He's wearing a radio collar so we'll be able to find him."

As JW was proudly recounting "his" management of Niko's reintroduction, big Alicia stepped out into the darkness with the radio receiver and antenna. The signal was loud and clear: Niko had settled into the top of a nearby mango tree for the night.

Chapter 52

Macumba

Ira decided that Niko's recapture could wait. The priority now was monitoring the Brookfield group. He asked Tina at breakfast to lock the cage if she saw Niko inside, and then the four headed back to Fazenda Santa Helena.

Somebody had set three shallow, fire-blackened clay bowls on the ground by the gate. The bowls were surrounded by empty sugar cane liquor bottles. There were burning candles in the bottles and in one of the bowls. Another bowl held a headless chicken, lying in its own viscous blackening blood, and the third bowl held the chicken's head, also steeping in blood. A large needle penetrated one of the chicken's eyes.

"What is that?" asked Ira.

"Macumba," said Alicia, stepping over the mess to open the gate.

"What does it mean?"

"We'll tell you later."

When they arrived at the tree with the cooler, the micos were already out, eating scraps of yesterday's food.

The assistants lowered the two food bowls and carefully weighed all leftover food, They cleaned and refilled the bowls with food that Erika had cut and weighed in the morning, and raised them back up into the tree near the cooler's entrance hole. They rinsed and refilled the water bowl in the stream, and raised it back up too.

Erika and Alicia began to collect data on Emily's and Sandy's behavior. Ira and William observed Opie and Petie. The micos were soon venturing out about 5 meters from the cooler, and Erika and Alicia found themselves standing alone, out of earshot of the men.

They had a chance to talk between observations.

"So what's with you and Senhor Mauricio?" asked Erika with her characteristic bluntness.

"As I told you, he's asked me to marry him."

"And......?"

"He's 50 years older than me. I'm only a few years older than his grandson."

"Does he love you?"

"I think so, and he's very sweet. His wife died about five years ago. I've never been in love, so I don't really know if I love him."

"Believe me, you'd know. If you don't sweat when you see him, you're not in love."

"I don't sweat when I see him."

"If you married him, your mother would never have to clean houses and sell meat pastries on the street again. Your brothers and sisters could go to school, even to university. You'd be the mistress of a fine ranch, and never have to work again."

"But I wouldn't have *earned* it."

"Sounds like you're going to turn him down."

"My family is pushing me to accept."

"It's your life Alicia. Are you worried that you'll never find another man that wants to marry you?"

"Actually I don't really care if I get married or not."

The men were also having a talk. "What's with the dead chicken?" Ira asked.

"It's macumba, a form of voodoo brought by slaves from Africa. Almost all of us Brazilians have some slave ancestors, and many Brazilians, even those that count themselves as Catholics, still practice macumba."

"Are the bowls and chicken some sort of curse?"

"More a warning of bad things to come. The candles were still burning when we arrived, so somebody is trying to tell us something."

At that moment, it began to pour.

Ira and William put on their raincoats. "Well," said Ira, "if this is the bad thing, we'll survive."

"Never take macumba too seriously, but don't take it lightly either," cautioned William.

Sandy, Opie, and Petie headed for the cooler to get out of the rain. Emily, inexplicably, headed in the other direction. She walked steadily, with apparent determination, to the top of one of the hills surrounding the forest cathedral, and started down the other side. It reminded Ira and Erika of Mom's behavior last year, when she climbed the cliff and was never seen again. But this year Emily wore a radio collar, and Alicia could follow her. Ira and Erika followed Alicia, leaving William to stare at a cooler box in the driving rain. He soon rigged a poncho as a shelter, and settled back in relative comfort.

Erika and Ira were struggling up the hill, slipping on wet roots and slimy mud. Their boots and pants were soon wet and dirty. When they slipped they instinctively grabbed for bushes or tree trunks, many of which had spines, leaving their hands bleeding. Licks of their hair were plastered to their foreheads and rivers of rain poured over their faces, despite the hoods of their raincoats.

They found Alicia and Emily on the far side of the hill. Alicia too had rigged a poncho as a shelter. Emily had stopped about 3 meters up in a small tree, and simply sat, hunched over in the cold rain.

Erika showed a peeled banana to Emily but she was not interested. Ira baited and set a small live trap on a branch below her, and she showed no interest in this either.

"She's probably not hungry," said Erika. "She ate less than an hour ago."

"At least she stopped running," said Ira. "She'll get hungry soon, and then we can lure her back to the cooler tree."

The rain picked up, and the temperature began to drop. Ira checked the little thermometer attached to his raincoat zipper. By noon it had fallen to 59 degrees Fahrenheit. By 3 PM it was 57.

Neither Emily nor her observers had moved more than a step.

William arrived at 5 PM. "The others have eaten a little but are pretty much staying in the box."

Erika tried for the fourth time to interest Emily in a banana, but she ignored the fruit, simply sitting on the same branch in the same hunched position.

"I'm miserable and I have a raincoat," said Erika. "Emily should be desperate by now."

Ira started to shiver as the rain and cold seeped through his clothes. He looked down in despair and discomfort, and was shocked to see that his boots were as bright as the day he had bought them. Eight hours of driving rain had bleached out every trace of dirt and stain.

"Let's try to climb up and grab her," said Ira. "Otherwise she's sure to be dead by morning."

"But she might start running again," said Erika.

"We have to try."

Ira stripped off his raincoat, stepped on William's linked hands, and pulled himself into the tree's lowest branch. The next branch was an easy step up, and Ira began to balance himself to make the grab.

Emily jumped straight up, one, two, three branches and ended up 8 meters high in the tree, again sitting and hunched over, ignoring the banana he offered.

The light began to fade at 7:30, and it was too dark to see by 8:15.

"There's no sense in staying any longer," said Ira. "She's not going to move now."

They walked dejectedly to the bus. As they locked the gate on their way out, Ira noticed that the rain had washed the chicken blood out of the bowls. Emily would surely die this night, either from exposure or in the jaws of a predator. Was this the "bad thing" that macumba had predicted?

Chapter 53

One Cold Monkey

There was no need to take showers. The driving rain had left the team with scoured, shriveled skin. They began to recover after donning warm dry cotton sweatshirts and sweat pants. Tina served boiling black beans and rice. Ira, Erika, and Alicia just picked at their food. William ate heartily, but all four were devastated by Emily's demise, so soon after being reintroduced. Ira and Erika drank too much wine. Peter offered support and shared the wine.

"The rain must have scared her," said Ira, "and she took off. Because of the boot camp, her locomotion was excellent, and she covered a lot of ground. But then, our post-release management failed. She just shut down, and would not allow us to rescue her."

The team arose early, donned fresh field clothes and still-wet boots and headed for Santa Helena. The rain had stopped but it was 55 degrees. The four trudged to Emily's last location. Her body lay on the ground where she had fallen from the tree during the night. At least she had not been attacked by a predator or scavenger. Ira picked up the body. She was soaked and cold to the touch. Her lips and tongue were blue. Ira cradled Emily tenderly, and then felt a heart beat! It was faint and slow, but she was still alive. Alicia immediately tucked Emily under her shirt, and they headed for the bus.

Ira asked William and Erika to stay with the group and feed the micos when they woke up. He and Alicia headed for Alicia's house, which was the nearest warm and safe place. Ira drove while Alicia snuggled Emily's nearly lifeless body. There was little traffic in the dawn hour, which was fortunate since Ira drove too fast and less expertly than Alicia.

Alicia's house was warm and only a few kilometers away, but it was not an ideal choice for treating a very sick endangered monkey. Alicia's mom shooed a half dozen kids away from their meager breakfast and cleared the table. She kicked three cats and a dog out of the kitchen. Kids and animals alike howled in protest. There was no alcohol for sterilizing the table or Ira's and Alicia's hands.

Alicia carefully removed Emily from beneath her shirt, with an unintended flash of cappuccino-colored skin. Ira took a thermometer from his emergency kit and took Emily's temperature: 93 degrees when normally it would be 100. Her breathing was shallow and ragged and her heart rate was down to 62 beats per minute from a normal rate of over 100.

"First job is to dry her and warm her up," said Ira. He wrapped Emily in a big fluffy towel that mom had taken from the "guests-only" supply, handed her back to Alicia, and sat down to wait. Mom served coffee.

Emily opened her eyes after ten minutes, and then made a soft peeping sound.

"She's not out of the woods yet," said Ira.

"I don't understand," said Alicia. "She's in my kitchen now."

"Idiom," said Ira. "Sorry. What I meant was that she could still die."

Emily began to struggle a bit after a few minutes, and mom put down a cup of warm milk. She kept an ever-changing menagerie of chickens, ducks, pigs, dogs, cats, and even a cow in the back yard, and had nursed many sick animals.

"Just put a drop on her lips," said Ira.

Emily licked the warm milk.

"Give her some more," said mom.

"Let's go slow, said Ira in his best Portuguese. He said to Alicia: "Tell your mom that Emily is really cold. Her internal organs will warm up more slowly than her external body. She could choke on the milk and get it into her lungs, and her kidneys are still too cold to handle the milk. We have to go really slowly now."

Ira injected small amounts of a prepared sugar and water solution beneath Emily's skin, and gave her a shot of antibiotics.

"Do we have an orange that she can lick? Milk is hard to digest"

Emily's recovery was miraculous. Within two hours she was sitting up in a tiny cage on the back porch, eating and drinking a little, and watching the children and animals launch their daily routines. Ira shuddered thinking about the other animals that may have occupied the cage, and at the vast pool of germs that now surrounded Emily as she recovered. At least she was alive. The exposure was a risk they would have to take. Since there were no wild micos on Santa Helena ranch, there was at least no risk to the wild population.

"Why don't you stay here for the day?" Ira asked Alicia. "I'll go back and share the news with Erika and William, and we'll pick you and Emily up this afternoon."

Chapter 54

Gummy

When the microbus rolled up to the Santa Helena gate the next morning, the chicken and its detached head were gone, probably having been dragged off by a scavenger. The bottles had fallen over and the bowls were full of rainwater. The macumba display no longer looked ominous. The rain had stopped, the road was drying, and a warming sun was rising in the east. Things were looking up.

Alicia had brought along a fully-recovered Emily, and Emily began to long-call from the little live trap before Alicia had even taken her out of the bus. Opie, Petie, and Sandy, still at the nest tree half a kilometer away, began to return the call. The micos met the team halfway up the trail. They were already venturing 250 meters from the cooler. Alicia released Emily at the base of the nest tree. Emily ran up to a branch just outside the cooler, reclined in a ray of warming sun, and enjoyed the grooming by all three of her kids.

She jumped up suddenly and peered attentively into the distance. All eyes followed her gaze. The two-leggers saw nothing unusual.

"Quiet," commanded Emily. "Looks like we have company. Get ready for a squabble."

"It's our territory now," said Opie. "Let's go get them."

"Wait," said Emily. "Let's see how big the group is."

But Opie couldn't keep his moth shut, and long-called in his loudest and most threatening voice. Petie joined in too. They took off in the direction of the mico they had spotted. Emily and Sandy lagged behind.

The intruder long-called in return, but it came out croaky and unmelodious. At least it gave the observers a clue about what was going on.

"Wild monkeys," whispered Ira.

"I see one now," said William. "By the way boss, we need some binoculars."

"Let's stay here. The intruders might be scared of us," said Ira, handing William his own binoculars.

Opie and Petie confronted the stranger, but there was no chase. The three sniffed each other. Opie and Petie looked back at Emily and Sandy.

"There's just one," yelled Opie, "and he's old."

Emily and Sandy caught up.

"What's your name?" Sandy asked the intruder.

"He can't talk like we can dear," counseled Emily. "I'm going to groom him as a way of saying hello and showing our good will."

The male lay on his side. Emily began to groom him. He was skinny and his hair was a knotted mess. His skin was covered with scabs and mosquito bites. His tail had been broken at some point in his life, and had healed with an odd kink. There were scars on his face and arms, signs of many battles.

"Help me Petie. This guy hasn't been groomed in years."

Opie, who had been spoiling for a fight, was disappointed but watched in amusement as Emily, Petie, and Sandy groomed their new acquaintance. The grateful intruder got up after ten minutes and began to groom Emily. He was looking better already.

"I was grooming his face," said Sandy. "He doesn't have any teeth in front."

"You be nice to him," said Emily.

"He seems to be old," said William. "He doesn't have any teeth in front."

William handed the binoculars back to Ira.

"You're right. All I can see are gums in his mouth," observed Ira.

"Monkeys chew gum?" said an astounded William.

"Uh-oh," said Ira. "Time out for a short English lesson. The word "gum" can refer to the pink flesh that helps hold your teeth in your mouth, or to the flavored sticks you put in your mouth and chew."

"So this guy is all gums, no teeth?"

"At least in the front of his mouth. He must be old."

"Let's call him Gummy," said William.

Ira rolled his eyes in resignation. There was no longer any hope for trying to use numbers and letters to name the micos.

Erika and Alicia distributed bowls of fresh food and water about 3 meters from the nest tree, and the Brookfield group headed back to eat. Gummy followed cautiously, keeping a careful eye on the four humans. He ate fruit voraciously but avoided the strange canned food.

Emily had made a decision, and announced: "Now that we've all groomed and eaten, let's take a nice nap together. We've had enough excitement this morning."

"Well, it looks like Emily has found herself a mate," said Alicia. "I wonder if she can be happy with such an old male." Alicia and Erika exchanged quick glances.

"Didn't you find it odd that Emily didn't lose any weight during the shipment and her brush with death?" Ira asked Erika.

Chapter 55

No Man's Land

Niko, having reintroduced himself to the wild, was also shopping for a mate. A two-year-old female from the Swamp group, S5, was lagging behind her group as they retreated across the swamp after an encounter with Niko. Niko was able to hold his own during these encounters, but he also had some unintended help. The Swamp group was wary of people, and pulled back when Tina and John Wayne came out of the field station. They wouldn't even approach when Peter and Carlos were coming and going. Niko of course was not scared of people. He was setting up a territory in the no man's land, or more precisely the no mico's land, around the field station. S5 and her sister S6 were starting to be threatened and nipped by their mother. It was time for them to leave their group and find mates. S5 seemed to have targeted Niko and the bananas and papayas that grew abundantly in his new territory.

Just as the Brookfield group was settling down for their first nap with Gummy, S5 followed Niko into the vine tangle at the top of the mango tree. They settled in for their first nap together.

Ira and Erika returned to the field station, having dropped Alicia at her house to enjoy Saturday night and Sunday with her family, and William at the bus so he could also have some downtime in Rio.

Ira located Niko in the mango tree, and noticed S5 for the first time. He and Erika showered and shared a beer on the veranda in the warm afternoon sun. They relaxed for the first time in a week, and then slipped off for their own nap.

Jorge pulled in at 5 PM for a beer and some company. Ira told him about the Brookfield group, Emily and Gummy. Then he pointed out Niko and S5, who were hunting insects on the hillside leading to the swamp.

"You mean he escaped, into the reserve?" asked Jorge.

Ira realized immediately that this would be trouble. "Yes, it was an accident. Remember he was quarantined at the National Zoo before he was shipped, so there is no danger to the wild micos."

"Maybe not," said Jorge, "but your import permit said that this group was to be reintroduced on the Santa Helena ranch, not into the reserve. I have to enforce the terms of the permit. You'll have to trap and remove him and, as I told you earlier, you can't take S5 out."

Ira answered: "It's not a crowding issue. They are establishing a territory in an area that no wild tamarin group would use because of the human activity around the field station. It's like you've increased the mico-usable area of the reserve by 30 hectares."

"Could be," said Jorge, "but I have to enforce the terms of the permit."

Erika had slipped away and hastily made some passion fruit *batidas*. She handed Jorge an icy glass of the drink and purred: "But look at the two of them. They're bonding so well. She might even be pregnant already."

After a few moments of silence to allow the *batida* glow to set in, Ira asked: "Could we request an amendment to the permit?"

"Sure." answered Jorge. "But with the bureaucracy it would take at least 30 to 60 days."

"And in the meantime......?" asked Ira.

"Try to trap him."

"To your health!" said Ira gratefully. They clinked glasses.

Ira wrote the amendment request on the next morning and dropped it at reserve headquarters. Then he and Erika fed and checked on the Brookfield group. Satisfied that the group was together and well, Erika and Ira headed for Alicia's house for Sunday dinner, at the invitation of her mother.

As they drove into the small town, only the bakery and a bar were open. Folks were walking home from the church perched high on the hill across from the town square. A few vendors sold watchbands, sunglasses, snacks, and pineapples near the square. Erika needed a new band for her Timex, so they stopped. The pineapple vendor caught their eye and summoned them over. He pulled back a tarp, revealing a large, coiled boa constrictor. It was dead, and its head and much of its body were missing.

"Where did you get this snake?" asked Ira in Portuguese.

"The cutters found it at the edge of a pineapple grove, somewhere near here. Only 50,000 *cruzados* a slice" (about 50 cents US Ira calculated), and the vendor whacked off a three-inch boa steak with his machete. "Delicious meat."

"We'll pass," said Ira. "You know, you're not supposed to kill wild animals."

"The cutters were scared," the vendor said.

" And you saw a chance to make an extra buck," Ira thought.

"Let's get out of here," said Erika. "I hope it wasn't the snake that…"

"Me too," Ira interrupted. "And I hope the snake is not on our menu today."

The kids were showered and spotless, dressed in Sunday best. Floors were meticulously swept, and plates and glasses sparkled. Cats and dogs were banished to the yard, but greeted Ira and Erika, at first suspiciously, and then with sloppy licks, crotch gooses, and sensual, purring shin rubs.

The house was redolent with garlicky black beans spiked with salted pork. Alicia's brother tended a grill in the back yard, with sausages, steaks, pork chops, and chicken crackling over the wood fire. Thankfully, there were no boa constrictor steaks. Glasses were filled with cold bottles of Brahma beer. No American had ever before eaten in this humble home, and Ira only yesterday was the first to have even entered. The family was pulling out all of the stops for Alicia's bosses.

Erika pulled coloring books and crayons out of her bag, and instantly won the undying affection of all of the kids. It was a big family, enlarged by foster children that Alicia's mother took in for some extra income. There was a child at just about every elementary school grade level, so Ira took the opportunity to practice his Portuguese with seven-year-old Angelina. It was a good match, and Angelina was eager to learn some English.

Alicia's mom commanded the kitchen like an admiral. The older girls bustled making salads and spaghetti. A hard look from mom usually sufficed for discipline, but she had a sharp tongue and quick hand for repeat offenders. A polished, well-used meter-long stick stood in the corner for use in the hardest cases. A lock had been welded on to the refrigerator door; it's not easy to keep a dozen hungry kids away from the food, 24/7.

There was no father in the home. Neither Ira nor Erika asked about it, but they did notice that the whole family deferred quietly to Alicia. The income and prestige from her job had elevated her to primary breadwinner. She was the family strategist. Erika wondered how her response to Senhor Mauricio's marriage proposal, accepted or declined, would affect this household.

Chapter 56

Weigh-In

Mondays were mico-weighing days. William and Alicia had been weighing the Olympia group and the Red River group, each now having four members, every Monday. They charged the electronic digital scale, carried it to the monkeys, set up the banana-on-a-string lure, and patiently tried to weigh each animal.

Hermes and Aphrodite were the most difficult, since they both stood on the scale and reached for the banana at the same time. Swamp 4 and O9 had overcome their shyness and were happy to get "free" bananas.

Ira and William dropped Erika and Alicia at the Brookfield group at Santa Helena ranch on Monday morning, and then set off to weigh the other two groups. Alicia seemed peeved, but Ira could not understand why.

After the men had driven off, Alicia said to Erika: "I actually enjoy seeing Mauricio and walking around on his ranch. I wish Ira had taken me."

When they got to the nest tree, they noticed that birds were visiting the food bowl. "We're losing a lot of food to birds, squirrels, and tegu lizards in the daytime and opossums, bats, and coatimundis at night," said Erika. "I can't get a good estimate of how much the micos are eating."

The women fed the monkeys and weighed the leftovers with a simple spring fishing scale that Ira had brought to Brazil.

"There's very little left, but we have seen them catch some insects and frogs, and eat some wild figs. The micos are not eating this much of our food. We need to think of a way to give them food and keep the other animals out."

The women separated to observe the monkeys, which were now traveling some distance, circling the nest tree on the hillsides that formed the forest cathedral. Sometimes the monkeys were 20 meters or more from each other, maintaining contact with little trills and an occasional long call. They ate some wild figs, drank water out of a hole in a tree, and even caught some grasshoppers. Petie found and ate her first frog. This morning, Gummy was sticking close to Emily. Erika and Alicia maintained contact with an occasional shout.

As William eased the microbus onto the highway, he pulled a large photograph from his jacket pocket and handed it to Ira. "I got this from one of my buddies at the space agency," said William. "Don't worry, sensitive areas have been cropped out and this version is declassified."

It was an aerial photo, without any titles or legends. Ira made out the highway, and then the broad area of forest that was the Poço das Antas reserve. The São João River, and then the Red River popped out at him, and he recognized the contours of the Rio Vermelho ranch. He was less familiar with the Santa Helena ranch but could speculate on its position as well. The forested areas were green, and fields and roads were red and yellow. The patches of green jumped out, thick and continuous in the reserve, smaller and patchy on the ranches. The forest patches looked like islands in a sea of red.

"This is unbelievable," said Ira. "When and how was it taken?"

"Last year, so it's reasonably current," said William. "It was taken from a satellite but I can't say more."

"Do we know the scale?" asked Ira.

"Yes, so we can do a pretty good job calculating the area of the forest patches. They're working on a tool to measure areas automatically and precisely, but I don't have the clearance to use it."

"This will do fine," said Ira. "I can already see where we could connect the forests of Santa Helena, Rio Vermelho, and Poço das

Antas by planting some trees. That connection is essential to the future of the Red River group and the Santa Helena group. Otherwise they will become inbred. I don't think there are many wild Gummys left to become unrelated mates."

They bounced to a stop at the trailhead leading to the Olympia group, and could hear the long calls of two mico groups. "There's an encounter underway," said William. "It will be hard to get their attention for weighing."

The encounter had ended and the intruders had withdrawn by the time William and Ira found the group. They visually located and identified Prometheus, O9, Venus, and Vesuvio, and began to clear a small area in which to set up the scale. Venus and Vesuvio pushed and jostled each other hilariously, but each managed to stand alone on the scale for a few seconds, allowing William to get their weights. Venus weighed 425 grams and Vesuvio 435. They were tamarin teenagers now.

Prometheus approached quickly and weighed in at 577. O9 was reluctant to approach the scale.

"We may have to retreat a few meters," said William. "It's tricky to stretch the string and keep the banana out of reach at this distance. Here, you take the string and give me the binoculars so I can see the weight."

It took Ira a few minutes to get the hang of adjusting the string to keep the banana at just the right height over the scale. But O9 was attracted by the dangling bait and walked cautiously to the scale. She scanned the area to see if she could reach the banana from a branch, and then reluctantly went to the ground, looked around carefully, and bounced onto the scale. William had the binoculars tightly focused on the read-out window; it stabilized at 563 grams.

"Wow, that's up," William said, consulting his neatly written notebook. "She was about 500 all year, and then started increasing. We didn't weigh her last week, but the week before she was 538. She's got to be pregnant."

He zoomed out a little, and only then saw the tiny heads peering from under O9's arm. "Babies", he squawked, too loudly. O9 bounded off with the piece of banana Ira had allowed her to grab after she had been weighed.

"Who first spotted Hermes and Aphrodite?" asked Ira.

"Alicia. She's got the eyes of a hawk."

"Then you get to name these," said Ira.

"Let's all work on it, but thanks for letting us use real names. I promise not to get overly attached."

Prometheus moved close to O9 and nuzzled the twins.

"We've got baby brothers," cheered Vesuvio.

"How do you know they're not baby sisters?" asked Venus.

"I saw their little whizzers."

"I could watch all day," said Ira, "but we'd better get to Red River ranch."

They stopped for lunch at a gas station on the highway, and ate greasy sausage sandwiches and drank Fantas.

"To their health," said Ira, raising his bottle. "Oly now has six micos and Red River has four. We started with eight last year. Maybe we've turned the corner, uh... started to improve."

Chapter 57

Beating The Birds

When they got together for their lunch break, Erika and Alicia were elated that the Brookfield group was moving all over the area, but finding each other and finding their way back to the nest tree. They were also happy that Gummy was being accepted by the group. He was in fact being groomed by six hands at this very moment.

"Ira's boot camp is really paying off," said Erika.

"But none of this would be happening if we had not been able to rescue Emily," said Alicia. "The soft release is working too."

"What's with the bamboo?" asked Erika.

Alicia had cut a piece of bamboo about 60 centimeters long. Bamboo is actually a thick grass. The stem is hollow, divided into separate sections by woody membranes inside the stem. Alicia had cut a nick into each section of the stem, making a separate entrance into each hollow section. It looked like a long green flute, but the inside was divided into sections.

"If we stuffed the food through the holes into the inside of the bamboo, the other fruit-eating animals probably couldn't get it. But the micos would micromanipulate, and pull the food out with their hands."

"That's brilliant," said Erika. "Suppose we made a square of four of the same-length pieces of bamboo. We could tie them together with vines. The micos could sit on it while they ate, and we could rig a vine hanger to attach to the rope."

The Bamboo Feeder

Photo by Benjamin Beck

They had completed a prototype by 2 PM. They found that they needed a diagonal piece for stability, which added even more holes for "hiding" the food.

"I can't wait to try it out," said Alicia.

"Bring down the food bowl, and we'll transfer the food into the feeder," said Erika.

"But Ira......"

"Alicia, this is a great idea. Ira will love it, and I'll take the heat if he doesn't."

At least the tamarins loved the idea and excitedly began to dig into the feeder holes to extract the very same food they had been ignoring only moments before. Opie had been first to catch on, Petie and Sandy learned the trick quickly, and Emily got it after an hour. Gummy and the birds were stumped.

"We'll have to go back to the bowl if Gummy doesn't catch on," said Erika.

A Cooler Nest Box with a PVC Feeder
Smithsonian's National Zoo Photo by Jessie Cohen

William and Ira were not able to weigh the Red River group. The micos had crossed the São João and were feeding on figs, high in a tree on the other side, inside the reserve. The observers were able to identify each of the micos, but headed back to the car with no new weight data. Then they had to spend a few minutes with a sad-faced Senhor Mauricio as he inquired about Alicia, trying to show only casual interest.

William drove to the Santa Helena ranch and turned the bus around at the head of the trail. He and Ira waited for the women to arrive. Ira sensed trouble when 30 minutes had passed.

"Bring the receiver and antenna. We'd better go find them."

Finding them was easy, and there was no trouble. Erika and Alicia lay on their backs on their ponchos, heads propped on their backpacks, staring up at the cooler box. Actually they were staring at a strange contraption, and giggling.

The feeder swung wildly as four micos jumped on and off, micromanipulating intently. Erika quickly explained what was going on. To the women's relief, Ira smiled broadly.

"That is simply brilliant. We stop feeding all of the animals in the forest, the micos are motivated to micromanipulate, and we can move the feeder as easily as a bowl."

"But it will get funky after a while," he continued. "How can we wash it out?"

"We could make one out of PVC pipe," said William. "They have it now in the hardware store in town. It's easy to cut, and will be easy to clean."

Gummy jumped on the feeder, stuck his arm in up to the shoulder, and dug out a grape. He shoved it into his near-toothless mouth, squished it, swallowed, and went back for more.

"We've also got some good news," said William.

Naming the new babies dominated the conversation on the trip back home and during supper. Ira and Erika shared a quiet glass of red wine on the veranda, celebrating the emerging success of the reintroduction program. Niko cheered too, with a macho long call as he settled into the mango tree with Nika (as Tina, now an enthusiastic self-appointed tamarin observer, had named her).

"We've got almost two more weeks in Brazil, and our work is essentially done for this trip," said Ira. "We beat the macumba."

Maybe we could take a few days of R and R at the beach," suggested Erika.

"Here's to that."

Chapter 58

Rude Awakening

The cooler box had been cut from the tree and lay at its base. The top had been pried open and it too lay nearby. Emily was screaming from a nearby tree. Gummy was even croaking angrily.

"*Meu Deus*," said Alicia. "Somebody tried to steal the monkeys."

"I see Emily and Gummy but not Petie, Opie and Sandy," said William, hastily unfolding the antenna and checking for signals. He directed the antenna in a full 360-degree circle, increased the sensitivity to maximum, and walked to the top of a nearby hill and repeated the whole process.

"Nothing. No signals except Emily's."

What had promised to be a lovely, peaceful morning watching the ever-wilder Brookfield group had turned into a nightmare.

"I'll never trust you two-leggers again," screeched Emily, though neither Gummy nor the people could understand her. "First you take away Rufous, and now you steal my kids. I'll never eat your food again, never sleep in your boxes again, never go in your traps again......," she railed.

In her grief and anger she was forgetting that people had recently saved her life. Maybe she didn't even know she had been almost dead. Now, all she knew was that she wanted to hide in the deepest darkest part of the forest.

"Take me away from here, Gummy." Emily actually took the lead and sped up and over a hill and disappeared. He followed loyally, though he would have liked a few bananas for the road.

"I'll follow her," said William, picking up the radio receiver and antenna.

"Let her go," said Ira. "She's traumatized and will think that we're trying to get her. We can always find her later."

"What do we do now?" asked William.

"Call the police," said Ira.

The Brookfield group of golden lion tamarins was technically the property of the federal government of Brazil. When the local police figured this out, they called the *Policia Federal*. The federal police were part of Brazil's military, and they were known for their ruthless pursuit and treatment of lawbreakers. Most of their work involved illegal drugs, weapons, armored car robberies, and bad guys who kidnapped wealthy people for ransom. But they were familiar with illegal smuggling of rare animals and plants, and knew that the same bad guys often trafficked in animals and plants as well as drugs and guns. They took this case seriously.

Two federal black-and-whites, Volkswagen Beetles, sped through the Santa Helena gate at 10AM. The team was headed by a man introduced simply as "Pedro". He was short, stocky, and rock solid. His massive bald head was balanced on top of a tree stump neck. His eyes were black pools in a giant unexpressive face. His small mouth barely moved as his greeted Ira, shaking his hand, or rather crushing his hand, in greeting.

"Tell me what happened here," Pedro said in Portuguese.

Ira asked William and Alicia to explain. Pedro and his team listened attentively. They examined the cooler, and looked up to where it had been attached to the tree.

One picked up a dirty rag from the ground, which was actually an old torn t-shirt with no markings. "What's this?"

Ira, barely able to keep up with the rapid Portuguese, said: "They probably stuffed it into the hole of the cooler to prevent the monkeys from escaping."

"How could the thieves have known the monkeys were sleeping here?" asked Pedro.

"We brought the farm staff and their families in to see the

monkeys last week," said Alicia, "as a gesture of friendship."

"How could they have gotten the monkeys out of the cooler?"

"They probably put the cooler into a big sack, pried off the top, shook the monkeys out, and then pulled out the cooler and the top. That's probably when the two adults escaped."

"There are thousands of monkeys in Brazil," said Pedro. "How can we identify the three missing ones?"

Alicia answered: "First, there are only about two hundred of these golden lion tamarins. Second, two of them are wearing radio collars. Third, each of them has a distinctive number tattooed inside their right leg," she said, innocently rubbing the inside of her right thigh. The investigators showed renewed interest.

"This is a good thing," said Pedro. He instructed his staff to go out and interview the farm staff and their families.

Within an hour, a farm worker had identified a former colleague who had shown undue interest in the monkeys, and who came from a local family that had long been thought to be involved in shady dealings. He had not shown up for work in the past two days.

"I know him," said Alicia loudly. "He and his family live in my town. They have a reputation for being mixed up in all sorts of crime. They live in a house surrounded by a high metal wall with barbed wire on top. Sometimes we can hear parrots calling inside, and my mother says she's heard loud growling too."

Pedro squinted, and said in a cold threatening voice: "I want to talk with this man. Let's go."

Ira was glad to be on Pedro's side, especially if Pedro wanted to "talk with you."

Pedro signaled to Alicia to get into the back seat of one of the Beetles.

Ira said, "No, I'll go. She and her family live in this town and need to stay out of this." Pedro nodded and Ira got in. Erika looked frightened as the black-and-whites sped down the dirt road and out the gate.

The cars stopped on the side of the road just outside of town. The five officers slipped on yellow bulletproof vests, stamped "Policia Federal" on the back. Pedro told Ira to put one on too. The officers pulled automatic machine pistols from the Beetles' trunks, and loaded them. A few spares were put in the back seat at Ira's feet.

"What's that?" asked Pedro.

"A receiver and antenna to check for the tamarins' radio signals."

"Good idea," said Pedro, "but we're going in anyway. You stay low and wait for us to come for you. Your job will be to identify the micos if we find them."

The cars raced into town and screeched up to the compound gate. The men began to kick it in. Ira pressed his head down on the seat, smelling the cool oil of the machine pistols. He wondered if they were loaded. Could he use one if there was a firefight? Ira was not a gun person, and he had not signed up for this. He turned on the receiver and it came to life with an audible signal. It was Opie's. He turned the dial, and picked up Petie's. Ira's hopes soared.

The gate fell open with a screech of metal and the officers poured into the compound. He could hear yelling, loud footfalls, and doors slamming but there was no gunfire. Ira snuck a look out the window and then began to climb out the VW's open door. Onlookers were gathering.

Ira peered into the gate entrance just as an officer was coming to get him. They startled each other. Nerves were jangling.

"No monkeys," said the officer.

"Yes, they're here," said Ira.

He ran up to Pedro, who held up two radio collars. Their bead chains had been cut with pliers, but they continued to transmit their signals. "Is this what you're looking for?" Pedro asked Ira.

The compound was empty except for a three-legged dog, a few chickens, and a sad old woman with dementia. There were a few small cages with tiny mesh and wood boxes where the micos had probably been held last night and this morning. Now they were gone, without a trace.

"We'll keep looking," said Pedro, "but they're probably being loaded right now on an oil baron's private jet, headed for his private zoo somewhere in the middle east."

Ira was suddenly exhausted, whipsawed between last night's elation over the project's growing success, this morning's shock at discovering the theft, the excitement of the raid, happiness at getting the mico's radio signals in the compound, and then the devastating discovery of the empty collars.

Ira rode silently back to Santa Helena in a police car. Pedro headed back to Rio.

Ira met his colleagues at the trailhead and reported on the raid.

"We found Emily and Gummy about a kilometer from the nest tree," said Erika, "and they kept running from us."

"Maybe they think we stole the kids," said Alicia.

"We stopped chasing them and left the feeder, filled with food, and some bananas," reported William.

"Should we take them the nest box?"

"I don't think they would use it and it's a red flag for thieves. They'll have to make it on their own."

Dinner was a sad occasion, in sharp contrast to last night's celebration.

"I think the police are going to give up," said Ira.

They all slept fitfully, thinking of the three tired, frightened, and hungry monkeys headed for the other side of the planet, if they were still alive.

Chapter 59

The Morning After

"We are going to have to reconsider using nest boxes in future reintroductions, if there are future reintroductions," said Ira over breakfast. "Who is going to fund us if the monkeys just get stolen?"

"We'll get the word out," said Alicia. "You and Peter spend thousands on salaries, gasoline, food, and car repairs around here. This area needs you, and we all need the monkeys. The decision makers will make it clear that there will be no more stolen monkeys."

"Speaking of getting the word out," said Ira, "I wonder if there has been any media coverage of the theft?"

Niko's long call brought instant smiles, and reminded them that they had work to do.

"Let's visit Senhor Mauricio and Senhor Nelson to discuss connecting the reserve and their properties with a strip of forest. Show us the photo William," said Ira.

William unfolded the satellite photo and watched as Erika, Alicia, and Peter really began to appreciate the power of a clear aerial view.

"I can sell the idea to Mauricio," said Alicia.

"I'm sure you could, but let's let William take the lead on this," responded Ira. Ira wanted Mauricio to buy into the idea for its merits, not as a gesture to impress Alicia.

One hundred and twenty kilometers away, in a swank neighborhood of the city of Rio de Janeiro, Opie, Petie, and Sandy were waking up. Actually, Petie had not slept because of the excruciating pain in her right leg.

"Where are we?" asked Sandy. "Where's mom, and Gummy?" "What happened last night?"

"You know as much as we do about what happened. Two-leggers came in the middle of the night, took the box off the tree, put it into a big bag, shook us out, and took us to those dirty cages." Opie was trying to stay calm and play the big brother.

"Was it *our* two-leggers?"

"No," answered Opie. "They sounded different and smelled awful."

"Where's mom?"

"I think she escaped out of the bag."

"Gummy?"

"Don't know."

"Is this a forest?"

"There are some tall trees and bushes, but there's a big wall over there," observed Opie.

"What's wrong with your leg Petie? It's twisted funny, and there's blood on it!"

"I think it's broken," said Petie, "and it hurts a lot."

A distinguished well-dressed man in his 70s, and a beautiful young woman of about 25 walked toward the tamarins' cage, hand-in-hand. They moved slowly, stopping to admire lush orchids and watch hummingbirds in the spacious garden.

"I have a present for you my beloved," said the man.

"Oh Louis, what is it?" squealed the girl.

"There are actually three presents." They stopped in front of the micos.

"They're beautiful!" she said, clutching her hands to her breast. "They are the rarest of the rare. I've wanted some for myself for a long time. French kings and queens used to keep them in their palaces." She wrapped her arms around the man, and kissed him.

"Can I hold them?"

Louis snapped his fingers and a caretaker stepped out of the bushes onto the path.

"Take one out for the lady to hold," said Louis.

"With all respect, sir, they are still quite wild and might escape or bite. They will need some time to become tame." The caretaker was frightened. Not many people dared to question Dr. Louis Bermant's orders.

"But the lady could feed them through the wire mesh," the caretaker added, handing her a grape from a bowl of fruit. "Mind your fingers, senhora."

Sandy was hungry. She jumped to the wire and cautiously took the grape. Neither Bermant nor the woman noticed the numbers tattooed on the mico's leg.

"Don't eat their fruit," hissed Opie.

"But I'm hungry," said Sandy.

Opie was hungry too, and his resolve weakened. He and Sandy were soon gobbling grapes and bits of papaya, banana, pineapple that they took from the young woman's long slender fingers.

"Look, she's got claws like ours," said Sandy, staring at the woman's long, brightly painted fingernails.

"Petie, you'd better eat something," said Opie.

"I can't," said Petie, curling up into a ball, with her twisted leg protruding.

"Here, I'll bring you some," said Opie, but Petie ignored his offerings.

"You have to eat!" said Sandy.

"That one looks sick," said Dr. Bermant to the caretaker.

"Looks like a broken leg to me," said the caretaker. "The poachers, ...uh suppliers, must have accidentally broken it."

"It looks so ugly," said the young woman. "Can you fix it?"

"No, we'll have to call our vet."

Chapter 60
Petie's Leg

D r. Louis Bermant had immigrated to Brazil from France in
1945, at the end of World War II. Many thought he had been
an escaping Nazi sympathizer. He arrived with a large sum of cash,
all in American dollars, and a trove of gold and precious stones. He
also brought with him an impressive collection of oil paintings by
18th and 19th century European masters.

The field of Dr. Bermant's doctorate was never revealed. He
did not practice medicine or dentistry, or teach in a university. He
founded a newspaper that quickly gained a national distribution,
largely because he printed stories slanted favorably toward the
country's military dictators and the Roman Catholic church. Lurid
stories about sexual scandals were avoided, to cover for the dictators and to insulate the bishops and priests from difficult questions
from their parishioners. Of course the public relished scandals, so
Bermant pandered to this audience by anonymously publishing a
sensationalist rag. Both papers were hugely successful. Bermant
purchased two national television stations, several radio stations,
and a share of the nationally subsidized airline.

Bermant contributed to the church, although he was not a prac-
ticing Catholic. Indeed he divorced his first wife in 1960; she now
lived in luxurious boredom in a high-rise condominium in Ipanema.
He also gave to hospitals, schools, orphanages, and children's sports
leagues. Bermant considered charity to be a business expense.

Shortly after his arrival in Brazil, he had purchased a large estate
in a gracious, secluded sector of Rio, at the foot of the mountainous
state park that bordered his property to the west. Here the ancient

forest still swept down the mountainside, providing cool shade and remarkable beauty to the wealthy homes below. Bermant could remember seeing wild golden lion tamarins in this forest in the 1950s. A remarkable inventory of wild monkeys, birds, orchids, and butterflies still lived here. Many visited his garden regularly. He had ordered the planting of a variety of fruit trees, and the installation and daily replenishment of dozens of feeders with seeds, nectar, or beef fat for the animals' satisfaction. He had built a stately home, with long corridors along which he hung his paintings. He had retained a team of gardeners and caretakers to harmonize the estate and maintain it meticulously.

Of course the homes in this lush neighborhood were prime targets for thieves. Bermant, like all of his neighbors, surrounded his grounds with a high concrete wall topped with broken glass. There were sturdy gates, front and rear. He upgraded electrical surveillance on the estate continuously but the key to his security plan was a small force of brilliantly conditioned and disciplined guards. Stories of their ruthlessness circulated freely. Equally disciplined Dobermans patrolled the grounds at night.

Bermant moved effortlessly in the halls of power and in the upper echelons of Brazilian society though his questionable history and addiction to attractive women tarnished his social reputation. He favored movie starlets when he was a dashing 40- and 50-year old, but he found in his 60s that the starlet set seemed to be attracted to younger and more virile companions. At this point his taste shifted to impressionable younger women with aspirations to wealth and standing. The Brookfield micos were a gift to the latest in this string of bimbos.

Bermant's veterinarian was a woman, but far from a bimbo. Dr. Claudia was a multilingual, Belgian-educated veterinarian whose practice served the pet dogs, cats and birds in this area of Rio. Over the years she had also treated a variety of wild birds and monkeys on Bermant's estate and several others nearby. She had suspected that some of these had been poached, but since she had no proof she treated the animals without questioning their origin. To do otherwise would have meant the loss of her lucrative practice. She was an excellent vet, and had successfully treated many animals with capture injuries, dietary deficiencies, and just plain, depression-caused lack of appetite and weakness. Many of these wild animals seemed just to lose their will to live after they were captured. Dr Claudia often wondered if they missed their wild homes and families.

She had never treated a golden lion tamarin although she had worked with more common species of small monkeys. She was struck with the flashing beauty of two of the micos in the cage at Bermant's estate, but recognized immediately that the third was in shock and suffering from a badly broken leg. The caretaker slipped into the cage and grabbed Petie without any resistance.

Dr. Claudia quickly injected Petie with an immobilizing drug, and set up an IV line with fluids.

"I'll have to take her to the clinic for X-rays," she told the caretaker.

"No, no, don't take Petie," screamed Sandy, but only Opie could understand her.

"More bad two-leggers," said Sandy to Opie.

"Maybe she is trying to help Petie," said Opie, trying to reassure his younger sister.

Petie died in Dr. Claudia's van on the way to the hospital. At least she was anesthetized and died painlessly.

Dr. Claudia usually just cremated dead animals, but she sensed that Bermant might question her. She decided to take X-rays of Petie's broken leg, just in case. As she stretched Petie out on her back on the X-ray table, she saw the tattooed numbers on the inside of the monkey's right thigh. This was clearly a poached wild animal, an endangered species. She remembered reading about the golden lion tamarin reintroduction in Dr. Bermant's newspaper, and seeing a feature about it on his television station. Dr. Claudia's pretense collapsed. Her professional ethics kicked in. She was obligated to call the federal wildlife authorities.

She took the X-rays, and some photographs as well. She put Petie's body into a freezer, and strode to the telephone.

Chapter 61

Busted

Jorge found Ira and the team in the restaurant at the gas station on the highway. They had bought two newspapers but neither carried a story on the theft. Ira thought this was curious.

The team was celebrating the minor victory of Senhor Mauricio's and Senhor Nelson's agreement to plant the forest linkage between their two ranches and with the reserve. The owners had even agreed to start a nursery and hire people to plant the trees. In just a few years the reserve would have a new 350-hectare "finger" of forest.

"We've got a lead on the stolen monkeys," Jorge said breathlessly. He declined a cup of coffee, looked at Ira, and said: "We've got to go to Rio. I'll explain on the way."

"More guns?" asked a worried Erika.

"I don't think so," answered Jorge.

Ira was in field clothes but the day had been dry and he was not too dirty. He grabbed his emergency pack and three of the small traps.

They breezed through the routine police checkpoints on the highway and arrived at the huge bridge leading into Rio in record time, at least for the lumbering Land Cruiser.

Jorge had explained that a vet in private practice in Rio had called the federal police about a monkey with tattooed numbers on its leg. She had identified it as a golden lion tamarin. The number sequence matched one that Alicia had given to Sergeant Pedro. The vet had been called to care for the monkey, but it died in her clinic.

"Where was the monkey when she found it?" asked Ira.

"On a private estate in an upscale Rio neighborhood."

"What about the other two?" asked Ira.

"They were still alive on the estate when she left."

"Who owns this place?"

"A mover and shaker, very well connected politically and socially. Every Brazilian recognizes his name." Jorge went on to fill Ira in on Louis Bermant's history.

"Have they arrested him?"

"No. The police are waiting for you to positively identify the monkeys as the stolen ones. We'll start at the clinic."

Dr. Claudia greeted Ira with a heavy heart. "I'm sorry about your monkey."

"Thanks for calling the police. Did the other two look OK?"

"Yes, but I did not really examine them."

"May I see the body?"

Dr. Claudia led Ira to the freezer and took out the body. Ira confirmed the four tattooed numbers. "Petie," he said.

"You give them names?"

"Yes, and right now I'm sorry we do. This would be easier if she were just 'B5'. She's 19 months old, and was just starting to adjust to life in the wild."

"Let's go," said Jorge, "before this guy gets wind of our arrival and dumps the other two monkeys."

"Can you keep my name out of this?" asked Claudia.

"I hope so," answered Jorge.

They made slow progress to the estate through the afternoon rush hour traffic.

"How can you keep her out of this?" asked Ira. "She'll have to testify in court."

"Maybe not," answered Jorge.

"What do you mean?" asked Ira.

"Maybe we won't have to go to court," answered Jorge.

Ira's mind raced: "mover, shaker, politically connected, won't have to go to court...."

"Why didn't you tell her to keep the body, the X-rays and the photos as evidence?" Ira asked.

Jorge snapped: "Look, you're in Brazil. Think like a Brazilian."

Ira brooded. There was no more conversation until Jorge pulled the Land Cruiser up to a reinforced gate with an armed guard in front.

"We're here," said Jorge.

"Where are the police? Where's Pedro?" asked Ira.

"You're going in alone. Dr. Bermant is expecting you. Don't worry, there won't be any guns or rough stuff."

Chapter 62

Rough Stuff

The guard patted Ira down, searched his backpack, and radioed for the gate to be opened.

Ira forgot the gate, guard, and gun as his senses were overrun with trees, bromeliads, flowers, birds, butterflies and running streams. The place was too neat and manicured to be a forest, but far too complex and natural to be a garden. The house itself was barely visible through the trees.

The guard escorted Ira around a flawless blue swimming pool and spa to a broad veranda that seemed to surround the house. Orchids and feeders hung from the eaves. Birds hurried to get the day's last meal, and a few fruit bats were already showing up at the nectar feeders.

A slender, distinguished, graying man strode confidently through the front door and greeted Ira amiably.

"Louis Bermant. Welcome to my home." Bermant's English was unaccented.

Ira refused his outstretched hand. "I want to see the golden lion tamarins!"

"In good time, of course. You know, in Brazil we usually have a coffee before doing business but it's too late for coffee. How about a drink?"

"No thanks. I want to see the monkeys, identify them as stolen property, and call the police."

"What then?" asked Bermant.

"You will be arrested for stealing endangered wild animals, federal property."

"Dr. Hornaday; it is 'doctor'?"

"Yes," answered Ira, ignoring the jab.

"Dr. Hornaday, look at me. I'm 70 years old and in no shape to be climbing trees and stealing monkeys. I could not have stolen them."

"You may not have actually stolen them but they ended up here. Technically you 'trafficked' in stolen property."

"Since you are so astute legally, you must be aware that I will testify that I was completely unaware that these monkeys were endangered or stolen."

Jorge had been wrong. Ira was not bleeding or broken, at least not yet, but this was rough stuff.

"What makes you tick, Dr. Hornaday? What do we need to do to settle all of this amiably?"

"I'm not feeling very amiable. Please take me to the monkeys."

Bermant ignored Ira and kept talking with an icy confidence.

"What makes me tick are power and money, and the women who chase men with power and money."

"The monkeys, please."

"You're probably an idealist and won't settle this for money, so I'll resort to 'influence'. Let's be honest. You *might* be able to get the federal police to arrest and charge me. The judge will be a close friend who owes me many favors. He will probably find me innocent. He'll decide that the monkeys were an impulsive gift from an old man to impress his young girlfriend, and find me innocent. This sort of male stupidity happens every day in Brazil. If he does convict me, I'll arrange to have a 'heart attack', and will serve my sentence in a luxurious private suite in one of the hospitals I have funded."

After a short pause to let this sink in, he continued: "Everybody will believe my story. I am a major donor to international conservation organizations, and have hosted fundraisers for them here in Rio. One time I shared the head table with a European prince who is the spokesperson for the world's best-known conservation group.

He walked in this very garden. It's inconceivable that I would know-ingly break Brazilian conservation laws. You can be sure that the media will support me."

Another pause. "If you're still not convinced, Dr. Hornaday, think about this: If you do bring charges against me, I'll make sure that you *never again* get a visa to enter Brazil. And that goes for your woman friend with whom you so charmingly share a tent, and all of your American colleagues. Your efforts in Brazil will be over. That's just one phone call away."

"Now, would you like that drink?"

"Would you agree never to buy endangered wildlife again?" asked Ira.

"Yes I will agree to that, although you're not in a place to en-force my promise. In return I want your promise never to identify me in connection with this sad story, privately or publically."

"I agree to that, although you're not in a place to enforce my promise," said Ira, searching to maintain a shred of dignity.

"I must correct you. I can enforce your promise as long as you want to do your work in Brazil."

"Please take me to the monkeys."

Bermant signaled to the waiting guard, who escorted Ira to the cage.

"It's Ira one of *our* two-leggers," said Sandy.

"Don't trust any of them," cautioned Opie.

"Should I call the police?" asked Jorge as Ira walked through the gate with the two monkeys in live traps.

"Not necessary." said Ira. "Let's get these two back to the field station."

"Now you're thinking like a Brazilian," said Jorge, almost smirking.

Chapter 63
A Glass Half Full

They stopped for gas on the way home. Ira bought some good Argentinean wine. They arrived at the field station at 10 PM. Erika, Peter, Alicia, and William were still awake.

"Oh honey, you've got them," said Erika, embracing Ira warmly.

"Only two," said Ira. He handed the traps to William and Alicia. "Do you still have the energy to process them tonight?"

"We already have the table ready," said Alicia.

"Put a collar on Opie. Use your judgment about Sandy. I want to get them out of here early in the morning, before Niko discovers they're here."

Jorge turned the Land Cruiser around and headed out. Ira gave him a tired wave of thanks.

"Are you OK?" asked Erika.

"Physically, yes. Otherwise just tired and a little beaten down. How about a glass of wine?"

He told Erika the whole story, breaking his promise of confidentiality for the first and only time.

Opie and Sandy were awake at the crack of dawn. They crouched in the little traps on the field station veranda, waiting for the next step in this crazy adventure.

"You've got a collar again," whispered Sandy. "Why won't they give me one?"

"Shh," said Opie. "I think I hear some tamarin vocalizations – little contact chirps. Listen."

"Yes, you're right!" said Sandy. "Should we long-call?"

Just then, Niko long-called.

"Let's not answer," said Opie. "There's nothing we can do while we're in these boxes."

Niko and Nika called again.

"There's something familiar about that call," said Opie. "Listen."

"Is that Niko?" asked Sandy.

"You're right!" said Opie, and then he long-called loudly.

Within seconds, Niko was sitting on the low wall of the veranda.

"Hey guys. Are you OK? Where's our mom, and Petie? What have you been up to?" Niko had not spoken to a tamarin in a week. Nika of course had never learned to speak two-legger talk.

Before Opie and Sandy could answer, Ira rushed out of the house, scooped up the two traps, and put them in the bus.

William, Alicia, and Erika followed, dressing and pulling on boots as they ran to the bus.

"We need to get these two out of here, before they pull in the Swamp group and we have a battle on our hands. Besides, Sandy and Opie should really not have any contact with tamarins in the reserve because they may have been exposed to all sorts of diseases during the theft."

"Darn," said Niko as the bus roared out. "At least I know those two are OK. I wish I could have introduced them to my new girl friend."

Alicia slowed the bus to a safe speed. William said: "I forgot to bring a nest log."

"I think we should probably not use the cooler or a nest log," said Ira. "They make it too easy to steal micos."

"So how are we going to reintroduce them?"

"I'm thinking we should just find Emily and Gummy, and then release Opie and Sandy from the traps as close to them as possible," said Ira. "What do you all think?"

Erika answered: "It would be great if the four of them join up as a group again. If they stay as two groups, we have a collar on Emily and one on Opie, so we can monitor them until we decide what to do."

"Sounds good to me," said Alicia.

"So what really happened in Rio yesterday," asked William.

"I can only tell you that the three stolen micos were discovered in the home of a wealthy Brazilian. Petie had broken a leg and later died. The Brazilian decided to give back Opie and Sandy."

"Let me guess: he wasn't arrested," said William, looking directly at Ira.

Alicia answered for Ira: "We can be thankful that we have Opie and Sandy, or angry that the guy wasn't arrested. Don't you Americans have a saying about seeing a glass that's half empty or half full?"

"It's better than that," said William. "I've done a quick count. We've reintroduced 13 zoo-born tamarins from the U.S. in two years, and we have 12 alive now. And that's not counting O9, Swamp 4, and Nika, or the Swamp group that you rescued last year."

"Thanks you two, I needed that reassurance," said Ira, wrapping his arm around Erika and giving her a squeeze.

Chapter 64

Family Reunion

"I recognize this place," said Sandy. "Maybe the two-leggers are going to set us free again. Maybe we'll even find mom and Gummy."

"But we passed our nest tree," said Opie.

The team spent 45 minutes tracking Emily's signal as she fled from them.

"We're as close as we're going to get," said Ira. "Let's let them out here, and back off."

Opie understood, and long-called. Sandy joined in. William and Alicia opened the traps. The two micos bolted out and climbed to the top of the nearest tree. Erika hung some bunches of bananas nearby.

"Good luck you guys," said Ira. "You sure deserve some good luck." It was hard to walk away.

As they left, they heard the answering long calls.

"Where have you two been?" said Emily as she feverishly groomed Sandy. "Where's Petie?"

"Some stinky two-leggers took us away. First we stayed in a dirty place and then in a nice place, with pretty good food. Petie was real sick and hurt. They took her away. Ira came and got us and brought us back."

"We smelled the two-leggers that took us out of the box. Gummy and I got away."

"They weren't our two-leggers," pronounced Sandy.

"I think you're right, dear," said Emily.

"Is there anything to eat here?" asked Opie.

"Plenty. Gummy knows where there are good fruit trees and I've been learning where to look for frogs and crickets. Just follow him."

"Can Gummy talk two-legger talk?" asked Sandy.

"No, and he doesn't seem to want to learn," answered Emily.

"Is he going to be our daddy now?" asked Sandy. Opie stopped eating. All eyes were on Emily.

"There's a hole over here that we slept in a few nights ago. Come inside with me for a minute," said Emily.

Gummy had found the bananas and was too busy eating to care that Emily, Opie, and Sandy went into the hole.

"I was devoted to Ruf and I still miss him. But this male is a wild mico, so he knows this area and he knows how to find food," said Emily. "That will really help us survive, and your survival is my main goal now."

"And there's something else," she continued. "On our last day in Beaver Valley, Ruf and I took an afternoon nap in the cooler box while you were all playing outside. We rubbed a little. I think I'm going to have babies again, and we'll need help raising them. If I play this right, I think I can convince this guy that he's the father."

"Can I count on you all to be nice to him and accept him?" she asked. "He can't replace your father, but he seems sweet and kind. Goodness knows how long it's been since he's even seen another mico. He's starved for company."

"OK" cheered the two youngsters simultaneously, just as Gummy peered into the hole.

After walking for 10 minutes, the team sat down to rest. Erika passed out some granola bars. She always seemed to have granola bars with her.

"I think Emily looks pregnant," said Alicia.

"But she's only been with Gummy for a week," said William. "Oh," he added after a few seconds of thought.

After a few more seconds of thoughtful silence, William asked:

"Do you think Gummy knows he's not the father?"

"He probably 'assumes' he's the father," answered Ira. "Not that tamarins understand the concept of paternity, or can calculate the length of pregnancy. They probably don't even have an understanding of time beyond 24 hours."

"So he'll carry Emily's babies after they're born and give them solid food, even though Rufous is the genetic father," added Erika.

It won't be the first time or the last time that a female tricked a male into raising another male's kids," said Ira.

Alicia was quick to add: "Oh, and males have such a great reputation for fidelity."

"If all goes well, those babies will bring us to 14!" observed William, now the self-appointed project records keeper.

Erika looked up and saw a fragile, stunning pink orchid that had bloomed overnight. Most orchids had been poached from this region, so this was a real find.

"Congratulations!" she said as Ira's eyes traced to the orchid.

"To us all, and to the micos."

Postscript

By 2005, 149 captive-born golden lion tamarins had been reintroduced to the wild. Many survived long enough to reproduce. Today, there are about 1,700 golden lion tamarins living in the wild, of which approximately 600 are descended from the reintroduced captive-borns. Many live on private ranches like the Rio Vermelho and Santa Helena ranches.

We did an analysis of the relationship between pre-release training and survival in 2000. It showed that the free-ranging experience ("boot camp") made no difference in survival. What did matter was the intensive post-release management that kept the micos alive long enough to reproduce. The babies born in the wild survived as well as true wild micos, for reasons still not completely understood. They seemed to have wild brains. In retrospect, it was Erika's and Alicia's ideas about post-release support that made the program successful. The full reference to the published analysis is in the Introduction.

A team of talented and dedicated Brazilians took over management of the program in the 1990s. They formed a non-governmental organization called Associacão Mico Leão Dourado (Golden Lion Tamarin Association). The association's website is www.micoleao.org.br

Ira and Erika finally got married. Ira still spoils their dog hopelessly.

For the moment, golden lion tamarins have avoided extinction. But the threats never go away. The area is now a suburb of Rio and is under constant pressure to be carved into housing developments, roads, oil pipelines, and shopping centers. The Americans who started the program in the 1980s have now founded a North American non-governmental organization, called Save the Golden Lion Tamarin (SGLT), to collect tax-deductible donations to support the program in perpetuity. Donations are invested in the professionally managed Devra G. Kleiman fund. More than 99% of donations to SGLT are sent to Brazil to support the priority activities of the Associacão Mico Leão Dourado. To learn more, and to contribute, see www.savetheliontamarin.org

A portion of any profits from the sale of this book will be contributed to the Devra G. Kleiman fund.

Appendix 1

The story's golden lion tamarins. While based on the reintroduction of actual golden lion tamarins, these individuals and
outcomes are fictional and should not be used in scientific com-
munications. Accounts of the actual individual tamarins and their
outcomes will be provided on request.

The Olympia Family (as of June 1984)

O1: "Mom", female, 5 years old, released in the quarry area of the
Poço das Antas reserve on 7 December 1984, disappeared on
8 December.

O2: "Dad", male, 6 years old, released in the quarry area of the
Poço das Antas reserve on 7 December, Eaten by a boa constrictor on 9 December.

O3: "Pandora", female, 18 months old, introduced to S4 (see below) on 1 December, Released with S4 on the Rio Vermelho
ranch on 3 December, forming the Red River group. Gives
birth to twins in "late July" 1985.

O4: "Prometheus", male (twin of O3), 18 months old, released on
7 December in the quarry area of the Poço das Antas reserve.
He paired up with O9 (see below) on 12 December and is the
father of twins O10 and O11, born 16 October 1985.

O5: "Hera", female, 12 months old, released on 7 December in the
quarry area of the Poço das Antas reserve, Killed by bees on 11
December.

O6: "Hercules", male, (twin of O5), 12 months old, released on
7 December in the quarry area of the Poço das Antas reserve,

disappeared in a group encounter on 9 December, found dead of starvation on 12 December.

O7: "Venus", female, 4 months old, still suckling and being carried, released on 7 December in the quarry area of the Poço das Antas reserve.

O8: "Vesuvio", male (twin of O7), 4 months old, still suckling and being carried, released on 7 December in the quarry area of the Poço das Antas reserve.

O9: Wild female, about 2 years old in December 1984. Joined the Olympia group on 12 December 1984, pairing with Prometheus (see above). Mother of O10 and O11.

O10 and O11, born 16 October 1985 in the quarry area of the Poço das Antas reserve. Mother is O9 and father is Prometheus. Unsexed and not yet named.

Swamp Group

Swamp 1: wild adult female, rescued on 28 November 1984 from ranch outside Poço das Antas reserve, released on 29 November on a ridge overlooking a swamp in the Poço das Antas reserve.

Swamp 2: wild adult male, rescued from ranch outside reserve, released on 30 November on a ridge overlooking a swamp in the Poço das Antas reserve. Expelled Swamp 4 from group on 30 November.

Swamp 3: young adult female, rescued and radiocollared on 28 November, released 29 November on a ridge overlooking a swamp in the Poço das Antas reserve.

Swamp 4: young adult male, probably twin of S3. Rescued and collared 28 November, released 29 November on a ridge overlooking a swamp in the Poço das Antas reserve. Expelled by his father S2 on 30 November. Paired with Pandora (O3) on 1 December. Released with Pandora on 3 December on the Rio Vermelho ranch, forming the Red River group. Father of young born to Pandora in "late July" 1985.

Swamp 5, "Nika" female, probably one year old. Rescued 28 November, released on a ridge overlooking a swamp in the Poço das Antas reserve on 29 November. She pairs up with B3 (Niko) to form Niko's group near the field station in the Poço das Antas reserve.

Swamp 6, female, probably one year old. Rescued 28 November, released on a ridge overlooking a swamp in the Poço das Antas reserve on 29 November.

Red River Group

"Pandora" and Swamp 4 (see above)

"Aphrodite" (RR1), female and "Hermes" (RR2), male, born in "late July" 1985 on Rio Vermelho ranch. Mother is Pandora and father is Swamp 4.

The Brookfield Group (ages as of March 1985)

B1: "Emily", 6 years old, mother and breeding female of the group. A primary link to language transmission in zoo golden lion tamarins. Released in Beaver Valley boot camp in the National Zoo in "early May" 1985, and then reintroduced on the Santa Helena ranch in Brazil on 9 October 1985. Got lost on 10 October, rescued on 11 October, treated by field team, and re-released on 11 October. Later pairs with Gummy (see below).

B2: "Rufous", 6 years old, father and breeding male. Born at "Monkey Forest". Direct descendant from the first captive tamarins in the U.S. and thus has rare genes. Released in Beaver Valley boot camp in the National Zoo in "early May" 1985. He was later found to have been exposed to and survived a usually-fatal virus, and thus was removed from the group and not reintroduced in Brazil. Died in a biomedical research colony.

B3: "Niko", 2 years old, male. Released in Beaver Valley boot camp in the National Zoo in "early May" 1985. Separated from Brookfield group on arrival in Brazil 7 October 1985 to avoid mating with Emily, his mother. Escaped to the wild 9 October and found mate (Nika, see below) on 12 October, establishing Niko's group, which lives near the field station in the Poço das Antas reserve

B4: "Opie", 1 year old, male, Petie's twin. Released in Beaver Valley boot camp in the National Zoo in "early May" 1985, and then reintroduced on the Santa Helena ranch on 9 October 1985. Stolen on 15 October, recovered on 16 October and re-released on Santa Helena on 17 October.

B5: "Petie", 1 year old, female, Opie's twin. Released in Beaver Valley boot camp in the National Zoo in "early May" 1985, and then reintroduced on the Santa Helena ranch on 9 October 1985. Stolen on 15 October and died on 16 October due to injuries sustained in theft.

B6: "Sandy", 2 months old, female, still nursing and being carried by everybody in the family. Released in Beaver Valley of the National Zoo in "early May" 1985, and then reintroduced on the Santa Helena ranch on 9 October 1985. Stolen 15 October, recovered on 16 October, and re-released on Santa Helena on 17 October.

"Gummy": Old wild male, joins Brookfield group on Santa Helena ranch and becomes Emily's mate on 12 October 1985.

Niko's Group

B3: "Niko", see above. Escapes from cage at field station and reintroduces himself to the wild on 9 October. Pairs with Nika on 12 October.

"Nika", formerly S5 of Swamp Group (see above), pairs with Niko around field station on 12 October.

Appendix 2

Because this book is set in both the United States and Brazil, I have used the international metric system (favored by Brazilians and scientists) and the less common United States system (favored by Americans) to express weights, lengths, volumes and temperatures. I chose the system/term that seemed most natural for the character or context. For simplicity, and to keep readers from drifting onto their smart phones, the table below shows the page number and approximate conversion for every measurement term used in the book.

Page Number	Cited Measurement	Approximate Conversion
ii	1,000 feet	305 meters
10	50 feet	15 meters
11	10 feet	3 meters
13	3-foot section	1-meter section
22	2 inches	5 centimeters
22	5 inches	13 centimeters
23	100 feet	30 meters
28	20 feet	6 meters
29	60 acres	24 hectares
32	10 feet	3 meters
33	16-foot ladder	5-meter ladder
36	557 grams	20 ounces
36	26 grams	1 ounce

Page Number	Cited Measurement	Approximate Conversion
36	500 meters	1,650 feet, or about 1/3 mile
36	50 meters	165 feet
39	4-foot nest log	1.2-foot nest log
39	6 inches	15 centimeters
39	3 feet	1 meter
39	12 feet	3.6 meters
42	30 feet	9 meters
69	120 kilometers	75 miles
79	10 meters	33 feet
87	40-pound child	18-kilogram child
88	200 meters	660 feet
93	100 meters	330 feet
103	50 meters	165 feet
103	8 meters	26 feet
104	442, 445, and 20 grams	15.6, 15.7, and 0.7 ounces
106	30 meters	99 feet
113	392, 478 grams	13.7, 16.7 ounces
114	5 kilometers	3 miles
114	100 pounds	45 kilograms
117	535 grams	19 ounces, or 1.2 pounds
119	268 grams	9.6 ounces
119	between 40 and 50 grams	between 1.4 and 1.8 ounces
121	10 square inches	65 square centimeters
122	20 inches	51 centimeters
134	500 grams	17.9 ounces or 1.1 pounds
139	Ninety pounds	Forty-one kilograms
154	500 grams	17.9 ounces or 1.1 pounds
155	20 grams	0.7 ounces

Page Number	Cited Measurement	Approximate Conversion
155	several hundred hectares	about 750 acres
164	10 feet, 25 feet	3 meters, 7.6 meters
164	20 feet	6 meters
166	25 feet	7.6 meters
169	20 feet	6 meters
170	50 feet	15 meters
172	2X4s (2 inches by 4 inches)	5 centimeters by 10 centimeters
177	800 grams, 500 grams	28.6 ounces, 17.9 ounces
178	6-inch buck knife	15-centimeter buck knife
186	150 meters	495 feet
188	500 meters	1,695 feet, or about 1/3 of a mile
189	30 meters	99 feet
189	238 hectares	588 acres
191	3 meters	10 feet
193	2 meters	6.5 feet
196	5 meters	16.5 feet
198	3 meters	10 feet
198	59 and 57 degrees Fahrenheit	15 and 13.9 degrees Centigrade
199	8 meters	26.5 feet
200	55 degrees Fahrenheit	12.8 degrees Centigrade
201	93 degrees (Fahrenheit)	33.9 degrees Centigrade
203	250 meters	825 feet
205	3 meters	10 feet
207	30 hectares	75 acres
209	meter-long stick	yard-long stick

Page Number	Cited Measurement	Approximate Conversion
211	20 meters	66 feet
212	425 grams, 435 grams	15.2 ounces, 15.5 ounces
212	577 grams, 563 grams	20.6 ounces, 20.1 ounces
212	500 grams, 538 grams	17.9 ounces, 19.2 ounces
214	60 centimeters	24 inches
223	One hundred and twenty kilometers	Seventy five miles
230	350 hectares	865 acres

The Author

Benjamin B. Beck is a comparative psychologist specializing in animal cognition and biodiversity conservation. His research on problem-solving and tool use by primates and birds led to a frequently cited book, *Animal Tool Behavior*, published in 1980. A second edition, co-authored with Rob Shumaker and Kristina Walkup, was published in May 2011.

Beck turned his interest in cognition to management and psychological welfare of zoo animals in the 1980s, co-authoring a 1988 survey of zoo gorillas demonstrating the importance of mother-rearing and early social experience for adult sexual and maternal skills. Work on cognitive aspects of husbandry led to a study of adaptation to the wild by reintroduced captive-born animals. Beck coordinated the preparation, reintroduction and post-release monitoring of 149 captive-born golden lion tamarins in Brazil between 1983 and 2005. The reintroduced population has now grown to 600, about one third of the entire wild population. He is co-author of *Best Practice Guidelines for the Re-introduction of Great Apes*, published in 2007 by the Section on Great Apes of the World Conservation Union (IUCN) Primate Specialist Group. He served as director of conservation for Great Ape Trust from 2003 to 2011, coordinating an initiative in Rwanda to found a national conservation park in the Gishwati Forest and conserve a small chimpanzee population living there. In fewer than three years, the protected area of Gishwati increased from 2,190 acres to 3,665 acres, and the chimpanzee population grew from 13 to 20, probably the first time the population had grown in more than 40 years.

Beck studied at Union College (NY), received his MA from Boston University, and his PhD from the University of Chicago. He was Research Curator and Curator of Primates at Brookfield Zoo from 1970 to 1982, where he was a principal in the design and construction of "Tropic World", one of the first large-scale mixed species tropical forest zoo exhibits. He served at the Smithsonian Institution's National Zoological Park as General Curator and Associate Director from 1983 until his retirement in 2003. He designed the National Zoo's innovative free-ranging golden lion tamarin exhibit, and was project executive for "Think Tank", a pioneering exhibit on animal thinking that opened in 1995. He was on the negotiating team that brought giant pandas from China to the Zoo in 2000. Beck was appointed Scientist Emeritus in the Smithsonian Conservation Biology Institute in 2010. He received an Alumni Professional Achievement Citation from the University of Chicago in 2003.

Beck is an author of more than 60 scientific papers and books, many popular articles and blogs, and has given over 100 presentations and keynote addresses at scientific conferences, colleges and universities. *Thirteen Gold Monkeys* is his first work of fiction. He is an Adjunct Professor at Drake University and Iowa State University, and a member of the Primate Specialist Group of IUCN. Beck serves on the Board of Directors of Save the Golden Tamarin, a U.S.A.-based conservation support organization for ongoing tamarin conservation in Brazil.

He lives with his wife and colleague Beate Rettberg-Beck and their dog Heidi on the Eastern Shore of Maryland.

CPSIA information can be obtained
at www.ICGtesting.com
Printed in the USA
JSHW040344180522
25996JS00001B/32